T0128109

DEATH IS THE FINAL RECKONING

A Sequel to *Solitary Vigilance*

Tim Drake

authorHOUSE®

AuthorHouse™
1663 Liberty Drive
Bloomington, IN 47403
www.authorhouse.com
Phone: 833-262-8899

This is a work of fiction. All of the characters, organizations and events portrayed in this novel are either products of the author's imagination or are used fictionally. It's a fictionalized story, dramatized from an historical viewpoint.

Published by AuthorHouse 04/19/2024

ISBN: 978-1-5462-3676-4 (sc)
ISBN: 978-1-5462-3674-0 (hc)
ISBN: 978-1-5462-3675-7 (e)

Library of Congress Control Number: 2018904102

Print information available on the last page.

This book is printed on acid-free paper.

Other Books by the Author:

Inherited Freedom

Solitary Vigilance

CONTENTS

"Death pays all debts."

William Shakespeare (1564-1616)

PROLOGUE

Darkness surrounded me. I was in a position that had become all too familiar to me. The solitary missions I had conducted before and during World War II had all run together, and I no longer kept count. The missions were similar; all that differed for me were the faces of the enemies I hunted. I completed each assigned mission without hesitation. The Nazi I hunted that night, Warren Weltzin, had maintained a vast number of Jewish concentration camps. He had delivered Zyklon B to the hundreds of concentration camps in Germany and surrounding countries. He had somehow eluded capture by the American and Russian forces when they converged on Berlin in May 1945.

I glanced at my watch; it was 11:17 p.m. I peered through my rifle's scope in the darkness, aided by the street lights that lined the road before me. I was tucked between two large rocks, approximately two hundred yards from the street, in an elevated position I had taken earlier that evening under cover of darkness.

Removing my eye from the rifle's scope, I watched a black, two-door Nash pull up and park about thirty yards down the street. The car cut its engine, and the street became eerily quiet. A man exited the car, his face hidden by his hat. He appeared to be about 5'9", Weltzin's reported height. I felt a wave of frustration come over me. I had not moved from my position in almost three hours. Finally, the man walked under a street light a few feet from his car. He removed his hat, pulled a handkerchief from his right front pants pocket, and wiped his forehead. The street light illuminated his face, and I saw it. He then replaced his handkerchief, pulled a pack of cigarettes from his shirt pocket, and lit a cigarette. At that point, there was no doubt that he was Warren Weltzin.

I pulled the trigger on my 1903 Springfield. The resulting blast echoed down the quiet street. Warren's head snapped back as it exploded and splattered against the outside wall of the bar. He dropped right where he had stood.

I quickly got up and disassembled my rifle as much as allowed, allowing me to conceal it in my duffle bag. After returning the weapon to my duffle bag, I went down from my perch above the street. It took me over an hour to reach the safety of Joaquin's house.

CHAPTER 1

A Lifetime of War

"Life is neither good nor evil, but only a place for good and evil."
Marcus Aurelius

My name is Allen Voigt. On the day WW2 ended, I peered over the deck of the USS *Nicholas*, a Navy destroyer, joined by its sailors. We had a front-row seat to Japan's surrender. The actual ceremony took place on the deck of the battleship USS *Missouri*, anchored only about one hundred yards away. General MacArthur and most of the United States senior military leadership were there. The Japanese dignitaries wore top hats and coattails, a strange sight. After the surrender papers were signed, naval gunfire erupted all over Tokyo Bay from the surrounding Navy ships. The sailors of the *Nicholas* and I congratulated each other and gave each other high fives and hugs.

The date was September 2, 1945. The war was finally over. At least, that is what I thought on that infamous day. I retired from the Army in January 1948, faithfully serving and defending my country for over twenty years. For the last few years of WW2, I served under General Donovan as a member of the Office of Strategic Services, or OSS. I participated in solitary missions throughout the European and Pacific war campaigns. After retiring, I spent thirty years as an Army contract employee. I trained young Army recruits headed off to the Korean War on counterintelligence and weapons. The Cold War escalated with the Soviet Union, and I was asked to train what is now known as Central Intelligence Agency (CIA) personnel on how to blend into society in foreign countries and maintain a false identity, even when under duress.

My last two years in the United States Army were classified until 1980. What I have never shared until now is what I was asked to do for the Army between April 1946 and January 1947. What prompted me to share my story now was a television news story about the death of Walter Rauff. He was a German Nazi SS officer who played a large part in the creation of mobile gas chambers during WW2. He was directly responsible for the deaths of thousands of Jews. When I saw news of his funeral in Santiago, Chile, I recalled my inability to capture him back in late 1946.

Death finally caught up with him at the age of seventy-seven in the form of lung cancer. I only wished that I had put a bullet in his head many years ago. I am now seventy-six and fully retired from any form of military service. I have never shared any of my mission activity during those last two years in the Army with anyone outside of my wife Alice, who heard the details of my last mission upon my return to the United States in early 1947. It is now time for me to share my story with everyone else.

In the weeks leading up to the Japanese surrender, I was a prisoner of war aboard a Japanese submarine. I was released when the submarine surfaced in Tokyo Bay the morning of surrendering. Upon my release, I got in a life raft and paddled to the *Nicholas,* where I stayed for two weeks after the surrender ceremony. It was nice to be back with my fellow military members, as most of my service during the war had been solitary.

I finally returned to Pearl Harbor in late September 1945 and went to Fort Meade, Maryland, in February 1946. A couple of months later, I was reunited with the love of my life, Alice Marie Davison. She was an Army nurse I had met for the first time almost fourteen years earlier in Zurich, Switzerland. She was injured late in the war while a prisoner of war in the Philippines. We spent a few weeks together in April of 1946 as she convalesced at her parents' home in Jacksonville, Florida.

Late in April, I received an urgent telegram that read: *"Captain Voigt, your presence is immediately requested back at Fort Meade, Maryland. Your service to your country is needed. You will be out of the country for a period of ten to eighteen months."*

My heart sank. It had been four years since I had last seen Alice during a mission to rescue her fellow nurses off the island of Corregidor in the

Philippines, and I had to leave again. I spent the next day with Alice and her parents and shared the news. As hard as it was for her to find out I was leaving again, Alice supported me and hugged me goodbye the afternoon of April 27, 1946, when I boarded a train at the station in downtown Jacksonville, Florida.

For the next twenty hours, as I sat in my seat and listened to the train rumbling north, I reflected on the missions I had gone on for the Army and the OSS. I had saved American lives by killing the enemy. I concluded this new assignment, whatever it was, would be different from my previous assignments because the war was over. There was no one left to kill. I eventually drifted off to sleep sometime at night and awoke when the train stopped in Wilmington, North Carolina. It was 4:30 a.m. I jumped off the train and found a young man selling newspapers, soft drinks, and snacks. I pulled out some loose change and bought a cold bottle of Coke and a Hershey's chocolate bar from him. By this time, my train was getting ready to depart. I promptly made my way back to the train and took my seat.

After the sun rose, I spent my remaining time on the train seeking out and talking with anyone in military uniform. I found a few Marines, Sailors, and Airmen. Without exception, all were headed home. Some had been injured and hospitalized for months after the war, while others had just gotten back stateside and were free to return to civilian life. I enjoyed the conversations and discovered many of them had been in the same general areas as mine during my missions. Speaking with them was therapeutic, as it helped me know that what we all had done during the war had made a real difference.

The train finally arrived at the Washington, D.C., train station around noon. I took a cab to Fort Meade, where I was dropped off at the front gate. The base was quiet, free of the volume of soldiers assigned there during the war. I checked in with the camp commander and confirmed that my small apartment awaited me. I had left a few uniforms and personal supplies there, so I knew I was prepared. As I left the commander's office, he handed me a telegram. This one was from someone I had never met before, General Robert Stiles. The telegram instructed me to meet General Stiles at his office on base the following morning at 8:00 a.m.

Before I retired that evening, I called Alice and told her I'd arrived safely and that I missed her. She begged me to be safe and contact her again when possible. As I hung up the phone, I wondered when that would be. I resented that I had been called back to active duty, but I was aware of my commitment to the Army, and I was determined to see whatever lay ahead of me through to completion.

Early the following day, I decided to run before breakfast. I added a few pounds during the last few weeks spent with Alice and her parents. I had eaten some fantastic home-cooked meals, but it was time to shed some weight. I needed to be in peak physical condition, regardless of the type of assignment that awaited me.

As I ran through the base, I noticed things mainly had stayed the same from my time there during the war. Mostly, I was struck by the fact that I only saw three other people during the entire five-mile excursion. America had ramped up its personnel and equipment to historic levels during 1941- 1945. Now that the war was over, things had rapidly slowed down. As I finished my last mile and returned to my apartment to clean up, an Army jeep pulled ahead and stopped. I slowed down, and as I did, the driver jumped out and turned in my direction.

"Captain Voigt, good morning," the driver said. "I'm General Robert Stiles. It's good to meet you finally."

"Thank you, Sir, it is a pleasure to meet you, as well," I replied. General Stiles asked if he could give me a lift back to my apartment, and since I was breathing heavily, I accepted his offer. After the General dropped me off, I quickly showered, ironed and donned a uniform, and rushed out the door for a quick breakfast.

When I entered the front door of the General's office building there on the Fort Meade base after breakfast, my mind flashed back to the day I had walked into the administrative building at Camp Pine during my basic training back in 1926. It was hard to believe that twenty years had passed. I'd been a lowly private back then, and I remembered being intimidated by the sight of three senior officers: Brigadier General Massey, Colonel Pruitt, and Lt. Yates. My drill sergeant, Sergeant Nolan, had been with me that day, encouraging me. Today, however, I was by myself.

I climbed the three flights of stairs to the General's office and knocked on the door at 7:55 a.m. General Stiles immediately invited me to enter and sit in front of his large oak desk. He was shuffling papers and he looked down, which gave me a chance to glance around his office. His walls were filled with black and white photos from his wartime experiences, and a picture of his family sat on his desk. He had two sons serving in uniform - one in the Navy and the other in the Army.

General Stiles finally looked up at me.

"Captain Voigt, I was just reviewing your twenty-year military career, and it's quite commendable," he said. "I'm a thirty-four-year Army veteran, having served in both world wars and during peacetime. I'm a close friend of Major Yates, an officer whom I believe you know very well." "Yes, sir," I said. "I first met Major Yates at Camp Pine, in upstate New York, in 1926 as a young private. I've always considered him my mentor."

General Stiles said, "Allen, let's call each other by our first names going forward."

Although I nodded and smiled back at him, I knew that would be a struggle, as I'd followed Army protocol for the last twenty years.

The General stood and walked around his office as he spoke. "Allen, have you been reading the newspapers? Are you aware of the Nazi trials that have been taking place in Nuremberg, Germany, since November 1945?"

"Yes, Sir."

The General paused, turned, and placed both hands on his desk. "General Donovan, whom you already know, is currently in Nuremberg, supporting the German war crime trials. Through various integration meetings with high-ranking Nazis, we have learned the possible locations of some of the Nazis that fled Germany at the end of the war. Martin Bormann, Rudolf Hess, Karl Donitz, and Hermann Goring have been very forthcoming with information. I do not have to tell you the atrocities that the Nazis conducted during the years 1939-1945, as you were witness to that. The Nazis who are currently on trial in Nuremberg will be justly punished, and many will be hanged for their crimes against humanity. It is the Nazis that escaped our grasp that must now answer for their crimes." He looked me straight in the eye and said, "Let me make this very simple for you, Allen. Your assignment, starting immediately, is to hunt down as many of those escaped Nazis as possible and to kill them."

Upon hearing that, I straightened in my chair and quickly gathered my thoughts.

I stood and faced the General and said, "Sir, I count it an honor and a privilege to be assigned this mission. The Nazi brutality and killing that I witnessed throughout Europe during the war stayed with me. The memories and images never leave my mind, and the smell of Jews burning in crematoriums still lingers in my nose. May I speak plainly, Sir?"

The General nodded, so I said, "Why don't we simply capture these escaped Nazis, bring them to trial, and allow them to be publicly sentenced, executed, or imprisoned?"

"Because they are all cowards and deserve to be killed and buried deep," he said. "This directive comes directly from the desk of President Truman."

I had yet to meet President Truman, although I had met President Roosevelt years ago. The sudden death of President Roosevelt hit both the nation and me very hard back in April 1945. President Truman helped fill the enormous void left by President Roosevelt and led America through the end of WW2. Truman had a reputation for being feisty and aggressive.

For the rest of the morning, General Stiles and I went through an exhaustive list of Nazis that had escaped capture at the end of the war. Some of the names I recognized, while others I had never heard. One particular name stood out, though: Walter Rauff. He and I had crossed paths briefly when I was at Auschwitz. He was responsible for killing thousands of Jews, as he had developed a mobile gas chamber that could be carried on a truck. My activity at Auschwitz had been undercover and consisted of construction work and gathering intelligence. Rauff had visited the camp one afternoon to gather supplies, primarily Zyklon B tablets. He'd cursed at the Jewish inmates who were working nearby and even spat on one of the prisoners as he'd waited for his trucks to be loaded. The most challenging aspect of my time spent at Auschwitz had been the grief I'd felt for the Jewish people and how useless I'd felt at my inability to save them. However, I had focused on the fact that the intelligence I gathered would ultimately save some of them.

General Stiles had lunch brought in for us, but I barely touched it because I had no appetite. Out of respect, I ate a few bites and swallowed some iced tea. I then shared my knowledge of Walter Rauff with the General.

Some of the Nazis that had escaped Germany included Adolf Eichmann, Franz Stangl, Josef Mengele, Erich Priebke and others. By early afternoon, we narrowed the list to four of the best possible targets for me to hunt and eliminate. Walter Rauff was on that list. The other three Nazis were Ekerd Jacobsen, Rickert Pagel, and Warner Weltzin. All four men had ties to the Jewish holocaust. The atrocities of the Nazis against the Jews and other groups had become fully apparent. It was estimated that over six million Jews had been exterminated during the war.

Ekerd Jacobsen and his death squad had been directly responsible for executing Jews in their own homes. During the last year of the war, the Germans had stopped transporting Jews via train and had entered their homes and executed them.

Rickert Pagel had selected young Jewish women just arriving at the concentration camps, taken them into German officer's or German soldier's barracks, and allowed them to be raped. After their abuse, the women had been brought back to the concentration camp and exterminated.

Warner Weltzin and his employees had been responsible for maintaining the concentration camps, including gas chambers, crematoriums, electric fences, and lighting.

General Stiles outlined my straightforward next steps. I was to fly to Berlin and meet with various contacts with direct insight and knowledge about the four designated Nazi targets. I was to learn about every aspect of these four murderers' lives, habits, family members, associates, and appearances. I was to study maps, possible escape routes, and countries to which these four Nazis had possibly fled.

It was expected that after four months of intense research and study, I would be ready to pursue my targets. Upon completing my initial review in Berlin and before returning to the States, I was to spend time with General Donovan in Nuremberg, Germany. I was not briefed on the content of this meeting with General Donovan, whom I had not seen in some time.

My time with General Stiles ended promptly at 4:00 p.m. I returned to my apartment and digested all the information I had received over the previous eight hours. As with my early days with the OSS, there was no debate when assigned missions and I did not question why I was chosen for my assignment. I knew what I was trained to do. The war was over; I needed to process everything I had heard and mentally prepare myself for a physically and mentally demanding mission. I looked at it as my last assignment, though. I was thirty-eight years old, and my body was beaten and tired.

I called and spoke to Alice after I got back to my apartment. I was frustrated that I could not share the details about my upcoming assignment. Our conversation centered on the fact that the Army was sending me back overseas on assignment. Alice still struggled with her memory and recalled very little about what I had done during the war, so she did not realize how similar this new assignment was to those in my past. I felt like the war was lasting a lifetime. Alice told me to be safe and contact her when I could, as she would miss me terribly.

I arranged with Fort Meade personnel to fly from the base to New York City the next day. From there, I would take a series of flights to Berlin. I was not afraid to fly, as I had done many times before, but I was not excited at the thought of spending forty-eight hours flying halfway across the world. I knew it had to be done, and it was the first step in constant travel. During the war, I had crisscrossed the globe, moving from one assignment to another to defend our country. Each trip seemed to get longer and longer.

On May 1, 1946, I left for Berlin, Germany. As I flew East, I recalled my first trip to Europe by submarine and the circumstances that had led up to that visit. The trip was in August of 1931 before Hitler assumed complete control of Germany. After basic training at Camp Pine, New York, I attended the Army War College in Harrisburg, Pennsylvania. Shortly after my graduation, Lt. Yates called me into his office in the administration building there on campus. We'd spent the better part of a day going over the role of an Army Military Attaché and the dangers and expectations associated with that role. As the clock on the wall in his office ticked away, Lt. Yates had told me where I would be assigned: Germany. Suddenly, it had all made sense. The four years of German language studies, geography and maps training, and all the combat and weapons training I had received all pointed to that assignment. By that time, I had been promoted to Lieutenant.

Lt. Yates had said, "Berlin is in turmoil, Lt. Voigt, and it will be your job to be America's eyes and ears over there. Your role will be to report to the United States Embassy in Berlin, which will allow you full access to the German government, present you with opportunities for intelligence gathering, and provide you with the unique ability to observe military build-ups. You will also initiate solo missions throughout the country; those missions will be made clear once you arrive in Germany. That is the good news."

Lt. Yates had paused for a moment. "The bad news is that after you leave this office, you cannot tell anyone where you are going or your new assignment. The issues you will uncover and participate in involve America's national security."

Soon after that meeting, I left for Europe. I fondly remember my first time crossing the Atlantic Ocean in a submarine. The submarine was the USS *Narwhal.* As I boarded the submarine, I noticed an American flag proudly waving from the stern. Two Navy sailors had stood guard at the entrance of the gangplank. I had walked up to one of them and said, "Reciprocity."

That was the word Lt. Yates had instructed me to say to whoever was guarding the submarine. He had also informed me that the response I was to receive as confirmation was "Perseverance." One of the sailors guarding the sub had responded with the correct word and motioned me to proceed up the gangplank and into the submarine. Other sailors performed miscellaneous tasks on the deck of the *Narwhal*, but they had paid no attention to me.

As I stepped onto the deck, I heard, "Welcome to the *Narwhal*, Lt. Voigt."

I looked up at the sub's conning tower and saw a man standing partially out of it.

"Thank you, Sir," I had responded as I walked in his direction.

The man soon joined me on the deck of the sub. "My name is Lt. Commander John Brown, Jr., I'm the skipper of the *Narwhal*."

Lt. Commander Brown had been proud of his sub and given me a quick deck tour. He told me the *Narwhal* was a brand-new submarine, commissioned a little over a year earlier, in May 1930. Lt. Commander Brown had not asked me any questions about why he was being asked to transport me across the Atlantic or about what I would do for the Army when I got to Germany.

I had followed Lt. Commander Brown through the small door in the conning tower and down into the submarine. It was dimly lit inside, but it was an active atmosphere, with sailors checking various dials, loading supplies, etc. I was like a kid in a candy store that day. I had never seen a submarine before, let alone been inside one. I'd been passed along to another sailor, who showed me my quarters, which consisted of a private room next to Lt. Commander Brown's quarters. I'd laid my suitcase down and waited for further instructions. The room was small, with several black and white photos on the walls showing some of the locations the sub had traveled. It looked like the *Narwhal* had been through the Panama Canal and portions of the Pacific already.

A little later, Lt. Commander Brown poked his head into the room and said, "Let's grab some chow."

That had sounded like a great idea since I was hungry. I'd followed him down the narrow corridor to the small galley where other sailors were already eating supper. Lt. Commander Brown said he tried to take his meals in the main galley with the men in his crew as often as possible. I had been introduced to the men in the galley as Allen Voigt without mentioning my rank or Army assignment. The skipper and I had enjoyed a good meal, exchanging small talk about where the sub had been during its first year.

We had left the safety of the New York City port sometime that night and headed out to the open water of the Atlantic Ocean.

During the seven days, I was on the sub, the crew was very open to my questions and put up with my stumbling through the small corridors and taking up space in the galley. On day five of our trip across the large expanse of the Atlantic Ocean, there was even one instance where we had come within a few hundred feet of a German submarine headed west as we were headed east. The radioman on the *Narwhal* had picked up the German chatter but couldn't understand it. Lt. Commander Brown knew I was fluent in German and asked that I report to the bridge immediately. I made my way to the bridge and joined the radioman and skipper. I listened for a few minutes on the ship's overhead speakers. The German sub was identified while we were submerged, nearing the western shores of France. The German submarine crew did not indicate that they knew an American submarine was off its starboard bow. Most of the German crew's conversation centered on what the crew would do when it reached its port of call, San Paulo, Brazil. I'd shared every word from the German crew with Lt. Commander Brown. He hadn't believed the sub was a threat because America was not at war with Germany, so we continued heading east.

We had entered the English Channel early on the afternoon of day six. The skipper surfaced the sub and allowed everyone to take in some sights, including the famous White Cliffs of Dover and the northern coast of France. The sub's navigator informed me that we would be docking at the port in Brugge, Belgium, around 11:00 the following day. That evening at dinner, I'd thanked the crew for welcoming me as a fraternity member.

At breakfast the following day, I had sought out the skipper and thanked him for sharing his insight into what he felt lay ahead for America and its Armed Forces. We had docked as scheduled on August 18, 1931, at the port in Brugge. At the time, the farthest I had ever been from western New York was when I attended the Army War College. I was about to be in a foreign country where I knew no one. I had shaken Lt. Commander Brown's hand, and he had wished me Godspeed in my upcoming assignments.

As I reflected on those past assignments on the plane, I thought about how they were monumental and critical to America's ultimate victory in the war. My new assignment seemed more personal. It would not be nation against nation but man versus man.

The sound of the plane's propeller engines drowned out any conversation on the plane. I was on an Army Douglas DC-4 occupied by several Army men and women flying out of Camp Meade for destinations unknown. I had been trained, while on assignment, to keep information about my OSS affiliation, current activities, or destinations private. I worried that my dealings with other military members often came across as rude, but I had to keep my assignments secret. My self-imposed silence was frustrating on this flight because the flight time was long, and I wanted to ask my fellow servicemen and women where they had served in the war.

However, I couldn't share my activities, so I remained silent and sat there, looking out the window.

Our plane finally crossed into France after a few stops to refuel. The number of occupants on the plane had dwindled to just a few by then. Looking out my window, I saw that the French landscape was dotted with craters left behind by the Allied bombing campaigns just before and during the Normandy invasion back in June 1944. I also saw hundreds of burned-out tanks and trucks littering the roads. Although most buildings were burned out and missing portions of their roofs, some were still in perfect condition.

As the plane's twin engines hummed, I reflected on all the missions I had conducted throughout France late in the war. I had killed German officers without mercy and provided countless pages of intelligence back to senior American military leadership in advance of the Normandy invasions. Although I was tired of war and the killing, I knew my duty and was committed to my new mission. I only hoped it would be my last. After one last stop in Paris, we lifted off again and headed for Berlin.

The Eiffel Tower was lit up, and people milled about below. The sun was setting behind us as we flew above the clouds. I had been flying for three days and was eager to get to Berlin.

On the final approach to Berlin's Tempelhof Airport, I saw only devastation out the window. In addition to the burned-out buildings, scattered about were hundreds of damaged vehicles and tanks. It was eerily like the devastation in France I had seen earlier, but on a much larger scale. My time in Berlin in the mid-and late 1930s did not compare to now, as back then, there had been open restaurants, gardens with blooming flowers, and hundreds of people moving about freely.

When I departed the plane, I noticed several German fighter planes parked around the airport runway area. I recognized a few Messerschmitt Bf 109s and Focke-Wulf 190s. They had been captured after the war. I was shocked that they appeared to be in perfect working order and had not been destroyed by the Allies or even the Germans as they neared their surrender in May 1945.

The contacts I was provided were German citizens who had worked for the Allies during the war. I was eager to meet them and not only learn more about my Nazi targets but also about these citizens individually. I had a strong feeling their roles were like mine during the war. I had been provided with an address, and as I was familiar with the layout of the city of Berlin, I felt confident I knew where I was going.

I had planned to walk to the address, but as I exited the airport, a young Army Private stopped me and asked if I wanted a lift. I accepted his offer, hopped into his Jeep, and threw my luggage into the back seat.

I handed him the address I'd been given, and as we left the airport, said, "Private, I see from your patch that you're a member of the 101st Airborne Division. I jumped with them on the eve of D-Day, during the early morning of June 6, 1944."

The Private's eyes widened. "I got to meet a few of those guys in London about six months ago," he said. "They sure had some stories to tell. My older brother, Fred, jumped on that day with the 82nd Airborne but died a few weeks later on the outskirts of Paris."

I shook my head and said, "I'm sorry for your loss, Private. What's your name?"

"John, Sir."

As we drove through the streets of Berlin, I took in the devastation of the once-beautiful city. John carefully avoided burned-out civilian and military vehicles, fallen debris from bombed-out buildings, and rotting animal carcasses. We had to back up and take a different street on several occasions. After a few miles, I was glad I had accepted his offer to drive me. Walking would have been a nightmare.

John eventually asked me what my role had been during the war. I felt comfortable telling him I had been in counterintelligence, but I didn't tell him I was an active member of the OSS.

Surprisingly, John did not ask me much more, not even why I was in Berlin. His job was to shuttle Army officers to and from their destinations, so he had probably been instructed to ask only a few questions of his passengers.

After about forty-five minutes of making our way through the bombed-out streets of Berlin, we arrived at our destination. John pulled the Jeep up to a simple, five-story apartment building on the northeast side of Berlin. We said our goodbyes, and I went into the building.

My contacts were Jonas and Anna Fischer. All I had were their names and address: Apartment #15. I had no facial descriptions or individual backgrounds. I walked up three flights of stairs and down a narrow, dim hallway. I found apartment #15, and before I even knocked on the door, I thought back to my first apartment in Berlin in August 1931. My assigned apartment back then featured two large windows with a great view of the Ministry of Justice and the German Chancellery buildings. That apartment had served me well in the years leading up to the start of WWII.

I knocked on the door three times, and to my surprise, no one came. I had been instructed to provide a password of "Victory" and to expect a reply of "Defeat." I knocked again, still waiting for someone to come to the door. I evaluated my options. Just as I was about to head back down to the lobby of the apartment building, a young woman exited the stairwell. She turned in my direction with her arms full of groceries. She noticed me, stopped, and stared at me for an eternity. I quickly assumed that I was standing in front of her apartment.

"May I help you with those groceries, ma'am?" I asked with a smile. She then walked toward me, saying, "Defeat."

"Victory," I replied.

I could see the relief in her eyes. I walked to her and helped her with the grocery bags.

"You must be Anna," I said as we stood in the hall.

"Yes," she answered. "Jonas is my husband; he should be home any minute."

"My name is Allen. I was told you were expecting me."

Anna smiled, inserted her key into the apartment lock, and opened the door. I followed her into the apartment and laid her two bags of groceries on the kitchen counter. Anna then told me to make myself comfortable while she put away the groceries.

I casually walked about the small apartment. I looked out the window as the sun set and finally sat in the living room. The apartment was small but appeared to have two bedrooms. I needed clarification on my living accommodations for my time in Berlin.

Anna didn't say anything and soon began to cook. I felt awkward sitting there in silence, so I broke the ice and told Anna where I was from and all about Alice. I spoke German to put Anna at ease. She was surprised at my German vocabulary, and she soon opened up and filled me in on where she and Jonas were from, where they met, and how they came to be in Berlin.

The story she shared was one of sheer perseverance through tragedy. It turned out her maiden name was Haber. Anna had been born and raised in Dusseldorf, Germany, the daughter of Jewish bakers. The Nazi persecution of her family had begun in the late 1930s, the likes of which I had witnessed firsthand while in Berlin and surrounding cities. Anna and her family had been forcibly moved out of their apartment in Dusseldorf in August 1942 and into temporary living quarters with many other Jewish families just outside of Munich, Germany. They, along with hundreds of other Jews, had been forced to live in cramped quarters. They'd been told they would resettle in southern Poland. In the winter of 1943, at the age of nineteen, she, her two younger brothers, and her parents had been shipped by railcar to Auschwitz-Birkenau in Poland. The railcars had been so complete that the occupants could only stand; they'd had to sleep or use the bathroom where they stood.

At that point in her story, I heard keys in the apartment's front door lock. Seconds later, the door opened, and a tall German man, presumably Jonas, stood. My fingers were crossed that he would not be alarmed at another man being in his apartment while his wife cooked.

I stood and greeted him. "Jonas?"

He replied in perfect English, "Yes, I am Jonas. I assume you are Allen Voigt?"

"Yes," I said. "Thank you for inviting me into your home."

We shook hands, after which Jonas greeted Anna in the kitchen with a kiss on the cheek and a hug. He then came over and sat in a chair beside mine while Anna kept cooking. The delicious smell of the food reminded me of the fine German cooking I had enjoyed during my previous time in Berlin.

Jonas and I exchanged small talk, and soon, Anna told us that dinner was ready. Jonas and I joined Anna in the kitchen at a small table. Jonas grabbed a short bench from a back bedroom and placed it beside the table for me. The dinner Anna had prepared looked and smelled terrific and included bratwurst, sauerkraut, potatoes, carrots and an assortment of bread.

The conversation around the meal ranged from Jonas and Anna's passion for Germany to their utter contempt for the former Nazi party and everything associated with it. Jonas, being a former German soldier, had been forced to join the Nazi party back in 1941, but he'd despised it every second he had been a member of it. After we finished our meal, we sipped our wine and continued our conversation.

It had been early December 1943 when Anna and her family arrived at Auschwitz-Birkenau in Poland. They had been in their railcar for eight straight days, stopping only once to exit the train so that human waste could be cleaned away and dead bodies in the railcars could be removed. The people had then been forced back into the railcar. They had arrived at the camp in the middle of the night, but the German Shepherd dogs had still been out in full force. They'd barked loudly and helped corral the thousands of Jews getting off the railcars. Snow had fallen heavily, and the temperature had been well below freezing.

I told Anna and Jonas about my covert work at Auschwitz-Birkenau back in March of 1942. I explained to them that my job had been to scout the camp and gather intelligence, all the time posing as a construction worker while reporting all my findings directly back to President Roosevelt. I told them how, in March of 1942, when I had come upon the camp, I had found its sheer size intimidating. It looked like a small city in the middle of nowhere. What immediately caught my eye was a large sign in German over the main entrance that read, "Arbeit Macht Frei." *Work sets you free.*

I also told them I had met the camp's Commandant, Camp Commandant Rudolf. Despite his relatively short height, he'd been in his early forties and had a commanding presence. He had reviewed with several of us the details of the final construction phase of the adjoining camp, Auschwitz II-Birkenau. The reasons for the second phase of construction soon became apparent. The second phase of the camp was much larger than the first, evidently because Auschwitz was overrun. They had to do something to ease the congestion of Jews, as over 2,000 were arriving every day.

I explained to Anna and Jonas how I had worked extremely hard not to show my anger and desire to kill the camp Commandant where he sat that day. He had laughed as he discussed how other categories of prisoners, like gypsies, the mentally disabled, and Soviet and Polish prisoners of war were also arriving. The trains that delivered the Jews and other prisoners rolled right into the camp. The prisoners were unloaded from the railcars in which they had been imprisoned for several days. The Nazis unloaded the prisoners off the train, forced them to remove all their clothing in the cold weather, and then directed them to large rooms where they were told to shower. Once all the prisoners were inside, airtight doors were closed. The Nazis then dropped Zyklon-B tablets into pipes located inside the walls. As the tablets hit the water, they released cyanide gas, eventually filling the room. The occupants of the room breathed in the poisonous gas and died within seconds. Once the gas chamber grew silent from the screams of its occupants, the Nazis forced other prisoners to remove the bodies and place them in large crematorium ovens where the bodies were burned. The bodies had been burned as quickly as possible. I told Anna and Jonas that I had been sickened by the laughter of the camp Commandant during that conversation.

Once I had left the Commandant's office, I'd been escorted to a little room on the camp's perimeter that became my temporary residence. It was a small room with a wood-burning stove in the middle. A bathroom was shared by four other people in adjoining rooms.

Later, we were given a driving tour of the first phase of Auschwitz. I'd seen hundreds of prisoners wearing gray and white striped uniforms with a yellow star sewn on the left side of the shirt. Despite the snow that had covered the ground, none of the prisoners had worn coats. Most prisoners had been men, but I'd noticed a few women and young boys.

Our car had passed over the train tracks used to roll in the trains filled with prisoners. I'd noticed a train off to my left that was a recent arrival; smoke was still billowing out of its coal-burning engine. I had seen hundreds of Jews disembarking the railcars. A long line had formed, and camp personnel had split the newly arrived Jews into two lines going left and right. Families had been divided, leaving women and children screaming.

In the distance, grayish-colored smoke had drifted from the chimney of a large, white building. A terrible smell had permeated the car as the car had drawn near.

The German officer driving the car had noticed my reaction to the smell and hollered out, "That is the smell of burning Jews!"

As we continued through the camp, the smell had begun to dissipate, but new horrors awaited me. Upon our arrival at Auschwitz II-Birkenau, I'd seen a mound of naked bodies stacked twice as high as our car. The German officer told me that those piles meant that there were fewer Jews left in the world. The people had been gassed, and soon, any trace of them would be destroyed when their naked bodies were tossed into the nearby crematorium.

We had exited the car, and I'd followed the German officer toward the additional crematoriums under construction. We'd been asked to inspect the masonry work, checking for any cracks in the workmanship. We then inspected some of the newly constructed barracks that would house more Jews when they arrived. We counted bunks, some as high as four levels, and checked the flooring and plumbing. To wrap up the day, we were led through a brand-new gas chamber resembling a shower facility in any gymnasium locker room or military barracks. The only difference was that cyanide gas had come out of the showerheads instead of water.

I finished my story by recounting how I had killed many German soldiers late at night during my time at the camp and had buried their bodies in the nearby woods. I also shared with them how I'd helped three Jewish prisoners escape back to England so they could tell their stories about the Jewish holocaust.

Anna and Jonas were shocked at my experiences at Auschwitz. Before my arrival that day in Berlin, neither of them had heard much about my background.

We continued our conversation deep into the night. Jonas explained to me how, as a German soldier, he'd arrived at Auschwitz in July of 1943. His role had been to monitor the fences, patrolling both the inside and outside with a German Shepherd. He had done that for four months, learning every inch of Auschwitz and Auschwitz II-Birkenau. That knowledge, I found out, had later helped Anna escape.

By November of 1943, Jonas had been assigned the role of guarding the barracks where the female Jews were housed at night. He also made sure the Jews leaving the barracks in the morning were counted and that the same number returned later each night. The Jews housed in these barracks had been spared the gas chamber and forced to work outside the camp in local factories, mines, and farms.

By March 1944, Anna had long been separated from her family. Through various sources, she'd heard the grim news that her entire family had been sent through the gas chambers shortly after arriving at the camp. They had been selected for death due to their ages: her parents had been considered too old, and both her little brothers had been deemed too young. It had been devastating news to hear, and she'd had to bear that news while struggling for survival in the camp.

Jonas had been assigned the job of escorting the female Jews to their assigned work each day in April 1944. He, too, had become disgusted and appalled at the mass killing of the Jewish population. He'd noticed Anna in early April; even in her disheveled shape, she had drawn his attention. He had wanted to help her and her fellow female Jews survive. He told me that he had often slipped the female prisoner's extra food rations and water, giving up his meals so they could eat more.

The owner of one of the farms on which Anna and some of her fellow prisoners worked was sympathetic to the Jewish plight. His farm had supplied food to Auschwitz. That owner, Hans Weber, had felt comfortable enough to approach Jonas one day as he was guarding the women picking vegetables in the fields. Hans had observed Jonas for a few weeks and had seen both his compassion for the women and his fondness for Anna. After multiple conversations with Jonas, Hans had devised a plan to convince the Auschwitz camp commandant that he needed three Jewish women to remain permanently at his farm to help care for the house and tutor his three young children. Hans's wife had died just before the war broke out, and he had no one to help him with the farm or his children. With Jonas's help, Hans had arranged for Anna to be one of the three women chosen for that assignment. Anna had grown fond of Jonas and had been excited to be able to spend time with Hans' children, as they'd reminded her of her two brothers.

By the time the Soviet Army liberated Auschwitz in late January 1945, Anna had been working at Han's farm for a while. She had regained much of her lost weight, and her hair had grown full again. When Jonas had been told that the Soviets were near the camp, he had gone to Hans's farm and burned his German uniform and worked as a day laborer alongside Anna. The Soviets had gone through the farm like ants, but they had mostly been courteous, grateful to have solid food. Jonas had heard how the Soviets had burned villages and raped women as they marched west, but he had not let anything happen to Anna.

Germany had surrendered in May 1945, but Anna had possessed no family or home to which she could return. Jonas's parents, who lived fifty miles west of Berlin, were also sympathetic to the Jews. Their home was in the American-controlled section of Germany, so Jonas and Anna had decided to make the arduous journey there.

During this entire evening of conversation, I could not stop wondering what this couple's connection could be to my assignment.

The evening ended with Jonas and Anna answering that lingering question. The answer I got was surprising and unexpected.

CHAPTER 2

Numbered Days

"The object of war is not to die for your country
but to make the other bastard die for his."
General George S. Patton, Jr.

The possible whereabouts of the escaped Nazis I was assigned to locate and kill were ultimately linked through Jonas' mother, Maritza Fischer. She had been a secretary to German General Hans Krebs. General Krebs had been with Hitler during his last days and spent considerable time in Hitler's bunker up until the day Krebs killed himself when the Soviet Army descended on Berlin.

Krebs had left behind his entire briefcase and some personal effects. Out of respect for her boss, Maritza had taken them with her when she'd escaped the bunker. Somehow, through the chaos and turmoil in Berlin, she found her way home and back to her husband. Maritza's original plan had been to return Krebs's personal items to his family, but she'd had no way of knowing where they were in the city or even if they were still alive.

Soviet shelling had been consistent day and night. There had been no power in her small home, but candles had provided enough light for Maritza to organize General Krebs's paperwork to occupy her mind. Going through the various pages, she noticed a piece of paper with Hitler's signature and the official Nazi seal on it. The paper listed twenty high-ranking Nazis who Hitler had authorized to flee Germany and keep the

Nazi Party alive and organized. Walter Rauff, Ekerd Jacobsen, Rickert Pagel, and Warren Weltzin were among the twenty names.

Maritza, like many other German citizens, had been directly opposed to what Germany had become under the leadership of Adolf Hitler. She'd served under General Krebs for over ten years and witnessed the deterioration of Germany and its inhumane treatment of the Jews. Because of her direct service to General Krebs, she possessed intimate knowledge of the high-ranking Nazis on the list and their roles during the war. Maritza had decided to provide this valuable information to the American Army, which had arrived in Berlin in early July 1945 and occupied the southwest section of Berlin near her home.

That wealth of verbal and written information provided by Maritza had made it to General Eisenhower's desk and later to President Harry Truman. That was the link I was looking for; I finally understood why I was sharing a meal with Jonas and Anna.

That evening, after a satisfying meal and stimulating conversation, Jonas showed me where I was to sleep for the evening, and possibly longer, if my temporary apartment in Berlin could not be secured quickly.

When I looked at my watch, it was 2:17 a.m. Berlin time. I was dog-tired, both mentally and physically, from the long trip. I was also frustrated that I had to be back in Berlin and that the war was technically not over for me just yet. I knew my German enemy well, as I had spent so much time in Berlin before and during the war, fighting them aggressively on all fronts. It was May 1946, however, and I fought to stay motivated and engaged for yet another assignment.

The following day, Jonas and I had breakfast at a nearby café that had managed to stay open amongst the debris in the city. Unbeknownst to me, a third party, General Ernest Harmon, was to join us that morning for breakfast. I had heard of him but never met him before. At the war's end, he had been appointed commanding General of the American sector in Berlin.

While the three of us ate outside the café at a small table that morning, worn-down and tattered Berlin residents mulled about the street, pulling carts behind them and carrying baskets as they searched for food and items to sustain them for another day. It was a sad sight to see. I thought to myself how incredible it was that one man, Adolf Hitler, had driven the German population into such chaos and despair.

After a few bites of breakfast, I said, "General Harmon, congratulations on your Berlin appointment, Sir."

He smiled in my direction and said, "Thank you, Allen. It's a pleasure to meet you officially. I was briefed on the missions you have completed before and during World War II. I was also given some of the detailed reports you gave President Roosevelt and other members of senior military leadership during that timeframe. Those previous accomplishments are why you were handpicked for this new assignment."

"Thank you for your vote of confidence," I said. "Honestly, I never thought I'd be back in Berlin, let alone coordinating my next assignment."

"The end of the war here in Berlin was a crazy time," the General said.

"I wasn't happy when General Eisenhower allowed the Soviet Army to occupy Berlin. I'm worried the next decision - to annex Germany and Berlin itself - could cause ramifications for future generations."

I thought for a second. "After being imprisoned in a Japanese submarine for weeks, I would've liked for the Americans to take Berlin."

After some deliberation, Jonas looked at me and said, "Allen, I only met you last night, but based on our conversation, I feel confident enough to ask you this. Would you mind sharing with us what your last few weeks of the war were like being captured by the Japanese? I've never met a Japanese person before, and the entire Pacific portion of the war fascinates me. We were given very little news on the activity there."

I looked at the General, seeking his permission to share my story. He nodded his approval. I didn't understand why Jonas was interested, and I wasn't in the mood to revisit that time, but because he and his wife had been so generous to me the previous night, I felt obligated. As the General and Jonas ate breakfast, I put my fork down, gathered my thoughts, and shared my story of the last few weeks of the war. I gave them both a little background first on my connection with General Donovan and Captain Givens before getting into the details.

"By June 20, 1944, I was back in England. I met with Captain Givens and General Donovan, who expressed their appreciation to me regarding my recent mission to France and gave me a full debrief on the success of Operation Overlord. I was relieved that the beaches I'd identified turned out to be the right ones. My relief was short-lived, however, as I was immediately briefed on my next mission.

"My briefing lasted for the next two days. I would be heading back to the Pacific to kill a Japanese General who had been assigned to shore up the defenses on some godforsaken island in the Pacific called Iwo Jima. The day after my briefing, June 23, I prepared to leave England and officially left on June 24. I spent the last week of June and most of July traveling back to the Pacific theater of war and the Japanese. "America and its allies had made much progress fighting the Japanese in the last two-and-a-half years I had been back in Europe. The island-hopping strategy was working. Since the battle of Guadalcanal, the Marines, with the support of the Army and Navy, had worked their way up to the Mariana Islands and were close to flushing the Japanese out of the Philippines. My assignment was to report to Saipan, the largest island in the Marianas. In June of 1944, the Marines and Army's 27th Infantry Division landed on Saipan and drove out the Japanese Army. Thousands of Americans had died during that month-long campaign. The island was vital for the Army Air Corps to use as a staging area for bombers, specifically the newest American bomber, the B-29. We were close enough now to Japan to use this long-range bomber to force the Japanese into submission.

"During my trip back to the Pacific, I met a lot of young American military personnel who were headed off to war for the first time. I was thirty-six years old, twice the age of some men I traveled with. When I entered the Army in 1926, some of these men had just been born. The younger men peppered me with questions about my long tenure in the Army. Considering my secret position in the OSS, I answered the questions as best I could.

"I hitched a ride on a brand-new B-29, the *Enola Gay*, flying from Seattle, Washington, to Honolulu, Hawaii. After a few days in Hawaii, I continued to the island of Saipan on that same B-29. It was a beautiful, fully pressurized plane manufactured at the Boeing aircraft plant in Seattle. The *Enola Gay* touched down on Saipan on August 3. I was assigned to an Army officer's tent near Obyan Beach, on the island's southern tip. As beautiful as the beach was, the devastation on the island was staggering. The Marines and 27th Infantry had landed on the island from the mid-western shores and flushed out the Japanese from the southern and central parts of the island. They then pushed north and completed the job after a few weeks. Everywhere I looked, I saw burned-out tanks, trucks, and buildings. The smell of rotting Japanese corpses permeated the air. The Navy Seabees were pushing the Japanese bodies into mass graves and burying them as quickly as they could.

"I spent the next seven months on the island. To keep my body in shape and my mind sharp, I joined the 27th Army Infantry soldiers, who were flushing out the remaining Japanese hidden in caves on the island. During that time, during the Saipan campaign, I received word that I'd lost a cousin from New York. I located his grave on the northwest corner of the island in the 2nd Marine Division's cemetery. My cousin's name was Thomas Staines, and he had been a member of the Army's 27th Infantry. I had not known him well, but he had been only twenty-four years old when he'd died on June 29, 1944, about the midway point of the Saipan campaign.

"In late December, I was directed by my OSS superiors to begin training for a nighttime encroachment onto a beach. I was introduced to the Navy's Frogmen, officially called Underwater Demolition Teams, or UDT. They taught me how to swim in the ocean using a new underwater device called an aqualung. It allowed me to swim underwater for long distances at various depths. That was a whole new experience and helped me pass the time. Within a few weeks, I could leave the safety of a Navy vessel anchored three miles offshore and swim to the beach in less than one hour.

"The military brass showed up on Saipan in early January 1945. The final planning phases of the invasion of Iwo Jima were underway. Due to my rank and position in the OSS and my ultimate mission to the island, I was told the details of the invasion, which was set for February 19, 1945. I was to wait in reserve off the island in a submarine until they determined the approximate location of a Japanese General in charge of the Japanese troops.

"The Marines that were to invade Iwo Jima left primarily from Hawaii. I trained with the UDT team and left Saipan on February 13. We boarded a Navy submarine, the USS *Redfin*, during the early morning hours.

The sailors on the *Redfin* were not quite sure what to think of us when we boarded the sub with all our diving equipment.

"Our travel to Iwo Jima took four days. We surfaced off the island, surrounded by numerous other Navy vessels of all shapes and sizes. The Navy had been shelling the island from their large battleships anchored nearby. Each time a shell was fired, the entire sub shook. It was a sound like nothing I had ever heard before. In addition, the Marine and Navy single-engine fighters were flying over the island, strafing and dropping ordinances at will.

"Late in the afternoon on February 18, the Navy frogmen I had trained with left the sub and surveyed the beaches around the southern end of Iwo Jima; this was the designated landing spot for the Marines. The divers removed various mines and obstacles, clearing a path for the landcraft. They returned to the *Redfin* late in the evening.

"The invasion of Iwo Jima began on February 19. From my vantage point on the *Redfin*, I watched in amazement as the landing craft proceeded to the beach, which was black as a piece of coal. I heard bursts of explosions and small weapons fire coming from the beaches. I had never witnessed anything like that during my time in the Army. The courage it took for those Marines to take those beaches was genuinely astounding.

"The next day, the *Redfin* submerged and began its scouting mission around Iwo Jima. The sub patrolled the entire island seven times to ensure no other Japanese Navy ships were dropping off reinforcements on the island's backside; none came.

"I was getting restless. I had not had active engagement against the enemy in over eight months. I had trained hard, and I was ready to reengage and kill some Japs. My time finally came on the evening of March 22. The battle raged on Iwo Jima, and the Marines were getting impatient. Thousands of Marines had died in the now five-week-old battle.

"The plan was to essentially cut off the head of the snake so the body would die. I was shown a picture of a Japanese General commanding the troops on Iwo Jima and told he was on the island's southeastern corner. I was not even given his name, only a picture. I had six hours to find my target, eliminate him, and return to the *Redfin*. The sub surfaced to periscope depth, and I exited it from a flooded rear hatch using my aqualung equipment.

"It was so dark in the water that night; there was no way I could swim underwater and keep my sense of direction. The water was frigid, and my rubber wetsuit didn't do an excellent job keeping it out. I surfaced and saw the island off to my right, approximately one mile away. Explosions lit the night here and there on the island, and a few campfires glowed on the very backside of the island.

"I swam underwater roughly fifty yards and resurfaced, repeating this until I reached the beach. I pulled myself up on the black sand and crawled to rocks near a cliff. I pulled off my diving equipment and hid it behind the rocks. My attire at this point consisted of only shorts and a t-shirt. I also had some Army boots tied around my neck. I had no choice but to put on the wet boots. As I climbed up the rock face, the only weapon on me was my trusty knife, sharpened especially for this mission. The climb up the cliff to the General's location was uneventful, and when I reached the top, I quickly hid behind some large rocks.

"I listened intently for any Japanese. It did not take long before I heard Japanese soldiers off to my immediate right. I worked my way around to their location. Two soldiers lay on the ground with apparent wounds to their upper bodies and heads. I carefully eased up behind them and quickly killed the first Jap by slitting his throat from one ear to the other. As he bled out, I put my arm around the other Jap's head and neck and placed my bloody knife close to his left eye. He was in no shape to fight back, so I knew I had the advantage.

"I whispered to him in his native tongue, 'Where is the General?' "He didn't answer. I asked a second time, and still, he refused to answer.

I pressed my knife slowly into his left eye and muffled his scream with my other hand. He then gave me what I wanted, telling me the General was about fifty yards behind me in a cave. I asked how many soldiers were with him, and he said only two. I felt confident that he had spoken the truth, so I slit his throat and left him to die.

"I worked my way up the sloping backside of the island, searching for the cave. The island looked as I imagined hell to look. Everything was on fire, trees had their tops blown off, and there were no signs of life anywhere. Large bomb craters dotted the landscape, which was littered with the bodies of dead Japs. I could hardly breathe due to the smell of rotting flesh and smoke.

"I finally found the cave, but no guards were posted nearby, which aroused my suspicion. I slowly and carefully approached. I didn't hear any voices, but what I did hear surprised me. Coming from deep in the cave was the sound of music, a Japanese song. It sounded like Japanese children singing about the brave Japanese men fighting on Iwo Jima. Easing into the cave, I spotted a Japanese rifle propped against the wall. I confirmed that it was loaded and ready to fire. Because I was counting on three Japs to be in the cave, I figured a rifle was my best option, considering the tight quarters.

"The music got louder as I neared the rear of the cave. I also started to see some illumination, so I knew I was getting close. I overheard three men speaking in Japanese about committing *hara-kiri*, a Japanese ritual for suicide that they considered honorable. The Japanese reportedly refused to surrender, feeling it was a disgrace to do so, choosing to kill themselves rather than surrender. I remained out of sight, and in less than a minute, I heard the first Jap gasp and shout, 'Long Live the Emperor!' I then heard another Jap do the same. I'd had enough. I knew they were committing *hara-kiri*, and I wasn't going to let the Japanese General die with honor. I sprinted around the corner with my Jap rifle raised. The General was sitting on his knees, holding a huge knife. He was startled to see me standing there in my shorts and wet boots. Before he could move, I fired, striking him right between the eyes. The backside of his head blew out, and he collapsed onto the dirt floor. The radio nearby was still playing; I fired another shot and silenced it.

I had been instructed to kill the Japanese General and remove his body from the island, the idea being that the remaining Japanese troops might believe he had deserted them. I laid the rifle down and dragged the dead General out of the damp cave. Upon exiting the cave, I picked him up and slung him over my shoulders. I carried him down to the rocky edge of the cliff face and unceremoniously threw him over the edge and onto the beach below. I then climbed down the rocks and located my diving equipment. I put on my diving flippers, oxygen tanks, and mask. Finally, I filled the General's uniform with hand-sized rocks that would force him to sink into the cold, dark Pacific Ocean.

Using all my strength, I pulled the body out into the water with me. Once we cleared the beach, the body immediately began to sink. I held his body up by wrapping my right arm around his neck. Blood was still oozing from his head, or what was left of it, as I dragged him further out into the water.

"I pulled him out about two hundred yards offshore and let him sink, watching as he disappeared into the blackness. I immediately looked for the familiar red light on the sub's conning tower and located it approximately half a mile away. I swam toward it, mainly on the surface, and upon reaching the *Redfin*, I tapped on the outer hull three times to signal to the sailors that I was back. The sub surfaced, and I climbed up a metal side ladder. The conning tower hatch opened, and a young Navy sailor greeted me.

"As I removed my diving equipment and handed it to him, he asked, 'Did you have a good swim, Sir?'

"I told him, 'As a matter of fact, I did, sailor. Mission accomplished.'

"I followed him back into the sub, and the *Redfin* returned beneath the waves. I detailed my mission to the sub's Captain, who transmitted the information via Morse code to my OSS superiors in Hawaii. A few hours later, the instructions from Hawaii were for me to remain on the sub and await further orders.

The war against the Japanese soon turned in our favor, and fewer missions required the OSS. The *Redfin* was instructed to go to Japan and survey Nagasaki, a city on the southern end of Japan.

Word reached the *Redfin* on March 26 that the Japs on Iwo Jima had officially surrendered, and the island was secured. The B-29 bombers, for the first time, had an island they could land on in the event they encountered damage or mechanical problems on their return from bombing cities in Japan.

I spent the next five months with the *Redfin* and its crew. The UDT divers were still on board, as well. I always stayed in the sub during those five months. The only respite I got was when the sub surfaced each day to take on fresh air, at which point I walked the sub's deck. We found out in May 1945 that the Germans had surrendered in Europe. Only the Japanese were left, and we were intent on making their surrender happen soon. We were all eager to get home.

By late July, the *Redfin* had successfully navigated Japan's southern tip and eastern shores. The sub managed to avoid the mines that the Japs had laid in the bay near Nagasaki. On the evening of July 30, 1945, the *Redfin* got within five hundred yards of the port of Nagasaki. The sub surfaced to periscope depth, and we all took turns looking at the city's lights. Most of us wondered why we were there. Later, I found out about the atomic bomb that we dropped on the city.

Word came down that the Navy wanted the UDT frogmen to plant explosives on as many of the Japanese Navy destroyers anchored in the bay as possible. I asked if I could join them. It took little to convince them since word had spread about the details of my Iwo Jima mission.

The same exercise that deployed me from the sub at Iwo Jima was repeated for the UDT frogmen and me. Nine of us exited the sub that night, each carrying magnetic explosives that could be attached to a ship's outer hull and set with a timer.

"Not long after we exited the sub, the UDT frogmen had gotten about one hundred yards ahead of me when, out of nowhere, a Japanese patrol boat cut the water between us. They opened fire from their deck machine guns and sprayed the water where I had last seen the frogmen. The firing continued for over a minute, and I assumed the worst. I looked back, and the *Redfin* was gone, having escaped beneath the waves to avoid any depth charges from the Japanese patrol boat. The information the sub secured over the last five months could not be compromised. I was on my own, floating in the port of Nagasaki. I swam over to a Japanese destroyer and clung to the side. I bobbed up and down, cold from the water and the coolness of the night.

The Japanese patrol boat left the area a short time later. After it pulled away, I saw my American brothers floating in the water, some face down and others face up. All were dead.

I had limited options for the first time in my military career. I had to get out of the water, but if I stepped foot on Japanese soil, I was a dead man. There was nowhere to hide. After bobbing in the water for over two hours, I was preparing to take my chances on land when I saw a submarine surface conning tower in the middle of the bay. It looked like the *Redfin* was back. I immediately swam in the direction of the sub's conning tower. As the sub surfaced, I saw it was not the *Redfin* but a Japanese sub with the identification of *I-401*. My heart sank, and I promptly turned to swim in the opposite direction.

"Immediately, I heard the crack of gunfire, and bullets pierced the water all around me.

"I stopped swimming and heard a voice shout in Japanese behind me, 'Halt! Swim toward me now.'

"I turned around and saw a Japanese sailor staring down the length of a machine gun at me. I could sink beneath the waves, figuring I could swim a mile underwater with my diving equipment and escape. I placed my mask on my face, but the Jap sailor immediately fired off another volley of bullets in my direction. I knew then that I had to follow his instructions if I wanted to survive.

"I swam toward the Japanese sub. I removed my diving equipment and climbed aboard the submarine by way of a metal ladder, my anxiety increasing with each step. Once I reached the deck, the sailor motioned me to enter the sub through the open hatch. I placed my legs down into the hatch first, at which point he took the butt of his machine gun and cracked it over my head. I blacked out, and my body fell into the sub.

"I woke up hours later to find myself chained to a torpedo rack at the rear of the sub. The compartment was dark and damp, with puddles of salt water on the floor. A small red light shone about ten yards before me, illuminating a door hatch. For two whole days, I saw no one and received no food or water.

"On my third day of capture, a Jap sailor awakened me with a kick to the head. He held a metal cup in one hand and a rice ball in the other. After throwing the rice ball on the floor, he handed me a cup of water. I worked around my handcuffs and got the cup up to my mouth. The water was not salty, but it was not fresh, either, meaning it was most likely recycled salt water. Regardless, it helped quench my thirst. The sailor abruptly took the cup and left the torpedo room, slamming the door behind him. I couldn't reach the rice scattered on the floor.

"Over the next two weeks, I was treated a little better, with a few balls of rice placed in my mouth. I slept a few hours each day and tried to keep my mind sharp by speaking to myself in German and Japanese, recounting as many memories as possible. I struggled to keep track of how many days, I had been handcuffed in the enemy sub. My mind wandered, and I wondered if I would ever see home again.

"The days passed.

"One day, the hatch to the torpedo room opened suddenly with a resounding clang. A brilliant shaft of light blinded me, and I blinked rapidly, desperately hoping my eyes would adjust. I recognized the outline of a Japanese Lieutenant walking hurriedly through the door towards me. He stopped directly in front of me, knelt, and silently began to unlock my handcuffs. After the cuffs fell away, he turned to the locks on the chains holding my feet. For what was now sixteen days, the cold steel bonds had held me prisoner there in the rear compartment of the Japanese submarine, and I heaved a shaky sigh of relief as the chains and cuffs were released.

"The stern face of the Japanese Lieutenant told me he was distraught as he impatiently motioned for me to stand. I had lain in an awkward position for over two weeks, so it was tough to move, let alone stand. Nevertheless, I gathered my legs beneath me and prepared to defend myself from what I expected would be an execution. When I rose, the Lieutenant placed his hand on his semi-automatic pistol but did not remove it from its leather holster. Instead, he gave me a belligerent shove toward the hatch door, where another Japanese sailor awaited us. I stepped through the narrow hatch with an immense feeling of relief, but I remained on my guard as we proceeded down the small corridor.

"I was astonished when I saw twenty or more Japanese sailors lined up at attention on either side of the narrow passageway. As I walked forward with the Japanese Lieutenant directly behind me, several of the sailors cursed at me in Japanese and spat at me. I was motioned over to the sub's cunning tower, and we paused momentarily as the Lieutenant and the submarine's Captain spoke in calm voices. I glanced over surreptitiously at the sub's depth gauges. The two men concluded their brief conversation and bowed to each other, with neither man looking in my direction. The Japanese crew did not know I had understood their conversations throughout my internment. I grasped the whole meaning of the readings on the depth gauges and the exchange between the Lieutenant and the Captain. I knew that the sub was rising rapidly. I also knew the subject of their conversation, which meant we would soon be exiting the sub, and I would be released. My mind raced, and my heart began to beat even faster.

"A Japanese sailor walked up the ladder to open the outer hatch. I watched him intently as he turned the dial and slowly opened the hatch. I was jolted backward by a sudden rush of cool air, starkly contrasting the humidity I had endured in the sub. Saltwater dripped in, splashing my face. Bright rays of sunshine lit up the sub's interior, and I squinted, looking up at a brilliant blue sky. The Captain shook my shoulder and briskly motioned me to proceed up the ladder after the Japanese Sub-Lieutenant. Even though I had overheard that I was to be released, I remained on my guard to defend myself if they decided to shoot me topside and throw me overboard. I exited the sub and was momentarily blinded by the sunlight. I gulped down the fresh, salty air.

"As my eyes continued to adjust, the Captain exited the sub behind me and motioned me to the back of the vessel. I set my shoulders with grim determination and started toward the back. Even though I had understood the conversations, I still expected the worst to happen.

"Suddenly, my eyes adjusted entirely to the sunlight, and my vision cleared. I looked around and was astounded by what I saw. The Japanese sub had surfaced behind a mighty flotilla of American Navy vessels. I saw battleships and destroyers, heavy and light cruisers. There were frigates and even submarines. The glorious American flag flew on each vessel, snapping proudly in the wind. It was at that point that I knew my life was spared.

"The Japanese submarine Captain turned to me and, speaking in clear English, said, 'You are free to go.'

"To his surprise, I thanked him in Japanese. 'Domo.'

"The Captain then directed my attention to a small inflated life raft that had been prepared for me and was now tied to the submarine's side. I carefully worked my way down the slippery rungs of the small ladder on the submarine's side and eased myself into the raft. I was cut loose from the vessel by the same Lieutenant who had just moments earlier released me from handcuffs and chains. I hastily picked up the two oars left in the raft and rowed toward the nearest American Navy Ship. I estimated the closest one was approximately four hundred yards away. My progress was painstakingly slow.

"My only sustenance for the last sixteen days had been a few cups of water, a few small balls of rice, and a slice of bread. I was tired and weak. I managed to row farther away from the Japanese sub, and as I did, I looked up and noticed a single white flag secured to the top of its cunning tower. I tried to increase my pace, but my legs and arms protested with every single stroke. The wind was against me, and the waves were choppy, but the sky was mostly clear. I turned my head around constantly to check my progress. I tried hard to keep my course steady as I fought through the waves. The Navy ship got closer and closer. After an agonizing forty-five minutes, I finally reached the starboard side of the anchored destroyer, the USS *Nicholas DE-449.*

"When my raft bumped up against the destroyer's side, a Navy seaman peered over the railing and called down, 'You look like an American, but what are you doing in that raft?'

"Before I could answer, he said, 'Are you a pilot? You must have been adrift for a long time if you were shot down!'

"I answered him with my dry throat in as loud a voice as I could. 'I am Lt. Allen Voigt. I'm an Office of Strategic Services member, and I've just been released from the Japanese submarine *I-401.*'

"The astonished seaman quickly directed me to a set of collapsible stairs lowered for me on the destroyer's port side by some other sailors observing our conversation. I gingerly got up from the raft and started climbing slowly up the stairs, letting the Japanese raft drift away. A crowd of sailors gathered to watch my ascent. When I wearily stepped aboard the deck of the *Nicholas*, the sailors silently took in my tattered uniform, bare feet, and matted beard.

"I looked around and finally asked the group a question. 'What's going on here? Where are we? What is the date?'

"From the back of the crowd, a loud voice shouted, 'We're in Tokyo Bay! The Japs have surrendered!'

"Then, from another direction, someone bellowed, 'It's Sunday, September 2!'

"I looked at the faces around me in astonishment. I couldn't believe what I was hearing. Then, from over the ship's loudspeakers came an announcement that was perhaps the most surreal of all.

"'You all are about to witness the Japanese surrender to General MacArthur."

For the next five hours, the sailors of the *Nicholas* and I had a front-row seat to the surrender of the Japanese. We congratulated each other and gave each other high fives and hugs. The war was finally over.

By this time in the conversation, I was done talking about it. I picked my fork up and finished eating; by now, what was the rest of my cold breakfast? Jonas and General Harmon were stunned by what I had just shared.

As I sipped my recently refilled coffee, Jonas spoke. "Allen, I know now why you were picked for this assignment. I don't know the specifics, but it involves hunting my fellow former soldiers. Let me make one thing clear. They are not the German soldier I was taught to be, but brutal and evil men who committed terrible atrocities and killed millions of innocent people during the holocaust. I hope you find every one of them and send them to the deepest corner of hell."

By then, we had all finished our breakfast. General Harmon asked me to join him at his command office to learn the specifics of my next assignment. An Army jeep picked us up outside the café, and as we rode through the battered streets of Berlin, I recognized some of the locations I had frequented during my time there in the early 1930s. When we passed Brandenburg Gate and the Reichstag, I was staggered by the destruction both structures had taken during the war.

The defined sectioning of the city of Berlin had yet to be finalized, but our drive took us to the city's southwest corner. We passed by the Bendlerstrasse, where the German Army had been headquartered. This area was called the Tiergarten and, in its former days, had been a beautiful section of Berlin.

It was near this building where the German Colonel, Clause von Stauffenberg, along with many others, had been executed in July 1944. They had failed to overthrow Hitler when they'd staged an assassination attempt at Hitler's Wolf Lair in eastern Poland.

Our Jeep stopped at a building about a block from that original headquarters. We walked up the steps of the five-story building to General Harmon's office, and I sat in a chair facing his desk. The General was an intimidating soldier. He spoke with a deep, gravelly voice that demanded attention. For over an hour, he recounted the details of his graduation from West Point in 1917, participation in World War I, and reorganization of the Army's 2nd Armored Division after their humiliating defeat in North Africa in February of 1943.

While I appreciated his service and his story-telling, I was impatient to learn the details about my upcoming mission and how I was to find the four escaped Nazis. Although I was weary, I was also very passionate about exterminating the Nazis. I just needed to get started.

After over an hour of General Harmon going on about his service record, I finally interrupted him. "General Harmon, may I be so bold, Sir, as to ask when I may begin to eliminate these escaped Nazis? I've served in the United States Army for over twenty years, but I am tired of war. While I'm eager and willing to conduct this next mission, after that, I'm done. How do I get started?"

After a long pause, General Harmon looked up at me and said, "Captain Voigt, I respect your position. I, too, am tired of war and its demands. Let me cut to the chase, then. You'll spend the next six weeks here in Berlin learning all you can about the Nazis you'll be hunting. You'll be partnered with a group of Germans comprising civilians and the former Wehrmacht. Collectively, this group has the most intimate knowledge about these Nazi bastards. They know about their land holdings in Germany and abroad, family ties, habits, and possible locations."

"Thank you, Sir," I said.

We spent the rest of the day reviewing the names and locations of the German team members with whom I would be working. I discovered I would be living in a small, furnished apartment down the street from General Harmon's office.

After our meeting, General Harmon and I grabbed dinner nearby, and a young Army Private escorted me to my apartment. I felt better and slept well that night.

The following day, I rose early and grabbed breakfast at a nearby café. I then headed out to meet my new German contacts across the city. The team was not together in one location; that would have been too easy.

I assumed the reason for having the team members spread across the city was to avoid suspicion and to keep my activities covert. Thousands of Nazi loyalists were still spread throughout the city, and the last thing we wanted was for a sympathetic ear to get word of our plans to one of the escaped Nazis, allowing him to change locations or identities again.

All but one of my meeting locations was on the Western side of Berlin. The Eastern side had been practically wiped off the map during the Soviet advance in late April and early May of 1945. Berlin was completely different from how it had been during my previous time there. Most of the buildings were gutted completely. Many residents lived in makeshift camps and in the city's subway system. Most of the city's rail system had been damaged in bombing raids, leaving the subways open for residential shelter.

The next six weeks were long; I thought they would never end. I spent the better part of each day reading and rereading each escaped Nazi's biography, from his birth to the end of the war. The biographies included the names of the men's parents, spouses, children, and lovers, their cities and countries of birth, where they had grown up, schooling when they joined the military, where they had served, and their last known location.

I took the details I had been provided a step further, though. I sought information on those who had served under these men, their leadership style, and any other personal traits that might give me a head start on finding them.

My six weeks back in Berlin finally came to an end. I was assigned four of the infamous escaped Nazis. Their days were numbered.

CHAPTER 3

Faceless Man

"It is well that war is so terrible, otherwise we should grow too fond of it.
Robert E. Lee

My six weeks of research in Berlin pointed to one area of the world as the most likely hiding place for my targets: South America. Chile, Argentina, Bolivia, Brazil, Uruguay, and Venezuela were all sympathetic to the Nazis, and records showed all had provided a haven to them. Those countries also had been favorite vacation destinations for the German people for years, with many Germans permanently relocating there.

I would start my mission by going to Argentina. It was rumored in Berlin that Hitler had escaped his bunker via a system of vast tunnels under the Reich Chancellery and made his way to Berlin's Tempelhof Airport. Many felt he had flown to Spain and traveled to South America via a German submarine. I did not believe these rumors, nor did the American military. The Soviet Army's accounts of finding his burned body outside his Berlin bunker were well-documented. Many of the faithful Nazis inside Hitler's bunker on the last days of the war had witnessed his dead body being carried outside, along with the dead body of his mistress, Eva Braun.

The four Nazis I had personally been assigned, Walter Rauff, Ekerd Jacobsen, Rickert Pagel, and Warren Weltzin, would be hunted by me for as long as it took. My orders were clear: find them and eliminate them. Their crimes against the Jews and other minority groups had been brutal.

On June 21, 1946, I left Berlin on a flight to Rome, Italy, but not before changing into civilian clothes. I didn't want to risk being seen in my United States military uniform in the event I encountered one of my targets. In my military career, I had probably dressed more in civilian clothes than military uniforms due to my undercover operations. Clothing for my upcoming trip to South America was okay, though, as I had purchased a few outfits in Berlin.

My assigned route included several flights on American military aircraft. Those flights would take me to Casablanca, off the west coast of Africa. I would board a French ship, the S.S. *Athos II*, which would take war refugees to South America for resettling. My goal was to assimilate with this group and look for leads on my four Nazis. The refugees traveling to South America would be from different countries, economic situations, and walks of life. I was told they had been vetted thoroughly, but there was still a risk that the group could harbor Nazi sympathizers.

After six long flights, I landed at night in Casablanca. My entire time in the Army, I had never traveled to Africa. However, my time in the city would be short, as my designated ship was due to leave port in two days. I checked into a small hotel in the middle of downtown Casablanca.

My overwhelming concern was my inability to speak Spanish, the predominant language in South America. I had never been unable to speak the local language on a mission.

The following day, I toured Casablanca by foot and by cab. The city was a central military hub for the Navy and the Army during the war. Significant portions of Operation Torch took off from Casablanca, allowing the American and British Armies to work through Sicily and Italy. Remnants of tanks, aircraft, and military supplies remained, but I saw no American military personnel.

The sunset that night was breathtaking, with orange, red, and purple streaks melting into each other across the sky. I missed Alice and had not spoken with her since leaving Fort Meade weeks earlier. The phone lines in Germany needed to be expanded and more reliable. I had not seen a phone in the twenty-four hours since arriving in Casablanca.

The following morning, I secured my ticket and boarded the *Athos II*. It was scheduled to arrive in the port of Buenos Aires on July 11, 1946.

The French flag waved briskly in the wind on the ship's stern. Seeing the flag as I walked up the ship's gangplank brought back memories of my time in France during the war.

The German occupation of France had lasted for years. For the last half of 1943 and the first few months of 1944, other OSS agents and I had run over thirty missions into occupied France and Belgium. The dangerous missions had been the same each time: to parachute in and be ferried out by boat across the English Channel. I'd infiltrated several German HQ offices and even secured a German officer's uniform after killing its owner in a dimly lit alley in Paris, France.

The information I obtained during those missions had been invaluable to the planning of Operation Overlord. The Germans, under the watchful eye of General Rommel, had secured the entire coast of France with pillboxes, anti-aircraft guns, and hundreds of tanks and personnel. German troop movements had clearly shown they expected an Allied invasion somewhere on the coast of France.

According to the information I had obtained in the German HQ offices, the Germans had not been faring well against the Soviet Union in Eastern Europe. They'd lost thousands of men each day. The Allied forces had been bombing Germany night and day. In March 1944, I'd watched as hundreds of American B-17 bombers flew overhead on their way to Germany, nearly blocking out the sun.

When I thought back to all the time I'd spent in Germany before the war, recalling the people I had met and the places I had visited, what struck me the most were the arrogance of the German people and their inhumane treatment of the Jews. Germany was reaping what they had sown.

In May 1944, I'd attended two weeks of closed-door meetings in England at a secret location. Generals Donovan and Eisenhower had both attended the entire two weeks for the final planning phases of Operation Overlord. The date of the invasion had been set for June 5, 1944. The information I'd provided to General Eisenhower and his staff had shown that the Normandy Beaches, located between the French cities of Cherbourg and Le Havre, were undoubtedly the best beaches for an Allied invasion. I'd seen pillboxes and gun emplacements along the beaches, but that location had appeared to be the best place to land men and heavy equipment. We'd known that German troop movements leaned toward the beaches closer to Calais, France, where they'd assumed the Allied forces would land. Based on my observations, the Normandy Beaches could be taken in under two days.

On June 2, I'd met with my superior, Lt. Colonel Yates, who had filled me in on my next assignment: jumping with the 101st Airborne into occupied France on the eve of the invasion. My role would be to assist the airborne troops as much as I could with navigation and to serve as an interpreter when German soldiers were captured. I had questioned the legitimacy of my role at the time, however. The 101st already had interpreters, and I knew they had studied the exact maps I had over the previous year. They hadn't needed my assistance.

The conversation continued, and the real purpose of my jump became clear. I was to hitch a ride back into occupied France and eliminate a high-ranking German officer. Upon the initial landing, I would offer navigation and translation services. Still, I would then take off and hunt down the German officer in the 12th SS Panzer Division, General Rudolf Fritz. The information I'd given General Donovan and Lt. Colonel Yates during my recent missions to France was that the 12th SS Panzer Division was one of the leading German Panzer divisions in and around Normandy. We expected the Germans to be confused immediately after the Normandy landings, and it was my responsibility to cause even more chaos by taking out one of their key officers. Once my mission was complete, I would hook up with the 101st Airborne near Caen, France. I was to allow the 101st to be the tip of the spear and do my best to keep up and stay alive.

I had spent the weekend in Devon, England, at Upottery Airfield with the 101st Airborne. Only a few of the senior offices knew my mission. The enlisted soldiers were told I was there to assist with navigation and interpretation. My short time with the 101st was special. None of the 101st had seen active combat yet; for many, the jump was their first into active combat. The 101st had been charged with taking out gun emplacements that could rain fire down on the invasion beaches and bridges, thereby preventing German tanks and equipment from reaching the invasion area.

I'd spent a few hours with the senior officers and shared a little about my time in Germany and the Pacific. I couldn't reveal much, but the officers I spoke with were amazed by the number of places I had been.

They'd asked me some questions about the Germans but, for some reason, were more interested in my dealings with the Japanese.

On June 4, we'd been called to the ready room to pack our parachutes and gear and prepare for our jump later that evening. At 3:00 p.m., the news broke that the jump would be postponed forty-eight hours. Operation Overlord was pushed to June 6 due to bad weather. We all understood but were frustrated, nonetheless. I had spent the next day resting in my temporary quarters, assuming sleep might be hard to find over the next few days.

In the late hours of June 5, we rechecked our parachutes and gear and proceeded onto the runway, where a large contingent of C-47 transport planes awaited us. I boarded a C-47 with twenty-five soldiers from the 101st and took my seat. I hadn't jumped from an airplane since diving out two years earlier over Guadalcanal. I hoped the coming jump would be smoother than that night's jump.

I had sat there on a C-47 in my French civilian clothes while the 101st members sported their recently shaved Mohawk hairstyles. They had painted their faces and held every combat equipment they could carry. They were an intimidating bunch. The men had enjoyed kidding me about my appearance, and since it helped distract them from being nervous on their first mission, I had let them say whatever they wanted and taken it in stride.

I'd had my parachute, my handgun, and my knife – the very same weapons I had used to kill the enemy and keep myself alive throughout all my years of military service. We had been given clickers to allow us to distinguish Americans from Germans in the dark. If we heard a click, we were to respond with two clicks.

Two hours after sunset, our C-47 had lumbered onto the runway, taking its place with the others. Shortly after takeoff, I looked out of the plane and was astounded by how many planes were in the air with us. There were other C-47s towing gliders filled with airborne troops from the 101st and the 82nd. We flew out over the English Channel, leaving the coast of England behind. When I looked at my watch, it was just after midnight, the early hours of June 6. We cleared the channel and approached the Normandy coast.

Flak from German anti-aircraft guns had started popping all around us. The flashes had lit up the sky, and the concussion from the explosions had shaken our plane violently. I'd watched with a feeling of helplessness as several of the C-47s were blown out of the sky and crashed in the Normandy countryside.

The flak had gotten so bad that the decision was made to jump immediately rather than wait for our designated drop zone to reduce the risk of being shot down. I was fifth in line to jump. I attached my cable to the jump line and approached the exit. I watched as the men who jumped before me suddenly disappeared behind the plane. Then it was my turn, and there was no time to take in the sights. I jumped into the darkness; the cable pulled my chute automatically, and I quickly orientated myself. I looked around and couldn't believe what I saw: hundreds of parachutes floating to the ground. I saw a C-47 explode in the distance, lighting the entire sky. My heart had sunk for the men who were aboard that plane, and my hatred for the enemy had grown even more significant.

I had landed hard. I hit the ground with my legs but started rolling end over end. Finally, my momentum stopped, and I sat up. I had survived the jump, and I still had my handgun and knife. I removed my parachute and came to my feet. No one else was around. How had that happened? I couldn't wait for anyone else. I had to find my target and kill him.

I had spent the next five hours walking east. Thanks to my numerous trips to France, I determined my location near the 12th SS Panzer Division headquarters. I estimated I had walked roughly twelve miles and was close to my objective. My plan of attack had been straightforward but extremely risky. Once I laid eyes on Rudolph Fritz, I would wait for the perfect opportunity to kill him in private.

The sun had finally risen. I'd secured my handgun and knife under my clothing and walked right into the town of Argences, a small town southeast of Caen. The 12th SS Panzer Division had been camped for months leading up to June, and I hoped they were still there. I knew they would soon be on the move once news of the large-scale Allied invasion reached them.

Walking into the small town, I saw dogs running aimlessly in the street and a few older men shuffling about. I had looked like an average French citizen, but I didn't speak French fluently. I had picked up a few words but would be in trouble if forced into a lengthy conversation.

I'd gone to the rear of the town and had seen that the German tanks were still there, all lined up in formation. I counted fifteen tanks, none of which had their motors running. I knew where the officers' quarters were, as I had impersonated a German soldier a few times to secure information.

I'd been standing next to a two-story building when a voice behind me had asked, in German, "What are you looking at?"

I turned and saw a German tank commander, half-dressed in his army uniform, with shaving cream all over his face.

I replied in German, "I'm just looking at all the tanks, Sir.

They're huge."

The officer, who was about my height and build, had laughed and continued shaving his face with the straight razor in his right hand and boastfully stated, "The Americans will be slaughtered when they invade." The alarms had sounded just then, and I knew exactly what that meant. The news had arrived that the Allies were invading. The German officer rushed back into his quarters, and I followed him. Thanks to the noise of the alarm going off, he didn't hear me when I came up behind him. Keeping clear of the straight razor in his hand, I shoved him hard from behind, forcing him to turn in my direction. I quickly stabbed him in the heart with my knife. As he stared at me, with his eyes glazing over, I pulled my knife out of his chest. He collapsed to the ground and died immediately. I raced to shut the officer's door. I removed the officer's pants and put them on over my civilian clothes. I found a clean shirt in his closet and hastily put that on, too, along with his jacket hanging nearby. He was a little bigger than I was, so his clothes fit perfectly over mine. Lastly, I removed my shoes and replaced them with the officer's black boots. I then found a map of the coastal area of France that lay on a nearby table, folded it, and placed it in the right front pocket of the officer's coat I was wearing.

The alarm had sounded throughout the headquarters area. I had very little time to find my target, Rudolf Fritz before he jumped into a nearby tank. I left the dead officer lying on the floor and exited his quarters. All I had to go on was the memory of a grainy, black-and-white picture of Fritz shown to me a few days prior.

The Panzer headquarters had been alive with activity at that point. Soldiers darted here and there, and tanks rumbled to life. I didn't see my target, so I went to a building that had previously housed senior-ranking German officers. The three-story brick building had a large Nazi flag flying from it. I walked right in and headed up the stairs, hoping to find Fritz.

By a stroke of luck, I had spotted him immediately when he walked out of a bedroom door.

I had spoken in German and said, "General, I have news about the Allied invasion. May I speak to you in private, Sir?"

He'd nodded and walked back into the room, motioning me to follow him. I'd pulled out the map I had placed in my newly acquired jacket and laid it on a coffee table, asking him to come over as I pointed to an area on the map. After he put on his reading glasses, he bent over the table and looked at the map. I quickly pulled out my knife with my left hand, the hand he could not see, and rammed it into the base of his skull with an upward motion. He had fallen immediately onto the table, breaking the table in half.

I had abandoned Fritz's quarters, hurried back downstairs, and walked away from the building at a steady pace. Germans were everywhere, hopping into tanks and trucks. I walked calmly into a French bakery and entered the storage area. I removed the German uniform I'd been wearing over my civilian clothes and threw it into a nearby trash can. I then darted out a back door and into a nearby alley. The town had been awoken by then, with French civilians running around in a panic. They'd known what was coming.

I had taken a bicycle propped up against a nearby building and hopped on it. I'd ridden right out of town, heading for Caen. It was about a sixteen-mile bike ride. Pedaling hard, I glanced back and didn't see anyone following me. After a few miles, some trucks filled with German soldiers sped by me on their way west toward the beaches.

The invasion, by then, had been in full force. The Allies had landed on five designated beaches around the Normandy area code-named Utah, Omaha, Sword, Juno, and Gold. The Americans had been taking the beaches of Utah and Omaha.

An American P-51 Mustang, a single fighter aircraft, had swooped out of the sky and strafed the road in front of me, hitting a German truck that had just passed me. The truck careened off the road to the right and flipped over into a deep ditch. A few German soldiers stumbled out but soon fell to the ground and shot up badly. The P-51 had then veered off to the left and out of sight. The Allies, it seemed, had controlled the skies.

My thoughts snapped back to the present day when I stepped onto the deck of the *Athos II.* Hundreds of people milled around the ship's deck, and I found it hard to make my way. I saw couples, couples with children, single mothers with children, old folks, and young adults. Some carried suitcases, while others held oversized bags slung over their shoulders. Still others pulled large travel chests behind them, occasionally assisted by the ship's deckhands.

It had been decided that I would speak only German during my entire voyage and upon landing in South America. The idea was that I would arouse less suspicion if I acted like an escaped or sympathetic Nazi. If I spoke English, I would immediately be identified as an American.

The ship's boarding process lasted most of the morning. By 11:30 a.m., I was settled into my tiny cabin on the third deck. My cabin had no window, and I found it a little claustrophobic. The room had a small cot and desk, with only a tiny lamp for illumination.

A little after noon, the ship's engines came to life. Even in my cabin, I felt the ship's momentum as it departed the Casablanca port. Over the years, I had crisscrossed the Atlantic and Pacific Oceans countless times, but this trip was different because we were in a post-war period. While my past missions had been challenging, I had felt more prepared for them than I did for my current mission. This mission would require me to cover thousands of miles, searching for men who were like ghosts. My new enemies would not wear uniforms and would be proficient at blending in and disappearing from the public eye. I would have to be extremely careful not to give away too much information about who I was or who I was hunting when interviewing people. I fully expected all four of the escaped Nazis to be surrounded by people sympathetic to their cause.

When the ship hit full speed, and we were several miles out into the Atlantic Ocean, I decided to go up on the top deck and catch the ocean breeze and a little sun. I hoped the environment would clear my mind and allow me to strategize about what lay ahead.

Reaching the top deck of the ship, I heard singing. The lyrics were German, and the singers' included men, women, and children. I had never heard the song before. I walked up to the group of singers and listened for some time. The upbeat song was about a farmer and his wife's tasks as they plant and harvest their crops.

I walked closer to the group, and as the song finished, an older gentleman looked at me and shouted, "Young man, join us!"

I replied, in German, "Sir, I may look young to you, but I'm thirty-eight years old. And I'm afraid I don't sing very well."

He grinned, looked around at the group of people, and, raising his hand, said, "That doesn't matter, and yes, thirty-eight years is young. I'm twice your age. I've been through two world wars and survived to sing about it. My name is Rudolf Hartmann. What is your name?"

I gave in to his invitation, walked closer, and replied, "My name is Fritz Greiner, and I'll join you."

Several people then embraced me as they pulled me into the large circle. I was posing as a German, using my assigned German name from back in the 1930s. We sang for over two hours. I recognized some of the songs, but I only knew some of them. Regardless, the group seemed to love having me join them, and I enjoyed the camaraderie.

The group dispersed, and Rudolf wrapped his arm around me as I walked away.

"Fritz," he said, "you sang better than I expected after you claimed you couldn't sing well. My family and I will have dinner in the second-deck dining room. Would you like to join us?"

I immediately replied, "Yes, Sir, I would be honored to join you."

Rudolph smiled and began to introduce his family to me. "Fritz, this is my wife, Elsa, and my two sons, Matthias and Holger."

I shook everyone's hands. Accompanying Matthias and Holger were their wives and small children. We all made our way to the second-deck dining room.

The dining room was spacious, and we found a large, open table near the ship's rear. Rudolph asked me to sit between him and Elsa, so I did. We eventually all settled in, and there I was, surrounded by a German family, sailing west across the Atlantic Ocean to a strange land. I was very comfortable, as I knew the language well and was experienced at keeping my German cover.

The dining room and menu exceeded my expectations. I had traveled under worse conditions before and during the war. The menu included German and Portuguese dishes, providing an assortment of meats, vegetables, rice, and breads. I knew I would not go to bed hungry that night.

We were about an hour into our meal when the questions started. Up to that point, the conversation had centered on various Hartmann family topics, and I had focused on eating and nodded periodically in the direction of whoever was speaking. Rudolf's daughters-in-law and children began to leave the table and go to their rooms for the night. I was left with Rudolf, Elsa, Matthias, and Holger at the table.

Matthias spoke first. "Fritz, what did you do during the war? What division of the Wehrmacht were you in? Holger and I were part of the 2nd SS Panzer Corp under Commander Wilhelm Bittrich. We both served in Poland and France."

The introduction could not have been planned any better. I looked at the conversation as an opportunity to dig deeper and possibly extract some leads as to the whereabouts of the four escaped Nazis.

I had four sets of eyes on me, awaiting my answer. My goal was to stick to the script and describe my German undercover role, in which I had served not in the Wehrmacht but in a more civilian support role. I was supposed to detail my duties leading up to December 1941, which had me performing construction, office, and warehouse roles. They couldn't know that those roles had been designed for me to gather intelligence and report back to the White House or that after 1941, I had served as a United States Army soldier conducting covert operations behind enemy lines. I would tell the truth about my activity but keep the secret of who I was and the reasons behind what I did.

"I did not serve in the German Army during the war," I explained. "I was diagnosed with a damaged mitral valve in my heart when I was a teenager, so I was a day laborer, working in various support roles. I was born in Villach, Austria, but by the early 1930s, I had moved to Berlin. During the war, I supported concentration camp construction, helping with the very first concentration camp outside of Berlin in early 1934. We built the camp near Oranienburg, just north of Berlin.

"When I first saw that first concentration camp construction site in early 1934, all I saw was a large tract of land devoid of any trees. Tree stumps dotted the land, dominated by two buildings resembling barracks in the final stages of construction. I paid the driver, picked up my bag, and headed toward the construction. A sign on the construction site's edge read, 'Attention! A construction project is underway. We are seeking skilled and non-skilled laborers. Apply at tent.'

"I knew I could pound a nail into a board, so I walked into the tent and found a middle-aged German man sitting behind a small table. He asked me about my business, and I told him I wanted to apply for a non-skilled position. "He then asked me to sit and fill out a brief application. I completed the application in German and handed it over.

"After looking it over, he asked, 'How did you find us here in Oranienburg?'

"I told him I was tired of working indoors and wanted to experience more of Germany. He appeared satisfied with that response and asked if I was ready to start. I immediately let him know that I was.

"We left the tent and walked toward a long row of tents partially obstructed by the barracks under construction. He assigned me to tent #3, then told me to drop my bag on a cot and follow him. Next, he introduced me to an older-looking man named Franz Kappel, holding a clipboard. He told Franz to use me as he wished.

"I stood there for a while as Franz shuffled through the papers on his clipboard, finally telling him I was a strong and organized worker.

"He didn't look up for a while but eventually said, 'Finally, here is someone ready to get his hands dirty.'

"He handed me a sheet of his paper and told me to follow it to the letter. He said if I completed the list of assignments to his satisfaction, he would let me keep my position. Over the next few weeks, my jobs involved shoveling dirt and cement in and out of wheelbarrows as I transported material to various buildings under construction on the property.

"January 1934 began bitterly cold. Snow fell frequently, but the construction of the camp didn't stop. Most camp workers kept to themselves as much as they could, which was a challenge given the cramped living conditions of our tents. Meals were served outside. The food was always abundant, so I kept my energy level up and remained in good health.

"Finally, on July 27, I approached Franz at dinner. He sat by himself, as he typically did.

"I asked if I could join him, and he said, 'Of course you can, Fritz, I've wanted to talk to you, anyway. You've been a reliable worker here at the camp. We're near the end of our construction, and I was wondering if I could give you a job reference or something.'

"I thanked him and told him I planned to give him my notice, as I wanted to return to Berlin. Franz didn't say anything initially, so we sat there and silently ate.

"Finally, he said, 'You know, you should stay another few days, as Vice Chancellor Hitler is planning on visiting the camp July 29 to conduct a complete inspection of our work.'

"I agreed to stay at the camp through July 30.

"Later, just before we finished our dinner, I leaned in close to Franz and asked, 'What is that large building on the edge of the camp going to be used for?'

"Again, Franz took his time, waiting until his last bites of dinner were finished before he said, 'The Nazis are gaining power every day. Soon, Germany will be in a much better position when Hitler gains full power. When he does, he will accelerate his plan to build a master race and rid Germany of the Jewish plague.'

"The morning of July 29, everyone assembled outside in front of the newly constructed camp commandant's office. Hitler and his motorcade were expected to arrive at approximately 10:00 a.m., and we were to greet him. Shortly after the appointed time, two large, canvas-covered trucks pulled into the camp and stopped before us. More than twenty-five German soldiers with 'S.S.' painted on the side of their helmets hopped out from the back of the trucks. They assembled in front of us with their rifles slung over their right shoulders. One of the soldiers announced that we would be searched for weapons and explosives. After being searched individually, we returned to our rows and stood facing the soldiers. A few soldiers fanned out across the camp, some taking up positions on the roofs and at the entrance to the camp.

"At about 10:30 a.m., we heard cars off in the distance. Soon after, Hitler's motorcade, including another truck of Nazi soldiers, pulled up in front of us.

"Hitler's motorcar pulled up right in front of where I stood. An officer who had ridden in the front seat of his motorcar opened Hitler's door. After exiting the vehicle, Hitler took several steps in my direction. He paused momentarily and then began to pace in front of our line, scrutinizing us intently.

"He soon returned to where I was standing, stopped, faced me, and said, 'What is your name, young man?'

"I calmly answered, 'Fritz Greiner.'

"Hitler then asked me where I was from and what I had done to contribute to the building of the camp. I told him I was originally from Austria but had lived mainly in Berlin. I also told him in detail what my contributions at the camp had been.

"'I, too, am from Austria, Fritz,' Hitler said. 'It is nice to have someone from my home country instrumental in the building of this first concentration camp.'

"Before Hitler walked away to visit with camp officials, he reached out to shake my hand and thanked me for my contributions.

"Hitler spent approximately two hours at the camp that day, inspecting each building and asking Franz many questions. What stood out to me the most during that entire visit was that Hitler spent over thirty minutes of his two-hour visit down at the remote building that contained the showers and ovens.

"At 12:45 p.m., Hitler and his motorcade left the camp as quickly as they had arrived. As they pulled away, Franz walked over to where I was standing and said that he wasn't surprised that Hitler had talked to me. Franz then said that he appreciated my good attitude and hard work."

Looking around at my dinner companions, I felt sick from remembering and discussing the camp. I did not want to continue recounting the details of my backstory.

Then Holger looked at me and said, "I saw Hitler once when his motorcade passed before our procession in Munich. I was close enough to touch him, but he was probably twenty yards away. I, like many other soldiers, was initially enamored with him and would have done anything for the Nazi cause. I now resent what Hitler and the Nazi party did to Germany."

The table became very quiet at that point. I fully expected Rudolf, Elsa, or Matthias to back up Holger by criticizing my work leading up to the war, but the table was silent.

I continued with my backstory.

"Berlin was a flurry of activity in January 1933. I was tired of outdoor manual labor and decided to find employment within the Reichstag. I first scanned the daily newspapers for classified advertisements listing any jobs within the Reichstag. I stumbled upon what I was looking for the second week in January. I was in the lobby of my apartment, just returning from the local market with some groceries. I overheard one of my neighbors complaining to another neighbor that a favored employee at the Reichstag had recently passed away, and he was unsure how he would fill the position. I quickly approached the man.

"'My name is Fritz Greiner,' I said, 'and I live here in this building. I'm sorry you lost your employee. I'm looking for work and can start immediately.'

"My aggressive offer surprised the man. He paused for a minute and asked, 'Do you speak English? This job requires some limited English translation.'

"Without hesitation, I responded, 'Yes, I speak English fluently, with practically no German accent.'

"The man said, 'My name is Albert Koch, and I work in the defense ministry. I need a runner who can cover the grounds of the Reichstag, delivering messages, paperwork, and the like. Let me hear your English, Fritz. Say something for me.'

"I paused, thinking what to say, and soon responded, 'Germany is a vast country, and opportunities abound for young entrepreneurs like me.'
"Albert smiled and said, "Meet me here at 6:00 a.m. tomorrow and we'll walk together to the Reichstag.'

"We shook hands, and I continued to my apartment with my groceries.

"The following day, I dressed and was in the lobby at 5:45 a.m., and to my surprise, Albert was already there, reading a paper.

"'Good morning, Sir,' I said. 'I'm ready to begin my employment at the Reichstag.'

"Albert folded his paper, tucked it under his arm, and replied, 'Not before a hearty breakfast. We'll grab something on the way.'

"The walk to work was about a mile and a half. We ate a quick breakfast at a diner right next to the Reichstag. Albert and I mainly chatted about politics. I was surprised he didn't mention Hitler during our breakfast conversation. We finished up and walked over to the Reichstag. It was an impressive building from my apartment window, but it was even more so up close. The building was incredibly ornate. The floors were primarily made of marble, cut into intricate patterns. Large paintings hung in the hallways. However, Albert's office was simple, with only enough room for two desks.

"After completing some employment paperwork, I spent the rest of my first day reviewing a detailed building map with Albert. He explained my duties: delivering and picking up written correspondence. Albert's office, it turned out, served as a repository center for all correspondence at the Reichstag.

"The morning of January 30, rumors circulated throughout the Reichstag that Hitler would be appointed Chancellor. Sure enough, at noon that same day, Hitler was sworn in as Chancellor. The ceremony took place at the Hindenburg's presidential palace. Cheers rang out throughout the Reichstag when the news arrived. I was in one of the main halls when I heard. People all around me were clapping, some were singing, and still others were standing in place with their right arms extended, shouting, 'Heil, Hitler!'"

I did not share with my dinner party that night how when the Hitler announcement had been made, and the crowd had started shouting his name repeatedly, I had felt a chill run up the back of my neck.

I continued with my story.

"Later that same day, when I returned to Albert's office, I saw him sitting at his desk with his head in his hands, starkly contrasting the actions of the other employees I had just seen. I said nothing as I laid a stack of papers on his desk. Hitler was now second in command, leaving only President Hindenburg above him. I have many news articles over the last year, many high-ranking government officials aligned themselves with Hitler.

"I spent the next four weeks running paperwork between offices. I often passed Hermann Goering, Joseph Goebbels, and Reinhard Heydrich in the hallway. On one occasion, I handed Martin Bormann a sealed set of documents.

"Late in the evening on February 27, 1933, sirens blared outside. I noticed an eerie glow around the edges of the curtain on my apartment window, so I pulled the curtain aside and looked outside. I was shocked to see that the Reichstag was on fire. Flames leaped out of the front windows and portions of the roof. Even though another building partially blocked my view of the building, I could tell the Reichstag was in serious trouble. I wore a thick coat and headed outside for a better view. It was bitterly cold outside. People hurried out of the surrounding buildings, all headed toward the burning Reichstag. When I walked closer, I felt the heat of the flames. The fire, by then, had whipped up, coming mainly out of the roof of the building. Watching the fire, I wondered if it was an accident or purposely set. I stood there for as long as I could. Fire trucks and emergency personnel arrived on the scene, and I decided to get out of the bitter cold and back into my warm apartment. It was hard to fall asleep with the sounds of the crowds below and the wail of sirens, but I somehow managed to catch a few hours of sleep. That ended my job at the Reichstag."

By that point in my story, I had undoubtedly eroded any good mood at the dinner table that night. It was late, and we all headed to bed. I left the table that night wondering two things. One, did I sell my backstory well enough, and two, what was the genuine sympathy of the Hartmann family?

I laid down that night, tired of having to be someone else. I had been in counterintelligence for so long that the truth and lies of who I was began to blend. My entire purpose of working at both Oranienburg and Auschwitz and in between at the Reichstag had been to gain intelligence for the United States and report it back to the White House and the Army. My work behind enemy lines had saved American lives and, hopefully, many Jewish lives as well. To me, those saved lives justified all the madness. The *Athos II* sailed on through the night. Despite my frustration, I slept soundly. The remaining six days at sea were filled with boredom.

I wandered the ship and listened to as many conversations as I could, hoping to pick up some clues about the direction or whereabouts of the four missing Nazis. I found it interesting that I never again encountered the Hartmann family during those six days at sea. It was almost like I had never met them.

CHAPTER 4

Alone I Stand

"Get there first with the most."
Nathan Bedford Forrest

The *Athos II* docked as scheduled in the port of Buenos Aires, Argentina, late in the morning on July 11, 1946. We'd had great weather and calm seas, but I was still happy to see land again. I felt somewhat unprepared for what lay ahead of me, however. I had been to many foreign countries before and during World War II, but I had known the primary language in those missions. This time, I did not. I was also apprehensive because I felt I needed a natural starting point.

I'd been to Buenos Aires before with the late President Roosevelt. On November 4, 1936, I had been invited to the White House to see President Roosevelt reelected. I'd joined the President on a South American trip the following week. My assignment had been to be his eyes and ears from a military standpoint. I had eagerly accepted the invitation.

We'd left Washington D.C. on November 21, 1936, and had returned on December 12. We traveled to the islands of Trinidad, Rio de Janeiro, Brazil, Buenos Aires, Argentina, and Montevideo, Uruguay. I'd been fascinated by the mountains in South America, which reminded me of the Swiss Alps. After returning home to the United States, the President asked if I thought South America would be an American ally if another world war broke out. I'd told him I was concerned about the Nazi sympathy I had witnessed in Argentina. We had agreed that none of the countries we visited had significant militaries and would, therefore, not be a threat to us if war did break out.

Here, ten years later, I was back in South America, hunting Nazis because of the continent's sympathy toward them.

As we prepared to disembark the ship that morning, Rudolph Hartmann suddenly put his arm around me and said, "Fritz? Or should I call you Allen? Are you ready to leave the ship and learn more about your mission?"

I couldn't contain the look of shock on my face. I immediately wondered how he had discovered my name and mission.

After taking a few seconds to absorb the surprise, I replied, "How do you know my real name and background, Rudolph?"

Rudolph just smiled and gestured for me to follow him. I followed Rudolph and his family off the ship, not knowing what to expect. As we neared the end of the gangplank, I noticed a familiar person waiting below on the dock, Lt. Colonel Yates. He had been my instructor at the United States Army War College in Pennsylvania. The last time I'd seen Lt. Colonel Yates was in June 1944. After working with the French Resistance forces in and around the D-Day invasion beaches just before the June 6th landings, I had just returned to London, England.

When I stepped off the gangplank, Lt. Colonel Yates was there to greet me.

"Hello, Sir," I said as I shook his hand. He was not dressed in an Army uniform, and I knew, due to the nature of my assignment, not to salute and draw Attention.

"Good to see you, Allen. I figure you are wondering why I am here and how Rudolph knows your real name," Lt. Colonel Yates said.

"Sir, I've never been this confused on one of my missions. I am truly hoping you can clarify," I said.

Lt. Colonel Yates nodded and led me toward a dilapidated public bus where Rudolph and his family were already loading their things. We boarded the bus, and I found a seat near the middle. Lt. Colonel Yates sat across the aisle from me.

The rickety bus soon pulled away from the docks. It was early afternoon, and the bus was uncomfortable due to its hard seats and the suffocating heat. Several of us opened our windows, allowing some fresh air to blow through the bus. My ride during my last visit with President Roosevelt had been in a Rolls Royce Phantom. This mode of transportation was quite a contrast.

Initially, nothing was said between Lt. Colonel Yates and me. The bus rolled through the downtown area of Buenos Aires. Some of the buildings looked familiar to me. As we exited the city's west side, the countryside started to open up. I saw large mountains in the distance, their tops blanketed in snow. Lt. Colonel Yates tapped me on the left shoulder and told me why he was in Buenos Aires and what role Rudolph played.

"Allen, the entire reason I am here in Argentina with you is to broker the relationship between you and Rudolph and to ensure you have clear direction on your critical mission here in South America."

I turned more in Lt. Colonel Yates's direction, almost sitting sideways in my seat. I tuned out all the noise of the bus and the other passengers.

The Lt. Colonel continued. "Rudolph and I first met in February 1945 in Berlin. I believe you know he is a German veteran of World War I, and both his sons fought in World War II. Soon after the war started, he became a secret dissenter of Adolph Hitler and the Nazi party. He raised his sons to love their country first, above any leader or politician. They all saw firsthand the brutality of the Nazi Party against the Jews and others deemed as less favorable."

It seemed Rudolph had crossed into American territory and shared information with senior Army leadership. He had provided maps and locations of hidden bunkers in and around Berlin. The most interesting fact that he shared, though, was that he had heard of numerous high-ranking Nazis who were fleeing Germany and heading to South America. Rudolph also told the Army that he had been born west of Buenos Aires and had inherited his father's home and surrounding property in late 1939 upon his father's death. The Army became very interested and immediately asked if he would consider letting the Army use the property as a base of operation if any future attempts were made to hunt down those escaped Nazis. Rudolph was willing and made it clear that if he and his family survived the war, they would relocate to his father's home, escaping Germany and all the fallout.

"At present," said Lt. Colonel Yates, "we are traveling to Rudolph's inherited home and will join him and his family for a few days. Rudolph has already reached out to his contacts in South America for support. As you learned during your recent time in Berlin, many of the citizens of Argentina and the surrounding countries are descendants of Germans who settled here years ago. Many of them are sympathetic to the Nazi party and cannot be trusted."

While I was astounded by all this new information, I felt much better about my current mission, knowing everything was tied together.

The bus rolled on for another two hours, with various passengers entering and exiting the bus. By mid-afternoon, the distance between towns and houses was vast. The landscape was made up of rolling hills, and the western mountain ranges came into view.

Finally, the bus came to a stop near a stone fence that was approximately six feet tall. In it stood an iron gate, which opened to a stone path that led to a large home back off the main road.

I looked at Lt. Colonel Yates and asked, "Is this Rudolph's home?" He said, "I believe it is, based on the pictures I was provided."

Rudolph confirmed it was his home and warmly welcomed us as we exited the bus.

Lt. Colonel Yates and I followed Rudolph and his family down the stone path. He had not visited this home since he moved to Germany with his parents as a ten-year-old boy over sixty years earlier. His wife and family had never seen it before. Several servants from the home joined us and insisted on carrying our luggage for us.

Giant sycamore trees dotted the property surrounding the home. The house had three floors and many windows, but what stood out the most to me were the white stucco siding and the dark orange roofing tiles. Two large Mastiff dogs greeted us when we got close to the house. Although the sight of the dogs was intimidating, one of them came directly up to me and allowed me to pet its massive head, which was level with my belt. The fantastic animal followed me until I entered the home.

Upon entering the house, I saw that Rudolph had control of the situation. He managed the home, property, and servants from afar, as everything was in order.

A female servant showed me to my room and told me that dinner would be in the main dining room at six o'clock that evening. My room was simple but very accommodating, complete with a private bathroom, a queen-size bed, fresh towels, a desk, a chair, and a lamp. The bed looked very inviting, and my eyes were heavy. I unpacked what little clothing I had and opted to take a nap. I looked at my watch; it was 3:00 p.m. I removed my shoes and crawled into bed, hoping to sleep for a few hours.

As I lay there that afternoon, my mind continued to wrestle with my ongoing frustrations, which centered on my long tenure in the U.S. Army, the countless missions, and my continued absence from Alice. It had been almost three months since I had seen her. There was no way for me to call her, and I couldn't send any written correspondence because there was a chance it could be stolen and expose my entire reason for being in-country.

I soon drifted off to sleep.

A persistent knock at my bedroom door suddenly awakened me. Opening my eyes, I tried to remember where I was. I arose from the bed, still half asleep, and wandered to the door. I opened it and found Lt. Colonel Yates standing there.

He laughed and said, "Allen, I guess you were sleeping. I'm sorry to wake you, but I hoped we could chat privately before dinner."

I looked at my watch; it was 5:10 p.m. "Sir, with your permission, can I grab a quick shower and change clothes?"

Lt. Colonel Yates said, "Allen, you don't have to ask for my permission, but I think that's a great idea."

I said, "Thank you, Sir."

"Meet me outside on the veranda no later than 5:30 p.m.," Lt. Colonel Yates said as I shut the door.

I then scrambled to shower, shave, and make myself presentable. I was ready to finish the mission and get home to Alice.

I met Lt. Colonel Yates on the veranda. The sun was setting over the western Argentina Mountains, and the temperature had dropped a few degrees, making the air outside more tolerable.

Lt. Colonel Yates appeared relaxed. He held a lit cigar in his left hand and a glass of bourbon in his right.

"Would you like anything to drink, Allen?" he asked. "I'll have what you're having, Sir," I replied.

With that, he motioned to a housekeeper, pointed to his glass, and then me. In less than a minute, I held a glass of bourbon.

Lt. Colonel Yates did not waste any time telling me what was on his mind.

"Allen, I am frustrated over the continued time away from home. You might remember my wife, Mary. I miss her. She has faithfully been by my side through my thirty-plus years of military service. I can only imagine how you feel. Your girlfriend, Alice, seems like a nice girl, and I'm sure you miss her terribly, too."

"Yes, Sir," I said.

"Regardless of your frustrations, Allen, I need you to complete this mission. I will return stateside soon, leaving you here to complete your assignment. As always, you will have my full support. We do not want to draw Nazi or Nazi sympathizer's awareness by having too many Americans wandering the streets of South America, making them wonder why we are here."

He took another sip of bourbon. "I will caution you to watch the staff here. You never know who might still be sympathetic toward the defunct Nazi party. Someone is hiding the Nazis, after all. We'll meet with Rudolph and his sons tomorrow to determine our next steps. Word has reached me that we may have a lead on the location of Warren Weltzin."

My adrenaline immediately kicked in, and I was eager to learn more, but I would have to wait.

We heard the call for dinner and joined Rudolph and his family in the main dining room. The room's large, oval table quickly seated twenty people. The Colonel and I were the last two to join the night dinner party. We had seats at each end of the long table. We would be thrown right into the midst of conversation that evening.

Everyone was there. Rudolph and his wife, Elsa, were seated next to me at one end of the table. Rudolph's sons, Matthias and Holger, and their families were scattered around the rest of the table.

Once seated, Rudolph stood and waited for us to quiet down before speaking. "I want to welcome you all here. This home has been in my family for almost seventy-five years. Fortunately, we've had caretakers to care for it and protect it during the idle years when no family members were here. I'm so happy to be back here with all of you. I thank God for protecting my two sons through the vicious war that ravaged Germany and took so many lives. I want to welcome Lt. Colonel Yates and Allen Voigt to my home. They are recent acquaintances, but I already consider them friends. Let's forget the recent war, death, destruction, and the thousands of miles we have just traveled to get here tonight. Focus on each other and the food that has been prepared."

While he spoke, servants poured wine for the adults, and as Rudolph finished, he raised his glass in a toast. We all raised ours and toasted with him. Rudolph sat back down, and a fantastic dinner was served.

I spoke mainly with Rudolph and Elsa that night. The conversation was light and easy, focusing on our backgrounds and family. I felt comfortable telling them about my childhood, family, and Alice. Rudolph and Elsa shared how they met in Berlin in 1921 and told me about their family. I learned about Rudolph's time in WWI, and we agreed that he and my father probably covered some of the same ground in France.

I was utterly relaxed that evening and thoroughly enjoyed myself. There was no mention of the awkward journey to Argentina from Casablanca and how Rudolph knew my real name as we departed the ship. There needed to be more conversation about my upcoming mission and how Rudolph and his family would support it. That would all come later.

By 9:00 p.m., Matthias, Holger, and their families had left the dinner table. It was getting late, but Lt. Colonel Yates moved down to my end of the table as he and I, Rudolph and Elsa, enjoyed a cup of coffee and some chocolate cake for dessert. We talked for another two hours about a range of topics. I was struck by the sadness in Rudolph's eyes when he spoke about Germany, describing the frustration of the German people after the First World War and how the door had been opened for Adolph Hitler and the Nazi Party to rise to power and influence the populace.

Elsa shared with us her sadness and disbelief regarding how the Jewish people and many of Germany's mentally ill were treated by the Nazis. She told us she had many Jewish friends who had lost their businesses, then had seen their families separated and shipped off to a concentration camp, never to be seen again. In the years leading up to the Second World War, I had operated undercover in Berlin and had firsthand knowledge of events like those Rudolph and Elsa described.

We finished our conversations around 11:30 p.m. and headed to our respective rooms. I was exhausted.

The following day came quickly, but I was eager to get going and learn more about the possible location of Warren Weltzin. Breakfast was self-serve in the kitchen, and once again, there was plenty of food. I grabbed some sausage and eggs, a few pieces of toast, and some coffee. I sat at a small table in the kitchen and devoured my breakfast. I was surprised I had such an appetite after the large dinner we had consumed the night before.

Matthias soon joined me, and we conversed over our breakfast in German. I asked him about his young family and what his plans were now that he was living in Argentina.

He didn't hesitate with his reply. "I never want to return to Germany, believe it or not. I am tired of war, and all that comes with it. My three children know nothing else, which is a shame. I want to help care for this property and raise my children in a peaceful environment. I'll be honest, though, I want to do all I can to help you find these escaped Nazis. I have been briefed and understand why my father is helping you. I want to help eradicate any form of the Nazi Party here in Argentina. Even though I was born in Germany, my family's roots are here, and I want to build upon that."

Later that morning, Lt. Colonel Yates, Matthias, Holger, and I followed Rudolph into his basement to hear about the next phase of my mission. The door that led to the basement was made of solid oak, approximately six inches thick. Its iron handle was so large that Rudolph had to grab it with both hands to push it open. The steps leading down were made of granite stone and were very wide and deep. I felt like I was in an old castle. When we reached the basement floor, the space opened onto a large room, approximately thirty by thirty feet. Dominating the room was a massive oak table covered with maps and photographs and lit by several lamps.

Approaching the table, I looked at the pictures and recognized several of the Nazis I had studied in Berlin. The maps on the table were detailed and appeared to be of every country in South America.

Rudolph stood across from me and started the conversation. "Allen, you have been introduced to my sons and me over the last week. Lt. Colonel Yates has since given you our background and has told you the limited role we will play in your assigned mission to eradicate escaped Nazis who most likely fled here to South America. Just before our leaving Berlin, with the help of Lt. Colonel Yates, we already put things in motion here in Buenos Aires, trying to locate as many escaped Nazis as possible." He held up a worn picture of a woman and three boys. "My sister, Lara, has three Argentinian sons born and raised here. My sister is five years older than I am. She moved back here in the late 1920s and married an Argentinian man who worked in wheat farming and exporting. Matthias and Holger's cousins have no Nazi sympathies. The U.S. Army corresponded with my sister about six weeks before our departure, around late May, requesting that her sons begin the initial hunt for our targets. One Nazi, who we think is Warren Weltzin, was quickly found in western Argentina, in the town of Tamberias. The city is on the western shore of the Rio De Los Pantos River, in a valley nestled at the base of the Andes Mountains. The distance between here and Tamberias is approximately 1,300 kilometers, and the town can only be reached by train, a ride of at least twenty-four hours, barring no train delays."

He motioned toward Holger, who stepped forward. "I suggest my son Holger accompany you. We will arrange for you to meet with my sister's oldest son, Joaquin, in Tamberias. We have heard that these Nazis do not remain in one location very long to avoid the risk of being detected. I urge you to leave soon to have any chance of confirming Warren Weltzin's identity and taking him out."

I replied, "Honestly, I'm surprised you could secure information quickly. It's even more impressive that your intelligence reach is that far. I've had a lot of training and even more field experience. However, coordinating a mission with a former enemy will be my first. I've witnessed the tenacity and perseverance of the German soldier, though, and I would be honored to have Holger by my side."

Despite that speech, I remembered what Lt. Colonel Yates had told me the night before. I would keep Holger at arm's length.

Lt. Colonel Yates spoke up, directing his conversation to Rudolph, Holger, and Matthias. "Let me be very frank. Up to this point, the support you've provided the United States Army is to be commended. We presently have more intelligence coming in that we can process. The real challenge before us right now is two-fold. First, the continent of South America is vast, and the challenge is pursuing these leads and finding our targets before these Nazi sons of bitches move to a new location. Second, Allen is and will remain in control of this mission from start to finish. I cannot be any clearer on that."

The basement then got very quiet, so it was uncomfortable for me to stand there in silence. I had to say something, so I turned to Holger.

"Holger, would you be prepared to leave first thing in the morning? I am."

"Yes," he replied. "I will prepare for us to travel by bus to the downtown Buenos Aires train station."

"Very good. I want to get some target practice in this afternoon. Can someone here provide me with a rifle, a pistol, and an area on the property I can use as a shooting range?"

Lt. Colonel Yates interjected. "Allen, you will be surprised to learn I traveled here with some of your favorite American weapons. I have a Colt 45 handgun, a 1903 Springfield rifle, and several hundred rounds of ammunition for you. These weapons are brand new, so your idea of some target practicing is good. Ensure they are broken in, and the sights are zeroed in."

"Outstanding," I said.

Rudolph had been silent for a while and finally rejoined the conversation by leaning over the table and touching it.

Looking at the maps, he said, "My family and I respect your position regarding Allen taking the lead role in this mission. You were the victors in both world wars. We Germans have made a mess of things across the world, and now others must fix it. We will honor the protocol and support Allen fully with his mission to eradicate these escaped Nazis."

There was another long, awkward silence, and then Rudolph smiled and walked over and put his arm around me. "Allen, I have just the spot on my property for you to break in your weapons. My property stretches east and west, totaling close to two thousand acres. A perfect hill for target practice is approximately two and a half miles into my property, heading west. You should take one of my Mastiffs with you. They are both males, named Cassius and Augustus. My feeling is that Augustus is more suited to join you, as he likes to eat more than Cassius and could probably use the exercise."

"Thank you, Rudolph. I will take you up on that suggestion. I had a dog in upstate New York named Bessie, a female Labrador who loved to hunt with me," I said.

I looked at Holger and spoke. "Holger, did you shoot any American weapons during the war? Regardless of whether you did, it would help if you tagged along. Please join me."

Holger replied, "No, I did not, but I would happily join you."

Before the meeting ended, Rudolph handed me a stack of folded maps of Argentina, Chile, and Bolivia.

We all walked back upstairs. Upon reaching the top step, Lt. Colonel Yates immediately pulled me aside.

"Allen," he said, "I cannot say any more than what I shared with you last night and what was discussed today downstairs. You know what needs to be done and how to get it done. I have the utmost confidence that you will carry this mission out to its completion. I won't be here when you get back this afternoon. I'm heading back to the United States and Fort Meade. I wish you the best of luck and safety."

With that, he shook my hand and told me my weapons and ammunition were already in my room waiting for me.

I returned to my room, reflecting on the morning conversations and interactions. I was a little angry over being in this position again, which I had faced many times before. Throughout the war, I had been asked to kill so many enemy soldiers I had lost count. Each killing was justified and conducted to defend our country, soldiers, sailors, airmen, and civilians. I was good at what I did, but it did not make my job any easier. I just wanted it all to end to get back to Alice and settle down.

It was time to break in my weapons. I changed into some outdoor clothing and inspected my gear. My weapons and ammo were secured in a civilian-type duffle bag, allowing me to transport them throughout the country without drawing Attention. The 1903 Springfield rifle was broken down into several pieces, making storing the long rifle in the duffle bag easier. Lt. Colonel Voigt had also thrown in a small toolkit so I could quickly assemble and disassemble my weapons and make necessary repairs.

I was ready to head out. I opened my bedroom door to see Holger walking down the hallway to meet me. He had a small duffle bag slung over his left shoulder.

I pointed to my duffle bag and said, "You heard earlier the names of the two weapons I have with me."

I then pointed to his duffle bag. "What is that over your shoulder, Holger?"

He replied with a broad smile on his face. "A surprise awaits you, my new friend. You'll have to wait and see."

I laughed, and with that, we were off. As we approached the house's back door, a female servant handed us a basket containing several sandwiches, some peaches, and two water-filled containers. We were both appreciative and thanked her for the lunch.

When we opened the house's back door, I saw the same Mastiff dog that had greeted me the day before.

A male servant working in the backyard spoke calmly to the dog, saying, "Augustus, go with these men."

That was all he had to say. Augustus immediately came over and stood by my side. The servant then asked Holger and me if we knew how to find the area Rudolph had designated for target practice.

"More or less," I replied.

"My name is Pablo, and I would be happy to show you," he said. "All I ask is that you pay attention so you can find your way back to the house."

"We'll take you up on that offer, Pablo. Thank you," I said.

Pablo laid down his shovel and joined our quest. Pablo spoke as the three of us walked away from the house, with Augustus trailing behind. "Your name is Allen, right? You are from the United States?"

"Yes, you are correct on both counts," I said.

He questioned me for the next fifteen minutes, asking me all about America.

I patiently answered all his questions, then asked him some in return. "Pablo, I assume you were born here in Argentina?"

"Yes, I have never lived anywhere else."

I then asked, "How did you come to work for the Fritz family?"

"I have worked for them since I was a teenager. I knew Rudolph's father and mother. My parents worked for them for many years. I'm fifty-three years old, but I'm happy to work here. The house was empty for many years, but we maintained it. We were recently notified of Rudolph and his family's arrival and made preparations for them. I am happy the house will be occupied now."

We reached the designated target practice area, and Pablo said his goodbyes. As he started to walk away, I opened my duffle bag. I could tell by the look on Pablo's face and the fact that he kept looking back at me as he walked away that he was curious. I stopped him from leaving.

"Pablo, would you like to shoot my weapons?"

The huge grin that came over his face was my answer.

I took out the pieces of the 1903 Springfield rifle and laid them on a nearby rock. I then removed the tools from my bag and assembled the rifle. In short order, I had the weapon put together and five rounds loaded into it with a stripper clip. I took out the Colt 45 handgun and loaded the clip with seven rounds.

From behind me, I heard Holger say, "Allen, are you ready for your surprise?"

I turned to face him as he removed the contents from his bag. He first produced a pistol.

"This is a German Walther PPK," Holger said. "I got it near Warsaw, Poland, from a fellow German soldier. I want to present it to you for the American victory in WWII and our new friendship."

I was surprised by his generosity and his kind words. In all my time in Germany, I had never seen a Walther PPK, let alone held one.

"Thank you, Holger. How soon can we shoot it?" I asked.

"Right now, if you like, but first, let me remove one more item I have brought."

He then pulled out a Hitler Youth knife. I had seen a few of these in Berlin before the war but had never held one.

"I would also like you to have this knife. It was given to me in late 1939 as part of my indoctrination into the Nazi Party. I want no remembrance of that time, and because of that, I would like to give it to you."

I didn't know how to reply to him. He had been a proud German soldier, but was ashamed of what the Nazis had done to him, his fellow soldiers, and the country he loved.

I took the knife and said, "Thank you, Holger. I fully understand." I placed the knife in my bag.

While Holger and I were speaking, Pablo set up some targets about fifty yards down range. They were about eight inches in diameter.

We decided to eat the lunch prepared for us before target practice. There was plenty of food; naturally, we shared our meal with Pablo. We spoke little during our lunch.

We spent the next two hours shooting all three weapons. Pablo had a great time shooting, something he told us he had never done before.

Before we left, I asked Pablo to set up some small rocks as targets, each approximately six inches in diameter. I asked them both to join me as I walked another fifty yards away from the targets.

My 1903 Springfield rifle had a scope on it, and I had zeroed in the sights and was comfortable with the rifle's performance. I asked both men to stand behind me and took my position lying on the ground. I loaded another five rounds into the rifle and located the rocks about one hundred yards away. I adjusted the scope slightly and took a deep breath. I fired the first shot and missed slightly to the left. I adjusted the sights, readjusted my position, and took another deep breath. I fired at the five rocks in succession, shattering each into small pieces.

"How did you do that, Allen?" Pablo asked. Holger said nothing.

"Lots of practice, my new friend, lots of practice," I replied.

I had seen the rocks shatter through my scope, but Pablo took the time to walk back to the rocks and inspect them for himself. He just shook his head. We collected all our spent cartridges and headed back to the house. It had been an enjoyable afternoon, but I took the time seriously and ensured all three weapons were fired correctly and in good working order. I would need them in the weeks and months ahead.

When we got back, Lt. Colonel Yates had left for home. I was prepared, though. I knew that the faster I found the Nazis, the quicker I could return home to Alice. I spent the rest of the afternoon cleaning all three weapons. The last thing I did was break down the 1903 Springfield and place all the weapons and ammunition in my duffle bag.

That evening, I was not in the mood to socialize. I had become more and more agitated by the entire mission. I was concerned my frustration might impair my judgment, Holger's, and my safety. I couldn't afford to make any mistakes.

Holger and I set off for our long trip west the following day. Rudolph had arranged transportation to the downtown Buenos Aires train station, where we would catch a train to Tamberias. All Rudolph would say about our transportation was that it would be a male driver in an old car and that he didn't speak English or German. We would have to trust him. Only a little was said between Holger and me as our unknown driver drove us toward Buenos Aires. Our driver dropped us off at the front entrance when we arrived at the train station. We went to the ticket office through the complex network of stairs, platforms, and tunnels. We purchased our one-way tickets to Tamberias, Argentina, via the cities of Rosario, Cordoba, and San Juan. Our route would take us northwest through rugged terrain. Even though I was frustrated to have to conduct this mission, I was looking forward to seeing more of the rugged landscape of Argentina.

After placing my suitcase in the overhead storage area, I settled into my seat. I kept the duffle bag containing my weapons and ammunition on the seat beside me. I was not going to take the chance of having that bag stolen. Holger sat directly across from me, carrying only his suitcase, no weapons.

Our journey would take about twenty-four hours and carry us across South America. The train finally left the Buenos Aires train station and began its journey northwest. Holger and I said little for the first hour but started conversing during the second hour. Breakfast had been served by that time in the Pullman car behind us, so we walked back and had something to eat. Before leaving my seat, though, I slid my duffel back deep underneath my seat and covered it with my jacket. I didn't expect any problems. The train was not overly crowded, and I wasn't suspicious of any passengers on board that morning.

A wide variety of delicious foods were available for our breakfast. Holger and I grabbed a table near the rear of the breakfast car, hoping we could converse in private. We wanted to go over what our plans would be once we reached Tamberias.

Our breakfast conversation that morning turned in a different direction, however. Holger brought up the previous day's rifle range activity and asked me where I had learned to shoot so accurately. I smiled and told him about my extensive training at Camp Pine in upstate New York, followed by my time at the Army War College in Pennsylvania. The driving factor, though, was my extensive field experience and constant practice. Holger told me he had not received anything close to that type of military training while he was a member of the German Army.

That led us to a discussion about locating Holger's cousin, Joaquin and coordinating the elimination of Warren Weltzin. Before our departure, Holger had been given a picture of Joaquin and his address in Tamberias. The picture was several years old, but it was all we had. We decided to go together to find him and secure Weltzin's last known location. We agreed it would be best if Holger stayed behind when I eliminated Weltzin.

We finished breakfast and headed back to our assigned Pullman car. We had neared the Argentinian town of Rosario, and upon our arrival, most passengers got off the train. Many new passengers boarded, and our stop lasted about forty-five minutes. We were soon on our way again.

Leaving the Rosario station, I ran through the various scenarios of how I might eliminate Weltzin in my mind. Not knowing the location or time of day I would come across him, I had several options. Would he be on a busy street in the middle of the day? Would he be walking down a dark street at night? Would he be sleeping in his bed, unaware of an American soldier sneaking up to slit his throat? The location and time of the kill would determine my choice of weapon. If the area was crowded, I preferred a knife; if we were in an isolated location, however, I wanted to use a rifle. I was completely comfortable with either situation.

By mid-afternoon, we reached the town of Cordoba. Our stop there was longer, so I exited the train and stretched my legs, remembering my duffle bag. Holger followed right behind me. The train engineer stated we would be in Cordoba for two hours as they had to take on more coal and load some cattle in the last two train cars. Holger and I decided to eat lunch in a small restaurant near the train station. Cordoba was a large city, but not as big as Buenos Aires.

While we ate, Holger and I watched the citizens of Cordoba as they walked by, going about their daily lives. Everyone had a destination and appeared to have no care in the world. The Second World War had not impacted South America. As I sat there observing, I looked intently for any German males that matched the description of the four Nazis I was hunting.

Holger noticed what I was doing and asked if I had pictures of the men with me. I told him I did have them and retrieved them from my duffle bag. I handed them over, and Holger looked at them for a long time, saying nothing. After a minute or so, he spoke to me in a low voice. He held up one picture and showed it to me.

"Allen, I believe I recognize this man. He is Ekerd Jacobsen." "You are correct, Holger," I said.

"He is directly responsible for Nazi death squads," Holger said. "He and his henchmen killed thousands and sent hundreds of thousands to the death camps. I recognize him because he recruited me early in my military career. I knew of his reputation and expressed my concern to my superiors, risking reprimand and possible demotion in rank. Fortunately, my superiors shared my concerns and convinced Ekerd to recruit another soldier. I was fortunate to be reassigned. He is an evil man."

We finished our lunch and returned to the train, boarding it just in time. The next leg of our journey would take us northwest toward San Juan and eventually into Tamberias. I settled into my seat to take a nap.

The train traveled all afternoon and into the evening. I woke up as the sun set and watched it disappear behind the distant Andes Mountains. I got restless and had to walk the long line of Pullman cars to stay alert. I returned to the cattle cars and tried to talk with the cowboys tending to the cattle, but they didn't speak English.

I later found the conductor and asked him when we would arrive in San Juan. He said it would be a little after three o'clock in the morning. He emphasized that we were gaining elevation, which slowed the train down. I walked back and forth the entire length of the train several times.

I saw a wide variety of passengers heading west with us: farmers, men in suits, women with small children, and even a few Catholic priests. No one paid much attention to me.

I eventually went back to my seat and dozed off again. I was awakened when the train stopped at the San Juan station. Most folks were still asleep. I looked over at Holger, who was snoring. I had to get off the train for a few minutes and get some fresh air.

I asked the conductor if disembarking was all right, and he permitted me. I exited the train and took a deep breath of the chilly, early morning air. The elevation change was pleasant. I looked down the right side of the train and saw a ramp placed up against the train. Very soon after that, the cattle transported in the last two train cars were unloaded and guided to a holding pen near the train station.

As I stood there watching the cattle, I smelled cigarette smoke. I glanced across the train station platform and saw a man in dark clothing, wearing a fedora, pulled low over his face. I found it odd that a man dressed like that was standing on a train station platform at almost four o'clock in the morning. I saw a portion of his face every time he puffed his cigarette. He was Caucasian, most likely of European descent. He finished his cigarette and promptly lit another one.

The train whistle blew; it was time to board the train. I turned and climbed the small stairs leading up into my Pullman car. I turned my head one last time and looked back in the man's direction. He was gone. I glanced at my watch as I sat back down; it was 4:05 a.m.

We were supposed to arrive in Tamberias at around 7:30 a.m. The train slowly chugged its way out of the San Juan train station. I was one step closer to my first target.

About an hour out of San Juan, the sun started coming up behind us, illuminating the ridge line and the Andes Mountains in front of us. It was a beautiful sight to behold. I have seen some fantastic sights across the world during my military career. The mountains of Switzerland and Argentina far outweighed the tropical paradise of the Pacific Islands I had seen during the Pacific Campaign.

I was charged and ready for our arrival in Tiberias. I couldn't sleep, so I looked out the window and ran through the various Nazi elimination scenarios in my mind. What a contrast to be looking at the majestic Andes Mountains as the sun rose, all the while thinking of how I was going to kill a Nazi.

By 6:30 a.m., we crossed the Rio De Los Patos, a large body of water on the eastern side of Tamberias. The wooden bridge shook violently as the train passed over. I knew how to swim but hoped I would not soon have to do so. In a matter of minutes, the train was safely across the water and quickly approaching our destination.

Holger finally awoke, clearing his eyes and yawning.

I laughed and said, "Good morning Holger. It looks like you slept well but missed some beautiful sights."

"Thanks, Allen. I did sleep well. Where are we now?"

I said, "We're approaching Tamberias and should arrive in less than an hour."

Holger gathered his things in preparation for our arrival.

The conductor walked the multiple Pullman cars and notified us that we were approaching the Tamberias train station. Holger and I soon exited our seats and walked off the train. We agreed that our priority was to find some breakfast before heading out to search for Joaquin, our sole contact in the city.

We hurried to a small café about five hundred yards outside the station and enjoyed a large breakfast of steak and eggs. Both of us were amazed at our appetites that morning. We were excited to be off the train and on solid ground, even though my body felt moving.

The city of Tamberias was much smaller than I anticipated. Sitting there eating breakfast, I wondered if Warren Weltzin was nearby. Would he see us and wonder why we were here? We were the only two people eating at the café that morning, which seemed odd.

When I asked the owner about it, he said in halting English, "It's too early for Argentinians to move about. Two hours from now, the café will be very crowded."

"Gracias," I replied.

I also asked him to take a look at Joaquin's address. He knew the approximate part of town where it was located and drew us a crude map.

Holger and I finished our breakfast. I suggested we walk to Joaquin's address to see how the city was laid out. I also wanted to observe the movement of people and various transportation options, as well as any areas where Weltzin could be working, residing, or simply hiding out, I needed to evaluate possible exit strategies once Weltzin was eliminated.

After walking about two miles, I saw that the city was in a grid pattern, with very narrow streets. We walked past a variety of bars, restaurants, and apartments. Soon, the narrow streets widened, and the buildings became fewer and farther between, with tiny, free-standing homes replacing them.

Finally, we came to Joaquin's home. It was a simple, square structure with a flat roof. Windows were set on either side of the front door; the curtains were drawn, and there was no evidence of movement. It was eerily quiet.

We were just about to knock on the door when it opened, and a man in his mid-twenties motioned us in silently. His appearance, although older, matched the picture we had been provided. We were directed to take a seat on some nearby chairs. It quickly became apparent that Joaquin didn't speak any English or German. I wanted to know how we were going to conduct the interview.

After some awkward silence, I pulled out my picture of Warner Weltzin and showed it to Joaquin. He looked at it, stood up, and walked over to a folder on a nearby table. He opened the folder and pulled out the same photo I had been provided back in Berlin, which Rudolph must have sent him. I pulled out the other Nazi pictures I had in my possession. Joaquin had copies of all of them and even some I did not have. I pointed to Weltzin's picture, Joaquin, and my eyes, hoping he would understand that I was trying to find out if he had seen Weltzin.

Joaquin began to say over and over again, "Si."

Now, we were making progress. Holger had never met his cousin Joaquin, and at this point in the conversation, he leaned over to me and did not hold back with his comment.

"Allen, how can Joaquin not know any English or German, being raised by my father's sister? Do you find that odd?"

"I do," I replied.

I handed Joaquin some paper and a pencil and made a writing motion.

He wrote "Descanso" and "Avenida Pío Baroja." The former turned out to be a bar, and the latter, a street. I had something to go on, finally.

Joaquin produced a crude map of Tamberias, pointed to the general area where the bar was located, and pointed to where we were on the map. The bar was on the opposite side of town, facing the Andes Mountains. I wanted to scout the location quickly but decided to wait until dusk. I hoped the location would allow me an elevated position, giving me a clean shot at Weltzin coming in or out of the bar. This all was predicated on the hope that the individual Joaquin spotted was, in fact, Weltzin and that he was still in the area and would continue to come to the bar. That was a lot that had to come together.

I spent the rest of the afternoon cleaning my 1903 Springfield and wiping down my ammunition. I was fully committed and determined to reach my target if it presented itself.

I asked Holger to remain at the house with his cousin while I scouted the bar. He just rolled his eyes as I left the house. By then, it was approaching dark, and the sun was low. I took Joaquin's map and started walking east. It took me about an hour to find Avenida Pío Baroja. It was a lonely street with few buildings. I walked down the street for about a mile, at which point the number of buildings decreased further, and the Andes

Mountains came into view. The rise from the street to the foothills was gradual, but there was enough elevation that I could get off a clean shot.

I found the bar named Descanso but stayed approximately one hundred yards away, hoping to avoid being seen by its patrons. I watched the bar door, but no one came in or out. I decided to head back to Holger and Joaquin immediately and finalize the next phase of the mission.

While walking back to them, I decided I would not wait. I would target Weltzin that night and over the next few nights if necessary. I had spotted a large grouping of huge rocks up in the foothills that would provide me with good coverage and an excellent sightline to my target.

The language barrier with Joaquin had become frustrating. I left Holger with instructions to get Joaquin to understand my mission and that I would return to his home upon its completion. The second thing I asked Holger to do was to devise an exit strategy for us to leave Tamberias as quickly and safely as possible.

Joaquin cooked us all some dinner, and I waited for nighttime. Eventually, after hearing Holger speak in German, Joaquin remembered some of the words he had heard as a child, and the language started returning to him. The two of them began to speak German back and forth, and I was astounded. After that, I felt better about our situation and knew we would be okay.

According to Joaquin, Weltzin usually reached the bar around 11:00 p.m. He kept to himself at the bar, drinking slowly and steadily until midnight. He always left precisely as he'd arrived – alone.

Finally, it got late, and I felt ready to leave. I said goodbye to Holger and Joaquin and left with my duffle bag slung over my left shoulder. I took my 1903 Springfield rifle and Colt 1911 handgun with me. I had to travel as lightly as possible. It took me just over an hour to reach my destination.

Darkness surrounded me. I was in a position that had become all too familiar to me. The solitary missions I had conducted before and during World War II had all run together, and I no longer kept count. The missions were similar; all that differed for me were the faces of the enemies I hunted. I completed each assigned mission without hesitation. The Nazi I hunted that night, Weltzin, had maintained a vast number of Jewish concentration camps. He had delivered Zyklon B to the hundreds of concentration camps in Germany and surrounding countries. He had somehow eluded capture by the American and Russian forces when they converged on Berlin in May 1945.

I glanced at my watch; it was 11:17 p.m. I peered through my rifle's scope in the darkness, aided by the street lights that lined the road before me. I was tucked between two large rocks, approximately two hundred yards from the street, in an elevated position I had taken earlier that evening under cover of darkness.

Removing my eye from the rifle's scope, I saw a black, two-door Nash pull up and park about thirty yards down the street. The car cut its engine, and the street became eerily quiet. A man exited the car, his face hidden by his hat. He appeared to be about 5'9", Weltzin's reported height. I felt a wave of frustration come over me. I had not moved from my position in almost three hours. Finally, the man walked under a street light a few feet from his car. He removed his hat, pulled a handkerchief from his right front pants pocket, and wiped his forehead. The street light illuminated his face, and I saw it clearly. He then replaced his handkerchief, pulled a pack of cigarettes from his shirt pocket, and lit a cigarette. At that point, there was no doubt that he was Warren Weltzin. He was a long way from home and squarely in my sights. After he took his third puff of his cigarette, I pulled the trigger on my 1903 Springfield. The resulting blast echoed down the quiet street. Warren's head snapped back as the back of his head exploded and splattered against the outside wall of the bar. He dropped right where he stood.

I quickly got up and disassembled my rifle as much as allowed, allowing me to conceal it in my duffle bag. After returning the weapon to my duffle bag, I worked my way down from my shooting position above the street. It took me over an hour to reach the safety of Joaquin's house.

CHAPTER 5

No End in Sight

"Evil gains work their punishment."
Sophocles

Hurrying back to Joaquin's house, I heard Spanish voices outside the bar where Weltzin lay dead on the sidewalk. I couldn't understand any of what was being said, but the voices were concerned over the fact a man was lying there on the ground, missing the back half of his head. As I got further from the bar, the voices faded away and were soon replaced with the distant sound of dogs barking.

It felt good to be back in the fight, eliminating the enemy, but at the same time, it felt strange, almost wrong, to be killing a former enemy during peacetime. My conscience was eased, however, when I considered what Walter Weltzin had done during the war. He had played a big part in sending millions to their deaths. The simple fact was that my superiors had ordered me to eliminate him, and in the Army, I was to obey without question.

I arrived back at Joaquin's house at 1:30 a.m. Before leaving the house earlier that evening, I had told Joaquin and Holger that I would knock three times, pause, and then knock four times to let them know I was back. I approached the door and went through my arranged knocking sequence. To my surprise, the door opened immediately. Joaquin welcomed me back, and I sat at his kitchen table. He quickly offered me water and a small meal of meat and potatoes.

Joaquin and Holger just stared at me as I ate ravenously, having worked up a healthy appetite. I said nothing to either of them until I had finished my meal. Their facial expressions showed they were anxious to hear about what had happened.

For the next hour, I shared with them every step of the mission. I felt like I was debriefing my superiors, something I had done countless times.

After hearing about my mission's success, they agreed it would be best if we slept for a few hours and then regrouped to discuss Holger and me's exit strategy. There was no immediate risk of being discovered.

Joaquin's house was small. He had no extra beds and only one small couch. I chose the hard floor. We all went to sleep quickly that night.

I was awakened a few hours later by a loud banging on the front door. Joaquin was the first to the door. I crouched on the floor and looked toward the door, still trying to clear my head. Joaquin motioned me to remain quiet. He then slowly opened the front door. The sun started rising, and the light broke into the room, but it did not illuminate me or the area where I was positioned.

Whoever stood on the other side of the door that morning was unhappy. I could not make out what was being discussed, but I could tell immediately from the stranger's tone that it was necessary. I assumed it had something to do with the Weltzin shooting outside the bar earlier that evening. Joaquin was firm and did not back down to the man's continued barrage of questions. Eventually, the stranger left, and Joaquin shut the door.

In a low voice, I immediately asked Joaquin if his conversation was about Weltzin's shooting a few hours earlier. He replied in broken German, so I couldn't understand completely, but I concluded that the man was a police officer and he was going house to house trying to find out any information on who killed Weltzin. That immediately put Holger and me at risk for arrest and interrogation if we were caught.

By that time, Holger was awake and trying to piece everything together. The police officer accepted Joaquin's explanation that he knew nothing and was the only one in the house. After a restless minute or so, Joaquin pulled back the curtain on his front window, ever so slowly, and peered out the window, looking for any signs of the police. There were none.

I knew Holger and I were on borrowed time and quickly hashed out an exit strategy with him. We asked Joaquin which routes out of the city were safe. I was still determining if the train would be a safe option out of the city, but I saw no other way to make it back to Buenos Aires.

After about an hour, Holger and I decided to wait until that evening to return to the train station. The last train to Buenos Aires left at 10:30 p.m., and we would be on it. We had our weapons and were resigned to the fact that if we had to, we would shoot our way out of the city. Both of us had been through a long and tiring war and survived. We were not about to be captured or killed in western Argentina. We spent the rest of the day counting the hours until we could leave. On two occasions, Joaquin left to secure some fresh food, which we appreciated. I must have cleaned my weapons three times because I was bored and the hours were long. During my time in basic training, I had been taught how to disassemble and reassemble many weapons blindfolded. I kept myself occupied by conducting this exercise on all three of my weapons in front of Holger. The first time I did it, he did not believe my eyes were closed entirely. I asked Holger to find something to blindfold my eyes with, hoping that would finally convince him. He quickly found a towel in the kitchen, and I wrapped it around my head. I repeated the exercise even faster. Holger was shocked, stating he had not been trained that way. I had only one comment for him in reply.

"That is why Germany did not win the war."

He smiled and graciously replied, "America was a formidable adversary. You are probably right."

The sun finally set, and the three of us finished off a meal of chicken and vegetables. Before leaving, Holger and I did our best to express our appreciation to Joaquin. He had sheltered us, fed us, and helped us avoid capture. I was forever in his debt. I then gathered my travel bag and weapons and exited out the front door, letting Holger and his cousin say their goodbyes in private.

I soon was joined by the two of them. I shook Joaquin's hand firmly, turned, and began to walk toward the train station, but I heard Holger's voice behind me.

"Allen, Joaquin feels it might be best if he goes with us to guide us through some back alleys and help us avoid capture."

I turned around and replied, "We're happy to have the company."

With that, Joaquin shut his front door behind him, and the three of us began to walk, with Joaquin in the lead. None of us spoke. We saw no one for the first mile and a half, but the streets became more crowded as we got closer to downtown Tamberias. There appeared to be some festival, and the streets were filled with people. Food and craft vendors had set up booths every few feet. The festival was a perfect cover for us. We walked through the crowd. We had vendors calling out to us, asking us to buy their wares. We shook our heads "no" while we continued to walk in the direction of the train station.

We eventually cleared the large crowd and could see the Tamberias train station ahead of us. The train was already puffing smoke, and people were beginning to board. Unfortunately, policemen had surrounded the train station and checked people's luggage and identification as they entered.

Joaquin, Holger, and I ducked into a nearby alley, out of sight of the police. We quickly assessed our options. We would have to go with the one that offered the least resistance and allowed us to board the train to Buenos Aires.

In German, I spoke in a low voice to Joaquin and Holger and laid out the only viable plan I could think of.

"Joaquin, Holger, and I will individually purchase tickets and attempt to board the train, and if successful, we will sit in separate train cars. We're going to give you our weapon bags. Please go down to the train tracks and position yourself at the rear of the train so you can throw the bags to us as the train leaves the station. I'll move to the rear of the last train car to catch them. Can you do that for us?"

Joaquin must have understood my instructions because he reached for our bags, shook our hands, and departed.

Holger and I discussed our exit strategy a little more before he left the alley and headed directly to the train station's ticketing office. The strategy was for each of us not to hide behind our nationalities. Holger would say he had been in Tamberias visiting his cousin and hoped the police officer that had knocked on Joaquin's door earlier that day was not the one he would run into while attempting to purchase a ticket.

My story would be that I was an extension of the United States government, scouting Tamberias for a possible vacation destination for

President Truman. I had spent enough time in the White House during the war that I knew some names to throw around to confuse an Argentinian police officer.

I peered around the corner of the building where we had all been hiding and monitored Holger's progress. I saw him just as he walked into the train station ticket office. He had not aroused any suspicion. It was my turn.

I stepped back into the street and walked toward the train station. I was neither nervous nor afraid; if anything, my adrenaline had kicked in, and I felt I was back in the war.

I approached the first police officer, checking people at the train station's front entrance. I was not even allowed to get the first word out when the officer spoke fluent English.

"Are you an American?" "Yes," I replied.

"Why are you in Argentina?" he asked abruptly.

The officer appeared agitated, trying to find the person responsible for shooting Weltzin. Little did he know the person responsible for sending the Nazi to his death was standing right in front of him.

In a very calm voice, I answered him directly. "My name is Allen Voigt. I'm here scouting out possible vacation spots for my President, Harry S. Truman. He has never visited your beautiful country. Our previous President, Franklin D. Roosevelt, visited Buenos Aires in November 1936 and found your country very inviting. I was with him on that trip. It is because of that previous visit that President Truman has asked me to come."

The officer was taken aback by my answer. "Where are you going now?" he asked.

"Buenos Aires," I replied.

With that, he motioned me to proceed to the ticket office.

I walked directly to the ticket counter, bought a ticket for Buenos Aires, and boarded the train. I spotted Holger in the second train car. I gave him a head nod as I walked past him and proceeded to the fourth train car. I took a seat that gave me a clear view of the officers stopping people from entering the station.

I had just sat down when the train began to lurch forward. I only had a little time to locate Joaquin at the train's rear. I had no idea how far down the track he had gone. I just knew the farther away from the train station he was, the more momentum the train would have, making the handoff of our weapons even harder.

As the train cleared the station, I jumped up from my seat and rushed to the train's rear. I didn't have far to go and quickly reached the last car of the train, which, to my surprise, was empty.

I opened the back door of the train car and was met by a rush of cool night air. There was no platform to stand on, so I held on to the door and leaned out of the car, hoping to see Joaquin. By then, the train was moving approximately fifteen miles per hour and gaining momentum. It was pitch black, and there was very little light except for the reflection of the full moon, which gave me just enough light to see fifty yards behind the train.

A few seconds passed, and there was still no sign of Joaquin. I feared he had been captured or didn't understand what I had asked of him. I had just begun moving back into the train car when I heard my name being shouted.

"Allen!"

I leaned back out of the train and squinted down the tracks. Joaquin was running at a full sprint from the right side of the train tracks with our weapon bags slung over his shoulders. I leaned out as far as possible with my right arm fully extended.

Joaquin reached the middle of the train tracks and ran as fast as possible to close the distance between us. He was so close I could see the sweat dripping off his forehead.

As Joaquin continued to run at full sprint, with one fluid motion, he dropped his shoulders, allowing the weapons bag to drop, and gathered both bags in his right hand. He pulled his right arm back and quickly flung both bags forward in my direction.

The weapons bags flew through the air, looking almost like they were in slow motion. They were coming in fast and straight for me, and hit me squarely in the chest with enough momentum that I fell back into the train car.

I immediately sprung to my feet. It felt like the train was moving much faster. I looked out the train door. The distance between Joaquin and me had widened considerably.

Standing on the tracks, he raised one hand and yelled, "Adios!" I answered, "Thank you, Joaquin!"

He waved to me as the train quickly pulled away.

I closed the door, sat in the last train car, and took inventory of the weapons bags. All the weapons were secure. I walked back to the train car where Holger was sitting. By then, we were clear of any watchful eyes, and I had no concern we were being followed.

Holger anxiously awaited my arrival, wondering if I had retrieved the weapons or if Joaquin had even met the train. He sat with his back to me, and as soon as he heard the train door open behind him, he turned and looked at me with a panicked look.

I sat across from him and placed the weapons bags under my seat. I took a deep breath as I pushed my back against the seat. Holger was anticipating my update as he leaned forward in my direction. I said, "Joaquin probably never had to perform that type of feat ever before in his life. While running as fast as he could, he took the weapons bags off his shoulders and threw them about fifteen yards up to me as I was hanging out of the back of the last train car. The bags hit me square in my chest and knocked me flat on my back. When I got back on my feet, the train and Joaquin were a long way apart. I waved goodbye to him. We have all our weapons. Your cousin is very resourceful."

Holger relaxed and sat back in his seat. His complexion changed, and he smiled as he offered me a reply. "Allen, I must admit, this is the most excitement I have had since the war. What happens next?"

I leaned forward in my seat and replied, "We kill more Nazis."

Holger had always denounced the Nazi party. He replied by slapping my left shoulder.

Our train back to Buenos Aires was moving along quickly as it lumbered down the tracks in a southeasterly direction. Due to the late hour, I did not expect a meal service on board the train, but I was starving and decided to venture out in search of anything to eat. There were very few people on the train that night, and I felt comfortable leaving the weapons under my seat.

Holger was hungry, too, so he joined me. I knew there was no meal car behind us, as I had just come from there, so we ventured toward the front of the train. Upon boarding the train earlier, I had entered the second car, so my only hope was that the first train car had food.

Passing through the cars that night, I noticed that the type of passengers on board was consistent with those on the trip we had taken up from Buenos Aires: a mixture of old folks and young singles. I saw no one that looked suspicious. Deep down, I was disappointed that none of my remaining Nazis were on board, sitting alone for me to kill them. That would have made my job much more manageable and gotten me home to Alice faster.

Soon, Holger and I smelled food being prepared. We were in luck.

Upon entering the food car, I saw something unexpected. Food was being prepared, but the car was full of Argentinian soldiers. Rifles were laid across tables, and all the soldiers had revolver pistols strapped to their belts. I did not even turn and look back at Holger, who was entering the car. I just found an open table and took a seat. Holger followed me and sat down across from me.

I was not intimidated, having been in many scrapes before and during the war years. I knew Holger, being a German soldier, could hold his own. I was glad I had decided to leave our weapons back in our train car, just in case there was a sudden inquiry from an Argentinian soldier.

A waiter soon came over and handed us two menus. Of course, the menus were in Spanish, but Holger could make out most of the words, which relieved me. I was famished. I found it amusing that I was more worried about ordering a late meal than I was over the fact that foreign soldiers surrounded us.

"Holger, just order me something, anything, and I will eat it," I said.

He laughed, offering a reply. "You must have developed a lot of faith in me, Allen."

The waiter stood by our table and waited for us to order. Holger tried to order in his broken Spanish, frequently pointing at the menu as if that would help get our order placed faster.

After about thirty seconds, the waiter put his hand up, telling Holger to stop talking. I chuckled.

The waiter then asked Holger if he would like to order in German. Holger tilted his head up from the menu and smiled, glancing over at me. He took a deep breath and began to order our meals in German.

I understood the entire conversation from that moment on.

Holger picked out a good meal for me: meat and potatoes.

We settled in and reviewed the last thirty-six hours. Our conversation quickly led to what could occur upon arriving in Buenos Aires.

I quickly concluded that Holger knew nothing about the whereabouts of the remaining three Nazis we were hunting. He and I assumed his father, Rudolph, had reached out to all his sources to provide me with the necessary leads for me to complete my mission.

My frustration was mounting because this was unlike all the World War II missions I had conducted. Those missions were organized, detailed, and well-planned by my superiors. The missions often required improvisation. I also had to be flexible and often waited for the mission's parameters to unfold. My current mission was frustrating because I had high-level orders: to find and kill four escaped Nazis. Outside of that, I was void of any other details. I had to consider that my superiors had complete faith in me, as I had served in the United States Army for twenty years, successfully completing missions every time.

Our dinner finally arrived. Very little was said between Holger and me as we ate.

The conversations by the Argentinian soldiers became louder and louder the more they drank. A few of the soldiers began to pull out their pistols and waved them about as they shouted to each other in drunken conversations.

I had been around a lot of drunken military members in my career, but this situation was different. We were locked in a train car barreling down the tracks at a fast clip. There was no way out in the event shots rang out.

Holger and I kept our heads down as we finished our meals, but always with a watchful eye on the soldiers' activities.

After I finished my meal, I laid my napkin on my plate. About that time, a young Argentinian soldier came by our table and bumped into me as I sat there. He carried a beer bottle in his left hand and a pistol in his right. In drunken Spanish, he tried to carry on a conversation with us, spilling his beer on me the entire time.

After about two minutes of mindless chatter from him, I'd had enough and stood up. The drunken soldier stepped back, stumbled, and fell on his butt, dropping his beer and spilling its remaining contents all over the floor. He did, however, manage to hold on to his pistol. His fellow soldiers, seeing him sprawled out on the floor and me standing over him, assumed I had pushed him down.

A few soldiers rushed to the drunken soldier's aide; the rest rushed Holger and me. In a matter of moments, we had gone from having an enjoyable dinner to having pistols stuck in our sides and pointed at our heads.

I quickly scanned the car and counted three soldiers helping the drunken soldier to his feet. Six more were huddled around Holger and me. That was a total of ten Argentinian soldiers upset with us.

The tension increased by the second. I was ready to grab the pistol of the soldier who had it pushed against the right side of my head. I was frustrated already, and this situation pushed me to my limit. On top of my frustration, I was dog-tired.

The original drunken soldier who had approached our table stood up and walked toward us, speaking rapidly in Spanish the entire time. The other soldiers backed away and let him through. He laid his pistol on the table and reached his right hand out to shake mine. With some hesitation, I reciprocated.

He laughed and spoke some more, putting his arm around me. I wondered what in the world was happening.

I looked over at Holger, who offered his best answer, as he could tell I was confused.

"Allen, the best I can figure out is that the soldier that fell, as drunk as he is, told the other soldiers that you didn't push him down and that he fell because he's drunk. I think they believe him."

At this point, our German-speaking waiter stepped into the middle of the meal car and spoke a few sentences in Spanish. He told the soldiers that we were Germans and corroborated the drunken soldier's story that we were not hostile to him, as he had witnessed the entire exchange.

From that point on, things changed dramatically. Holger and I took center stage, with the drunken Argentinian soldiers asking us lots of questions. The waiter interpreted the questions thrown at us in German, and we gave our answers, which he translated into Spanish. We were asked some wild questions. I let Holger take most of them.

Questions posed to us varied from, "Did you fight in the German

Army during World War II?" to "Did you kill Americans?" to "Did you ever see Hitler?"

I quickly realized that this interaction with the Argentinian soldiers gave me a chance to ask about my three remaining Nazis. I hoped that one of these soldiers had seen one, had heard rumors of their locations, or had even interacted with one of them.

There was a lull in the conversation, so I took that as my opportunity to throw out the big question.

"Holger and I are traveling throughout Argentina to enjoy the countryside and escape the destruction of our homeland. In your travels, have you met any other former German soldiers? We would love to meet them and talk with them."

The waiter translated my question into Spanish.

An awkward silence followed, and I assumed that all of the Argentinian soldiers understood the Spanish interpretation from the waiter and had yet to meet any other German soldiers on their travels.

Finally, a young Argentinian soldier spoke up from the back of the pack.

"I met an older German soldier in Tamberias a few weeks ago. We were stationed there for sixty days. I met him only because he came to our location asking if we wanted to buy a German Luger handgun. He had a box full of them, complete with holsters. He was only asking twenty pesos for each handgun and holster. I bought one."

At that point, the soldier reached into a bag at his feet. He pulled out a German Luger pistol and said, "In fact, here is the gun I bought from him."

"That is a fine weapon, sir," I said. "I had one during the war and used it many times. I would love to meet this German soldier if I ever return to Tamberias. Do you happen to remember his name?"

The Argentinian soldier paused for a moment before replying, "I don't remember his first name, but I believe his last name was Pagel. He said he was trying to raise money for a trip to Bolivia. He said something about wanting to buy a mountain cabin way up on the mountain of Nevado Sajama. He said he had lived in Austria and missed the mountains."

I couldn't believe what I was hearing. Rickert Pagel was on my list. I so much wanted to find the bastard and eliminate him.

We spent another hour with the Argentinian soldiers. One by one, they left the meal car to sit in one of the leading passenger cars to sleep off their hangovers.

It was almost 2:00 a.m., and I was exhausted. I continued to pick the brain of the Argentinian soldier who had bought the Luger pistol. I asked him what he knew about Bolivia and the topography. He admitted to me that he was surprised Pagel would want to live in the mountains of Bolivia, as there was very little rain in the northern part of Bolivia, and the landscape was full of scrub vegetation and rocks. He said very few people lived there.

His description made perfect sense to me. If I were an escaped Nazi trying to hide out in South America, I would go to the most remote part of the continent and live out my life in isolation. Unfortunately for Pagel, his days in Bolivia were numbered.

I thanked the soldier and bade him goodnight. Holger had left the meal car already, so I was the last person to leave. When I reached my seat, I saw that Holger was already asleep beside mine. I reached under the seat and grabbed a weapon bag, configuring it to form a pillow. I drifted off to sleep, encouraged that I had an unexpected lead.

Our train rumbled down the steel tracks all night. I woke up each time the train stopped at a station. The sun eventually rose in the east. When we were about six hours from Buenos Aires, I couldn't sleep any longer.

Holger was nowhere to be found when I stood up to stretch my legs. I headed straight for the meal car to find some breakfast. I passed what seemed like every Argentinian soldier, asleep or holding his head in his hands because of a hangover. I even had to step over some soldiers sleeping on the floor.

I finally entered the meal car. The same waiter was in place, and Holger was sitting at our table from the night before. He was already eating a delicious breakfast of scrambled eggs, bacon, and orange juice.

I sat down with him and quickly ordered the same breakfast. I soon got my meal and shared with Holger the intelligence I had received the night before about Pagel. We asked the waiter about the distance to Bolivia from Buenos Aires and the best mode of transportation.

What he described was arduous. We could take a train to the southern border but must secure a guide, horses, and supplies. There were not many roads to the base of Nevado Sajama.

For the time we had left, Holger and I figured we would return to his father's home west of Buenos Aires, regroup, gather the required supplies, and plan the best route to Bolivia.

In my mind, I wanted Holger to continue with me on these missions. I felt I could move and navigate faster without him holding me back. I did enjoy his company, however, and part of me thought it might be good to have someone with his military experience with me.

Our train lumbered into the downtown Buenos Aires train station on the morning of July 19, 1946. It had been a long trip but a rewarding one. Holger and I quickly disembarked and boarded a bus heading toward Holger's father's home.

Traveling over the western roads of Buenos Aires, I looked out the bus window and wondered how I would kill Rickert Pagel. He was in his early sixties, and I did not expect him to put up much of a fight. Regardless, I had to be careful and ensure my plan was sound. The movement of the bus rocked me to sleep, and I dreamt of my time back on Guadalcanal during early August 1942 when I was asked to survey the island in advance of the 1st Marine Division's assault on the Japanese Army and Navy, who had taken the island many months before. I had parachuted onto the island, but shortly after jumping out of the plane, piloted by my basic training buddy, Tom Beckett, the plane was hit by anti-aircraft fire from the island. Tom had crashed on the island. After finding the crash site, I concluded that Tom had survived the crash but had been captured by the Japanese Army on the island. I'd spent the next several days searching for Tom to mount a rescue mission. After three days, I was very close to the assigned arrival time of the 1st Marine Division.

I had found Tom but would have to kill several Japanese to rescue him.

On that third day looking for Tom, I looked at my watch; it was 2:18 p.m. I had just slept for six hours. My body needed the rest, but I felt guilty because Tom was imprisoned. However, I knew I had to build my strength to rescue him.

There could be no risk of the Japs discovering me, so I had to stay exactly where I'd slept. I ate a D-ration and a candy bar, washing them down with some water from my canteen. I had enough cover and room to move my legs and roll from side to side to avoid cramps. For the rest of the afternoon, I kept my eyes trained on the building where I hoped Tom was still located. I also surveyed as much of the camp as possible, trying to get a read on the number of men, types of equipment, and so on.

One significant development I noted was the large quantity of tanks, mortars, and howitzer cannons in one corner of the camp. From my position, I counted at least fifteen Jap tanks. There were stockpiles of ammo canisters everywhere. It looked as if the Japs were preparing for a significant American invasion. Little did they know that there was already an American on the island who was ready to administer retribution for their attack on Pearl Harbor. At 6:00 p.m., I finally had proof that Tom was still alive, but that confirmation was coupled with concern and even some uncertainty about our situation. Tom, shirtless and bloodied, was dragged out of the building by two Jap soldiers. I watched as he was pushed to the ground and kicked repeatedly. A senior ranking Jap officer screamed at him in broken English, telling him to kneel in front of him. From what I had witnessed thus far, Tom barely had enough strength to pull himself up. He finally got to a kneeling position, at which point the Jap officer kicked him back down with his boot. The officer screamed again for Tom to rise. Tom managed to get to his knees a second time, and the Jap officer just kicked him down again.

The abuse continued for over an hour. It was 7:00 p.m., and Tom was on his knees, with his hands tied behind his back. He was forced to sit like that for over an hour. By that time, the sun had set completely. A light from a nearby building illuminated the area around Tom. The Jap officer pulled his samurai sword from its sheath on his right hip and raised it above Tom's head, where he held it for several minutes.

Several times the Jap officer cut a swath through the air with the sword only to stop within an inch of the back of Tom's head. Tom stayed motionless.

After three false attempts with the Jap officer's sword, Tom picked his head up, turned in the direction of the Jap officer, and screamed enough for me to hear, "Do it, you Jap coward!"

Tom then lowered his head and stayed very still. The Jap officer was furious and instructed two other Jap soldiers to raise Tom to his feet. He told them to secure Tom by his arms and legs to two large posts. Tom was left in that 'X' position as the Jap officer, and his fellow soldiers reentered the nearby building. A few other Jap soldiers returned from patrol, walked by Tom, and spat on him.

I assessed my options for rescuing Tom. My best option was the one I had mulled over the day before. I would wait until after midnight and then work my way down to Tom, secure him, kill a few Japs, and head for the coast. The sub would be waiting; at least, I hoped it was. The fact that Tom never reported his landing or reported back to his superiors could have been interpreted by them to mean that I never parachuted and that Tom and I had simply crashed and died. Going for the sub was our only viable means of escape.

Midnight came. I surveyed the area all around me and listened for any movement. It was all clear. I prayed to God, asking Him to make my motions swift and sure and give me the strength to rescue Tom. I secured my backpack and inventoried my grenade count, ammunition, knife, and remaining food rations. I secured my last remaining canteen of water to my side, after which I removed my handgun from its holster, chambered a round, and rose to my feet.

I saw no one, other than Tom, within fifty yards in front of me. I left the secured area where I had been for over fifteen hours and slowly moved in Tom's direction. With relative ease, I approached him. I heard all the Japs in the surrounding buildings laughing and hollering, probably drunk with sake.

Tom's head was down, and he appeared to be unconscious, not surprising from the beatings and torture he had received over the last thirty-six hours. I holstered my handgun, took out my knife, and cut the rope holding Tom's arms and legs. As he fell, I caught him and hoisted him over my back. Carrying Tom, I headed toward the nearest patch of dark jungle. We made it about one hundred yards into the jungle without being seen. I was not going to leave just yet, however. Those Japs had ticked me off, and I was going to get a little retribution for Tom.

I gently laid Tom down on the ground and positioned his head and back against a palm tree, facing back toward the camp. He finally woke up.

He recognized me immediately and said, "Allen, what are you doing here? How did you find me?"

I gave him some fresh water from my canteen and replied, "It wasn't easy, but I came upon your crashed plane and saw the Japs had carried you off. We're one hundred yards from where you were a prisoner. It's probably not the best idea, but I'm going to leave you here and head back to the Jap camp for a little payback."

All Tom did was raise his head and say, "Especially the officer."

Time was not on our side, as we had a tiny window to make it to the sub.

I left Tom my handgun and an extra ammo clip for protection and said, "Tom, shoot first and ask questions later. You and I are the only two Americans on this island. When I come back, and I will be back, all I will say as I approach you is the word 'Freedom.'"

As I headed back to the Jap camp, I wondered if this was a good idea.

I had somehow lost the Jap handgun I had secured earlier, but I had my knife and three hand grenades. If overwhelmed by Japs, I would simply pull my grenade pins and take most of them with me in the subsequent explosion.

I paused as I cleared the jungle and reentered the camp's clearing. Surprised that I did not see even one Jap milling around the camp, I walked right up to the building where Tom had been kept earlier in the day. I peered into the single window on the right side of the building. All I could see were a small lantern in the corner of the room and two Japs lying on cots in the far corner. I carefully eased around to the front door of the small building and turned the handle. It was unlocked. I quietly entered the room, leaving the door slightly open behind me. The Jap officer was on the far cot. I knew this because his samurai sword and uniform hung nearby on a hook. I would kill him first.

The wood floor creaked slightly with every step I took. I stopped every step, looking for any movement from the two men lying before me. I decided to change weapons and borrow the Jap officer's samurai sword, mainly for the speed of killing and because it was much longer than my knife. As I approached the sword hanging on the hook, the Jap officer suddenly moved and turned over. The officer's samurai sword was hanging in such a way that I could grab its handle and pull it out of its sheath in one swift motion.

I paused, checked the position of both men lying there, and, with one quick motion, pulled the samurai sword out of its sheath with both my hands. I then turned it sideways and rammed the weapon into the right side of the officer's chest, pushing it into him until the sword came out of his body on the other side. The officer's eyes opened, and although he saw me, the force of the sword's blade ripping his heart apart left him unable to make a sound.

In my peripheral vision, I saw the other Jap that lay to my left rise when he sensed something was happening. I pulled the sword out of the dead Jap officer, turned, and with one quick movement, decapitated the soldier. He did not have a chance to shout or scream. The only noise made was his head hitting the wooden floor with a thud and rolling a few feet away. His body immediately fell back down to his cot. Blood pumped from his neck.

It was time to go. I wiped the Jap blood off the sword as best I could on the officer's blanket and returned it to its sheath. The sheath had a red cord that allowed me to carry the sword on my shoulder. This time, the sword was coming with me. I picked up a clean blanket for Tom on a nearby table.

Not knowing if my actions had stirred any other Jap movement outside, I approached the partially opened door with slight hesitation. I listened first but heard nothing. I then leaned partially out of the door and looked in both directions. The camp was dark, except for a few dim lights shining from nearby buildings and tents. I exited the building and headed back toward the jungle. I managed not to alert any Japs and made it back in the direction of where I had left Tom about thirty minutes before. When I arrived, I saw that Tom was still leaning against the palm tree, and his eyes were shut. My handgun was in his right hand. I moved closer and whispered, "Freedom."

Tom's eyes opened, and he turned in my direction and said, "Allen, glad you're back."

I knelt near Tom and said, "It's time to move. Can you walk?"

Through his parched lips, Tom said, "If it means getting off this God-forsaken island, I can."

I helped him to his feet and handed him the Jap blanket I had secured. "Tom, you hold on to my handgun because I'm going to need both my hands to get you out of here."

I looked at my watch; it was 1:45 a.m. We had just over four hours before the sub designated to pick us up would leave the area. With one of Tom's arms around me, we headed out. We did our best to maneuver through the jungle for the next ninety minutes, continuing in a southeast direction. We didn't want to encounter any Jap patrols, but we couldn't afford to slow down and go quieter because our window of time was quickly closing.

At 4:15 a.m., we saw the beach below us. We had about a half-mile walk to the beach, but it was steep. I kept Tom behind me as we made our way down. The rocks and thick vegetation gave us some footing and something to grasp. Tom had no shoes, and the walk had ripped his feet open. I told him to stop. I bent down, pulled him over my shoulders, and carried him down the rest of the way. It took us another twenty minutes to make it to the beach. We hit the soft sand and continued to the waterline. Tom sat down and let the salt water cover his feet. Even though it must have been excruciating, he kept his feet in the water, as it was the best way to clean his wounds. We both scanned the horizon for any sign of a flashing red light. We saw nothing. My heart sank. The time was 4:40 a.m., and we only had twenty minutes left. We knew we were on the right section of the beach because of the maps we had diligently studied back on Pleasant Island.

I pulled out my binoculars and scanned the water in a one-hundred-and-eighty-degree sweep. Still, we saw nothing that resembled a red light. I suddenly heard dead branches snapping behind us, back toward the jungle. Tom had given me back my handgun, so I pulled it out, got down on one knee, and pointed the gun back in the direction of the jungle. The snapping sound got closer. I still could not see who or what was coming toward us. I placed my gun in my left hand and with my right hand peered through my binoculars in the direction of the movement. I was shocked by what I saw. There stood two young Navy sailors. I put my binoculars down and walked over in their direction.

As I approached them, I said, "Go Navy! I am Captain Voigt."

One of the sailors replied, "Yes, Sir. We know who you are. We're here to take you to the sub. We saw you and the other man clearing the jungle just a few minutes ago. We were hiding in the shadows, hoping it was you. There is a raft to take us out to the sub. We didn't know what condition you would be in, so the Navy asked for two volunteers. We were the first two to volunteer. We were told you might not even make it back."

The sailor and I returned to the waterline and stood with Tom and the other sailor. We all scanned for a red light.

A few minutes passed, and then Tom said, "There it is."

We all saw it at that point. A red light flashed on and off every three seconds. The two sailors returned to the jungle's edge and removed a small raft hidden under some dead branches. They carried it out into the surf. One of the sailors told us to climb aboard.

I helped Tom into the raft, threw my backpack and samurai sword, and climbed in. The other two sailors followed suit. They grabbed the two oars lying on the raft floor, put them in position, and began to row with all their might. The red light looked hundreds of yards away as the raft bobbed up and down in the water. We must have been closer to the sub than I first estimated. Less than fifty yards before us, the sub suddenly rose beyond periscope depth to where half of the hull was exposed on the waterline.

The sailors rowed up to the sub. A large hatch near the conning tower opened, and three sailors climbed out to assist us. One threw us a rope, which the sailors in our raft used to navigate to a small ladder attached to the sub.

Tom was asked to go first. He pulled himself up and held onto the ladder with all his might. One of the sailors and I helped him get out of the raft and halfway up the ladder. The sailors on the sub took over from there and helped him onto the sub. I secured my backpack and samurai sword and followed Tom up the ladder. The two sailors that had rescued us then climbed aboard and let the raft drift away.

We hastily made our way into the sub. The last sailor down the hatch closed it and turned the handle, securing the seal tight. Because we had entered the sub from the forward compartment, we had to return to the control room, where we would meet the sub's Captain. As we returned to the control room, I felt like I had been in this sub before. I then heard a familiar voice shouting in our direction. It was Captain Dempsey. I was back on the *Spearfish.*

We arrived at the control room, and Captain Dempsey gave me a big bear hug and said, "When I heard the Navy was covertly looking for a sub to pick you up on Guadalcanal, I immediately volunteered our sub for the mission. The necessary repairs were made back at Pearl Harbor, and we are back out hunting Jap subs. It took us three days to get to you, but here we are, Allen!"

I shook my head in disbelief. I removed the samurai sword from my back and handed it to Captain Dempsey, and said, "Captain, please accept this sword as my appreciation for rescuing me twice from islands full of Japs."

Captain Dempsey took the sword in both hands, looked at it for the longest time, and said, "Allen, I have never seen one of these before. I see a little blood on it. Is that yours?"

I smiled and replied, "Not mine. The Jap that bled on this sword will not need it back."

The *Spearfish* soon disappeared below the waves and into the blackness of the ocean. Tom was taken to the sick bay, and his wounds were treated. As the sub traveled southeast, away from Guadalcanal, I spent the next hour with Captain Dempsey and a Marine Captain by the name of Stowell, poring over a map of Guadalcanal and pointing out the location of the Jap positions. I related the types of military equipment and ammunition I had seen. I pointed to the northeast corner of the island as the best landing spot for the Marines. I told Captain Stowell that although the beaches were narrow, the jungle widened, which would allow men and machines to pour onto the island.

I finished up with both men by saying, "The Japs will be very shocked in the morning when they find that Lt. Beckett is gone and several Jap officers are dead. The big surprise will be the landing of the Marines."

It was the early morning of August 6. The Marines would be landing in just over twenty-four hours. I wished them a good landing and hoped my time on the island would prove helpful.

I checked on Tom. He already felt better. The morphine helped ease the pain. A young Navy doctor told me Tom had two broken ribs and some deep bruising on his back, but otherwise, he would be fine.

I found some food in the sub's galley. Afterward, I went to the sub's rear, where several cots existed. I found an empty one, crawled onto it, and soon fell asleep. The *Spearfish* sailed for three days and nights in the direction of Brisbane, Australia.

When the bus suddenly stopped, I was jolted awake from my dreams about Guadalcanal and Tom's rescue. We had finally arrived back at Rudolph's home.

Pablo and Augustus were waiting near the road. It was good to see them. I had no idea how they knew we would arrive at that moment, but I did not put anything past Rudolph. He was connected. He had figured out where Warren Weltzin was and allowed me to eliminate my first escaped Nazi. I couldn't wait to tell him about what I had found out about Rickert Pagel.

Holger and I greeted Pablo. Augustus ran up to me and put his two front paws on my chest, trying to lick me in the face. I hugged the big dog and rubbed his back as he licked my face repeatedly. Our collective merry little band walked up to the house. I looked forward to sleeping in an actual bed.

CHAPTER 6

Run to the Hills

"Nothing endures except change."
Heraclitus

Rudolph, Elsa, Matthias, Holger's wife, and all their family members assembled in front of the house to greet Holger and me when we neared the front porch. We hadn't been gone that long, but everyone acted like we had been gone for years. The fanfare was clearly for Holger and not for me. While everyone was milling around Holger, Rudolph came over to where I stood by myself, shook my hand, and said, "Congratulations, Allen, on locating and eliminating Warren Weltzin. Joaquin called us and told us your mission was successful. The quality of the call was not good, but I concluded that you had taken out Weltzin and that you and Holger were safe and returning to Buenos Aires."

I replied, "Thank you, Rudolph, for helping us find him. Joaquin was more than accommodating. He performed exceptionally well under pressure and was instrumental in our success."

"That is good to hear, Allen, and I am not surprised," Rudolph said.

I started to share with Rudolph the news I had recently received on Rickert Pagel. I had just begun when Rudolph put his arm around me and suggested we all return to the house and enjoy a nice lunch. My update would have to wait.

The next few hours were taken up with tales of our train rides back and forth, our excitement about avoiding the Argentinian police on two occasions, and of course, my details about my elimination of Warren Weltzin, but only after Matthias and Holger's small children had left the table. I was uncomfortable answering the barrage of questions, especially in front of kids.

During the war, I had been required to debrief my superiors after every mission. The information I shared had always been top secret, and the audience had always been small. However, that days debrief was more like a show-and-tell like when I was in grade school. Life was funny sometimes. After lunch, Rudolph asked Holger and me to join him on the back veranda for cigars. For the next hour, we provided more specific details on our Tamberias activity to Rudolph.

"Allen, the details you provide will be sent to your superiors in Washington, D.C., as soon as possible. Lt. Colonel Yates will be eager to receive the update on your successful elimination of the first Nazi on your list," Rudolph said.

There I was, a Captain in the United States Army, relying on a German to assist me in notifying my superiors. It was a strange turn of events, for sure.

Although I was exhausted by that time of the day, I wanted to do something I had not done in a very long time, and that was to take a nice, long outdoor hike with a dog.

I was an only child, but my childhood in western New York was full of fond memories. I enjoyed playing in Cazenovia Creek, hunting in the woods with my grandfather, Henry, and playing in the fields and barns with my neighborhood friends. My family did not have much money, but I did not know any better, and life was good. A one-room schoolhouse in Boston, New York, provided me with most of my early education, but the best education I got was hiking in the woods with my first dog, Porgy. He died in 1928 while I was in basic training, but the times I spent with him growing up were exceptional.

I wanted to spend the rest of my day outside to clear my mind before leaving for Bolivia. I asked Pedro and Rudolph if I could take Augustus out for a long walk on the property, notifying them I would not be back in time for dinner.

By the time Augustus and I cleared the back door of the house, the dog was jumping up and down. I got the sense he knew he could run and explore.

We left and walked due East. I looked at my watch; it was 3:40 p.m. Scattered clouds drifted across a blue sky. I found it perfect weather for getting out and clearing my head.

Rudolph's property was vast and gave Augustus a perfect opportunity to run. He repeatedly sprinted twenty to thirty yards before stopping to catch his breath. We had walked about two miles when Augustus found a creek where he lapped some cool water. I went upstream from him and drank some water myself.

Before long, Augustus began to walk beside me, keeping perfect pace with me. As we walked deeper into the property, I was taken back to my time in western New York, long before I entered high school, the ROTC or Army boot camp. It had been an innocent time. War had not begun in Europe, Pearl Harbor had not been attacked, and hundreds of Americans had not died. Millions of Jews were still alive and together as families. It was nice to reminisce about the better days, if only for a few minutes.

When we had walked about six miles into the property, we came upon a rustic stone fence roughly four feet in height and ran to my left and right as far as my eyes could see. I concluded this was a border wall marking Rudolph's property. The sun was starting to dip into the western tree line behind me. I decided it was time for Augustus and me to return to the house. I had not taken a flashlight, but I knew the moon would provide some light as we started to walk back toward the house.

After we had walked for about forty minutes, the sun had set entirely. The property had become eerily quiet. I estimated we were still three miles from the house when Augustus suddenly stopped dead in his tracks and growled deep in his throat. I immediately dropped to one knee and put my right hand on his back. His breathing was slow, and his growl became louder. In my excitement to get out and clear my head, I forgot not only a flashlight but also to bring any form of protection. My weapons were back in my room at the house. For all I knew, Augustus and I were about to encounter some trespassers intent on inflicting bodily harm or, even worse, a wild animal that was out for a late-night snack.

I had encountered countless enemy soldiers over my military career and defeated them. This situation seemed a lot different. I was concerned about my safety.

Augustus's breathing suddenly stopped, and his growl ceased. He took off and disappeared into a small group of trees. Clouds covered the moon, so I could barely see the tree line.

I then heard what sounded like a vicious dogfight. The fighting continued for what seemed like an eternity, then suddenly stopped. I still had not risen from kneeling but suddenly decided to stand up and run toward the trees.

Augustus had sensed danger and opted to protect me. I had to know if he was all right. I cautiously approached the group of trees. The moon broke free of the clouds, and I could see a blood trail leading from the trees off to my left. I followed the blood trail and soon came upon a large mountain lion. He appeared to be dead; he had a large wound on his neck, and his head was lying in a pool of blood. When I got closer, I saw that his head was almost severed from his body.

I then heard heavy breathing that I knew must be coming from Augustus. I found him lying a few yards away, licking his right leg, which was bleeding. As soon as he noticed me, he stood and approached me, rubbing his head against my right leg.

I knelt and, with both hands, rubbed his head and back. I inspected his leg and determined he would be able to walk home. I wrapped his leg with a portion of my shirt that I tore off. I had no idea how I would have carried him back to the house if he had been severely injured.

Over the next ninety minutes, Augustus and I walked back to the house, stopping occasionally for me to check Augustus's leg. I felt sorry for him, but was also incredibly thankful for him. That mountain lion was slightly larger than he was and would have quickly taken me down if Augustus had not killed him first.

When we got closer to Rudolph's house, I saw Pedro approaching us with a flashlight to greet us. I told him what had happened, and he walked Augustus into the house and tended to his wound. I stayed with them for thirty minutes as Pedro gently cleaned and bandaged the wound. He also fed Augustus and gave him fresh water.

It was close to 11:00 p.m. I decided to go to bed. I had not eaten since lunch, but that was okay. I was glad Augustus would be all right.

Despite the encounter with the mountain lion, I found that I felt better. I drifted off to sleep that night, wondering how Alice was and how she was progressing in her recovery. I missed her.

The following day came quickly. A knock at my door awakened me. Before leaving bed, I looked at my watch on the nightstand. Surprisingly, it was 9:20 a.m., and I had slept for ten hours. My body must have needed it.

I got up, still half asleep, and managed to find the door. I opened it slowly and was greeted by Pedro.

"Augustus is eager to see you, Allen. Would you like some breakfast?" "I am so glad Augustus is doing well," I replied, "Yes, I would love something to eat. Let me put on some fresh clothes. I'll meet you in the kitchen, Pedro."

I splashed some water on my face, ran some more water through my hair, and tried to look presentable by putting on some wrinkled clothes from my suitcase.

I went to the kitchen and found a bountiful breakfast had been prepared. It was more food than I could eat, but I dug in and enjoyed every bite. While finishing breakfast, Augustus approached me and nudged his head against my left leg. I rubbed his head and gave him a piece of toast, which he ate in two bites.

After breakfast, I went back to my room. Augustus followed me and lay in the corner of my room as I showered, shaved, and put on some fresh clothes. I walked back out into the main common area of the house and was met by Holger.

We spent the next few minutes talking about my previous night's adventure as news of it had spread throughout the house.

Rudolph suddenly appeared from the nearby basement door and said, "Holger and Allen, please join me in the basement. I have news on our infamous Nazi, Rickert Pagel, and I cannot wait to tell you."

Holger and I followed Rudolph back into the basement, where Rudolph wasted no time sharing his news.

"Rickert Pagel is holed up in a cabin in western Bolivia and in poor health. Allen, maybe you can give him a quick death. My sources are solid. I have his approximate location and maps of the surrounding area. It will likely take you five to seven days to reach him.

I paused for a good thirty seconds before offering my reply. "Point me in his direction, and I will do the rest," I said.

Rudolph offered a smile, and for the next few hours, we pored over the maps on the table and spoke about the country of Bolivia. It had a dry and desolate landscape, situated far out in the western part of South America. Rudolph seemed to know a lot about Bolivia, but he admitted several times during our lengthy conversation that his information about the country was secondhand. This frustrated me, but at the same time, I had to appreciate Rudolph and all that he was doing for me.

Late in the afternoon, an older gentleman walked down the stairs and into the basement. Rudolph immediately introduced him.

"Allen, Holger, this man is Javier. He was a childhood friend of mine growing up here in Buenos Aires. Shortly after I moved to Germany, he and his family moved to Bolivia. For the last forty years, he has been living there. I got word to him, and he has traveled here over the last few days. He has graciously agreed to give us a deeper understanding of Bolivia and will escort you all to Bolivia."

I appreciated Rudolph's efforts to give us more firsthand knowledge of the country and told him so. I also thanked Javier.

Javier smiled at me and began to study the volume of maps on the table. He looked at the maps individually, putting them aside or tossing them on the floor. For the next fifteen minutes, we all watched Javier's actions. It was entertaining as Javier tossed away more maps than he kept on the table.

It turned out Rudolph's Spanish could have been better. This became apparent as Javier spoke rapidly in Spanish about the three maps he had left on the table. After about thirty seconds, Rudolph motioned for Javier to stop. Rudolph called for a female servant to come down from upstairs and perform the role of interpreter.

The servant soon came down and patiently translated from Spanish to German for over an hour. The servant had followed Rudolph and his family to Germany when Rudolph was a young teenager and had now returned with the family to South America. I had just noticed her.

Javier told us that we could expect limited transportation options upon reaching Bolivia. We might have to travel by car, horse, or even on foot into the southwestern area of Bolivia. He later told us that Rickert had picked the most remote part of Bolivia and was holed up in a mountainous area, approximately eighteen thousand feet above sea level. The high elevation was something I had not experienced during the war. The temperature would also be challenging, as we would most likely encounter snow when we got closer to Rickert.

At that point in the conversation, I had enough information to proceed with my mission. I had more planning than required, but my natural enemy in this mission would be the elevation and cold temperature. I had experienced cold weather in western New York, but this assignment would take it to a new level of discomfort.

The servant left us and headed back upstairs. I thanked her in German, and she smiled in return. Javier then sat in the corner of the basement, leaving Rudolph, Holger, and me to work out the final logistics of our trip to Bolivia.

The first leg of our journey would take us back along the same route we had just taken to Tamberias. In Tamberias, we would take another train northeast into Bolivia. The third leg would require us to find some form of transportation to the base of Nevado Sajaman, near the eastern border of Chile. It would be approximately thirteen hundred miles.

By this point, Holger and Rudolph agreed that we had enough information to find Rickert. Once we got close, we would have to improvise. While my military training and years of experience in the field had taught me how to adjust and use my surroundings, those factors still did not make it any easier to seek out the enemy in a strange land.

Holger assumed he would be joining me, and it made more sense that he did. Most of my military missions had been solitary, but at this stage in my military career, I welcomed the company.

I spent the rest of the day preparing for our long journey. I cleaned my weapons again, sorted out which clothing I would take, and studied the maps we had been given earlier in the day.

We shared a hearty dinner that night. Holger and I swapped stories about the war and debated into the late hours as to which country had the best-mechanized weapons during the war.

Holger and I agreed to get an early start in the morning. As I walked to my room, Rudolph approached me with a box.

"Allen, here is a brand-new pair of boots for your journey. I had one of my servants go into town today and secure a pair each for you and Holger. This mission will be more arduous than the last, and you must keep your feet warm the higher in elevation you go."

"Thank you, Rudolph," I said. "That is very kind of you."

Rudolph continued, "The distance you will travel will be great. As you and Holger make this journey, I will continue to expand my search and leverage all my contacts. I'll get word to Joaquin in Tamberias if I'm able to locate any more Nazis on your list. One could be closer to your next location, preventing you from coming back here to obtain more leads."

I paused a minute before replying. "In all honesty, Rudolph, I'm hoping to avoid spending more time in Tamberias since we barely got away the last time. With that said, what you are outlining makes perfect sense. Holger and I will make sure to get in touch with Joaquin before returning to Buenos Aires."

I shook Rudolph's hand and thanked him for all his kindness and hospitality. I then retired for the evening.

I awoke before sunrise and prepared to head to Bolivia the following day. The sooner I could accomplish that, the sooner I could return home to Alice.

Breakfast had been prepared for Holger and me, and we enjoyed every bite. As we prepared to be transported to the train station that morning by one of Rudolph's servants, Augustus found me and greeted me with a sloppy lick of his big, wet tongue. I rubbed his back and patted him a few times before heading out. I let Holger take plenty of time to say goodbye to his wife and children.

There was no discussion in the car that morning between us; we each had our own thoughts. I was thinking about every possible scenario related to Rickert Pagel. What type of structure would he be living in? Would he have any bodyguards protecting him? Would he be armed and able to put up any resistance? At what elevation would his cabin be on the mountain? The higher the elevation, the less weight I would want to carry.

Holger and I were soon dropped off at the familiar downtown Buenos Aires train station. We purchased our tickets for Tamberias, Argentina, and boarded the train. I found an open seat and settled in for the long trip. I had spent so much time on trains before and during the war that the rides almost became hypnotic. The noise of the wheels rolling down the steel tracks and the train's movement always put me to sleep or into deep thought. This trip was no different. I chose to sleep this time. I must have slept hard because I was awakened by the jolt of the train when it stopped at the first town along the route. This repetition continued for two days as the train lumbered northwest toward Tamberias. The monotony was grueling because I had spent so much time on trains over the last two weeks. By the fourth stop, it was dark outside, and I felt like exiting the train and walking the rest of the way. I knew better than to try walking to Tamberias, though. However, I stretched my legs and attempted to converse with the train engineer. After a minute or so, I was not making any progress with my limited Spanish, so I decided to get back on the train and find my seat.

Holger found me soon after that, and we talked the rest of the way to Tamberias. It was funny during this leg of the trip in that Holger finally relented and admitted the United States military had better vehicles during the war, citing examples of the Army's two-and-a-half-ton cargo truck and the famous Jeep. I agreed that the Germans had better tanks but needed to make more of them. Our conversations were entertaining, and the debate was endless. It helped bide the time and ease the boredom of train travel.

The second night, we finally arrived at the Tamberias train station. It was just after 1:00 a.m. This time, no police officers were patrolling the train station.

Shortly after entering the train station, we discovered that the next train for Cochabamba, Bolivia, was leaving at 5:00 a.m., so we had four hours to wait.

Holger and I rolled the dice and decided to seek out Joaquin and surprise him. We found a cab parked outside the train station, hopped in, and gave the driver Joaquin's address.

Riding through the streets of Tamberias early that morning, I saw no soul. I saw a hungry dog walking in an alley, looking for food.

Finally, the cab driver pulled up to Joaquin's house, but something did not seem right. One of the house's front windows was broken, and the front door was partially open. Holger quickly paid the cab driver and asked him to wait for us to return. We jumped out of the cab and rushed up to the front door.

"Joaquin, Joaquin?" Holger shouted. There was no reply from inside the house.

I shoved the front door open the rest of the way, and we sprinted into the house. I knew immediately that the news was not good. I had smelled death many times during my long military career, and there was no mistaking it. We found Joaquin tied to a chair in the kitchen. He had been shot in the left side of his head. His head and upper body were slumped forward. His hands were tied behind his back, and his feet were bare. He had been dead for several days and had been tortured before his death. His fingernails and toenails had all been ripped out. The nails and bloody pliers were scattered across the kitchen floor.

Holger became distraught, fell to his knees, and began to cry. He clutched Joaquin's thighs and apologized to him repeatedly.

"Joaquin, this is my entire fault. You didn't deserve this. I am sorry, cousin. I am sorry."

I dragged Holger away from Joaquin's body and sat him in a nearby chair. I knew Joaquin had probably been killed in retaliation for my killing Weltzin days earlier. I was not sure, but everything led me to this conclusion. Joaquin had been tortured to extract information regarding the Nazi's death and who killed him. I figured he had been captured after chasing our train and tossing us our weapons.

It had been a brutal death.

Time was not on our side, but Holger and I could not leave Joaquin in that state. I asked Holger to tell the cab driver we had a body to take to the nearest funeral home. I cut Joaquin's bonds, wrapped his body in a blanket, and secured it with some of the same rope that had initially bound him to his kitchen chair.

Holger returned and helped me carry Joaquin's body out of the house. The cab driver had backed his car up to the front door, allowing Holger and me to place Joaquin's body in the trunk. It was hard to close the trunk lid with Joaquin's body in there, but it was the only choice we had.

The cab driver spoke very little English and no German. Still, we got him to understand that we needed to transport Joaquin's body to the nearest funeral home.

After a short drive, we drove to a home on a residential street. The sign on the front door read *Funeraria Reinshagen*. I concluded we were in the right place but noticed the German last name.

Holger knocked on the door, and after a few minutes, an old man greeted us. The cab driver helped us explain our situation to the old man, who motioned for us to bring Joaquin's body into the house. Holger and I carefully removed his body from the trunk and carried it into the home and then down a nearby flight of stairs. The old man directed us to place Joaquin's body on a stainless-steel table.

We watched as the old man carefully removed the rope and blanket from Joaquin's body. There was very little blood on the blanket due to Joaquin's being killed days earlier. His body had become very rigid, and the smell of death permeated the room.

What happened next took me by surprise.

The old man paused from his review of Joaquin's body, turned to me, and said in perfect English, "You killed Warren Weltzin a few days ago, didn't you, son?"

The shock of his question caused me to fall back slightly, and my back hit the wall of the dimly lit basement. Holger glanced in my direction with a look of concern on his face. I quickly gathered my thoughts and tested the old man, feeling him out to see if he was a friend or foe. I said to him in German, "Warren Weltzin war ein Nazi-Verbrecher, der den Tod verdiente, den er erhielt." *Warren Weltzin was a Nazi criminal who deserved the death he received.*

The old man smiled and replied, "Er war kein Freund von mir und viele von uns alten Deutschen waren glücklich, ihn zu sehen getötet. Du bist nicht mein feindlicher Sohn." *He was no friend of mine and many of us old Germans living here were happy to see him killed. You are not my enemy, son.*

I was instantly relieved, as did Holger, who gave a massive sigh of relief.

I conversed with the old man in English for the next few minutes. "Sir, might I ask your name and where you are from?" I asked him. He said, "My name is Thomas Reinshagen. I am from Dusseldorf, Germany, but I have lived here in western Argentina since the end of World War I. I became a mortician, and I care for the cemetery nearby. My wife, Olga, passed away several years ago, and she is buried there. I knew you must have killed Warren because very few people could have killed him by taking a shot from that distance."

I replied, "Yes, Sir. That shot came from me. My name is Allen Voigt, and I'm a member of the United States Army. I have been ordered to locate and eliminate as many escaped Nazis as possible."

I then introduced Holger. Holger spoke up and offered our condolences regarding the loss of Thomas's wife. He told Thomas that the man on the table was Joaquin Garcia, his cousin.

"Holger, your cousin died a violent death, and all evidence points to the fact he was tortured for information, most likely related to the shooting of Warren. I am confident he did not give up any information, as the authorities know nothing. The noise on Weltzin's death has died down considerably over the last few days," Thomas said.

I spoke up. "Joaquin did die because of my killing Warren Weltzin. Joaquin helped facilitate our extraction from your local train station a few days ago. I am afraid he was probably identified as a supporter of mine and tortured because of it."

Thomas said, "Warren was a Nazi who refused to accept that Germany had lost the Second World War and that Hitler was dead. He continually spouted anti-Semitic rhetoric in restaurants and bars. I treated his body after you shot him. There was not much left of his head. He is buried in an unmarked grave in the cemetery nearby. He is not the only escaped Nazi that has passed through our city."

That comment caught my attention, forcing me to inquire further. "Thomas, do you think you could identify these Nazis if I showed you photographs? Would you consider being a resource for us in helping to locate them?"

Thomas was quick to respond. "I do not need to see any photographs as their faces are burned in my mind. I would be very willing to assist you. Walter Rauff, Ekerd Jacobsen, Rickert Pagel and Warner Weltzin all have passed through Tamberias. Walter Rauff appears to be the ringleader. I have not seen anyone besides Warren Weltzin in over six months. I have a strong suspicion that they have fled to neighboring countries."

Our time was limited; we had to return to the train station. I spent our remaining minutes allowing Holger to explain to Thomas how he wanted

Joaquin's body buried and remembered. Thomas understood Holger's wishes and promised to take good care of Joaquin.

As Holger and I exited the basement, I turned to Thomas and shared more information on where we were headed.

"We are leaving on the next train out for Bolivia in search of Rickert Pagel. Our sources tell us he is in Bolivia," I said.

"Happy hunting," Thomas said. "My son, Timo, will drive you to the train station. You do not need to create any more suspicion by walking the streets at this hour."

Not much was said between Timo, Holger, and me on the short ride to the train station. After we were dropped off at the station, Holger and I quickly secured our tickets for Cochabamba, Bolivia, and found our seats. I was exhausted, and our hours in Tamberias turned out differently than expected.

It was almost 6:00 a.m., and the sun was coming up on the right side of the train as we traveled northwest toward Bolivia. It was a beautiful sight. The Andes Mountains were off in the distance, highlighted by the rising sun. The sun's rays permeated the train's windows and warmed the train car.

Our travel to Cochabamba, Bolivia, would cover over fourteen hundred miles, approximately six hundred more miles than the distance between Buenos Aires and Tamberias. I was getting my fill of train travel.

About two hours into our trip, Holger and I decided to find the meal car and grab breakfast. Over breakfast, we talked about Joaquin and all the events we encountered during our brief visit back to Tamberias. Holger was justifiably distraught over the brutal death of his cousin but took solace in the fact that we had found him and that he would be given a proper burial. He worried about how we would get word back to Joaquin's mother and Uncle Rudolph. I did not see how that could happen any time soon.

We finished our breakfast and decided to stay in the meal car and sip coffee. Our conversation drifted into how we would go about finding Rickert Pagel, how I would eliminate him, and how we would eventually leave the mountain.

After four long days of train travel and uncomfortable sleeping arrangements, our train finally rolled into Cochabamba, Bolivia, and its small train station. It was 3:15 p.m., and there was not a soul around.

Looking out of the train windows, I saw no large buildings, houses, or trees. It looked very remote, with some rolling hills.

Holger and I gathered our limited belongings, which included our weapons, food stores, and water secured from the train's meal car. We exited the train in search of transportation.

I estimated we would have to cover almost three hundred miles traveling west toward the border of Chile. There are better methods of getting there than walking.

Stepping off the train offered some relief from the stuffy, smelly train. The relief was short-lived, however, as we walked into temperatures above ninety degrees and very high humidity.

The train station in Cochabamba was tiny, and only a few people were milling around that afternoon. Shacks were scattered around the station, but nothing looked remotely inhabitable.

A few other folks exited the train with us. Before long, the train left the station and lumbered north. Holger and I must have stood out that afternoon, appearing helpless. As we lingered there on the train station platform, pondering our mode of transportation, a weathered old man approached us. He was an intimidating individual. He had bullets strapped across his chest in a crisscross pattern. He also had an old Winchester rifle slung over his left shoulder and a big iron revolver on his right hip. He looked just like the pictures of the infamous Pancho Villa from Mexico.

In halting English, he asked us where we were going and how we would get there. As best we could, we told him we were looking to get to the mountain called Nevado Sajaman to do some hiking.

As our luck would have it, he was from Cosapa, Bolivia, only twenty miles from the base of the mountain. He told us his name was Arturo, and he would happily take us to his home. We could then leave for the mountain from there. He had arrived on a different train and he had been visiting his family in another remote part of Bolivia. That was the good news.

The bad news was that his truck, parked nearby, looked like it was on its last leg. The tires were nearly bald, and little paint was left on the truck to distinguish its original color. The truck bed was full of straw, where we would have to sit for the next several hundred miles. The only other option was to walk. Holger and I opted to accept the ride. Thankfully, Arturo had no chickens or pigs in the back of his truck that hot afternoon.

It took a long while for Arturo to start his old truck. When the truck's engine finally turned over, a puff of white smoke billowed out of the truck's tailpipe, choking Holger and me as the truck pulled away from the train station.

Our route was down an old dirt road. There were no paved roads in this part of Bolivia. Potholes dotted the road every few yards, and entire sections had been washed out, preventing us from making good time. Arturo occasionally had to leave the road and navigate around the washed-out sections. At the rate we were going, reaching Rickert would take us a week.

After about two hours of monotony and limited conversations with Holger, I lay my head back on the straw and stared at the blue sky. There were a few white clouds, but none covered the sun as it beat down on us. Other than my travel bag containing a few changes of clothes and my weapons, I had nothing to cover my face. I decided to cover my face with straw.

I must have drifted off to sleep because I was startled when Holger shook me to get my attention.

I sat up.

"Holger, what is the matter?" I asked.

"We are about to have some company," he replied.

I turned and faced forward. About one hundred yards before us were two trucks blocking the road. In front of the trucks stood six armed men with their rifles drawn.

As Arturo slowed the truck, I pulled Holger down, hiding behind the truck's cab.

"We are not going to be killed in Bolivia today, my friend," I said.

I reached for my bag and got my 1911 Colt 45 and a few ammunition clips. I pulled out my old Army knife and wedged it in my boot. Holger pulled out his handgun, as well.

As Arturo brought his old truck to a stop, I motioned Holger to exit out the back of the truck with me.

We both hid behind the truck as Arturo got out of the left side of the old truck and engaged the six men in conversation. It was hard for me to understand what was being said, but the tone of the man talking to Arturo told me that this encounter would not end well.

"When I move around the right side of the truck, you move around the left," I whispered to Holger.

Holger nodded that he understood.

Suddenly, a shot rang out. I dropped to the ground so I could peer under the truck. Arturo's body fell to the ground, dead from a shot to the head.

The fight or flight scenario was on. I chose to fight.

I immediately rose to a crouched position and worked around the truck's right side. As I cleared the front of the truck, I rose to a standing position and began firing at the six men. Five were standing, and one had just leaned down to take any valuable items off Arturo's body.

Holger had done his job, had worked around the left side of the truck, and was also firing by this time. Four men dropped immediately with mortal wounds. Holger shot the man leaning over Arturo. The sixth man managed to get a shot off; it missed me, but the bullet ripped past my left ear. Before the sixth man could pull his rifle's bolt back to position another bullet, I shot him in his right knee, forcing him to drop to the ground and drop his rifle. I dropped my handgun on purpose and, in a singular motion, reached for my knife with my right hand. I fell on the man, placing my left knee on his chest. I plunged my knife into his heart. I held the knife in his chest, and the life left his body. I just stared at him for a moment.

I felt Holger's hand on my left shoulder. "Are you okay, Allen?" Holger asked. "Yes," I said.

Here we were, on a dirt road in western Bolivia, with seven dead men surrounding us. These men were bandits bent on killing anyone they could come across, hoping to steal from those they killed.

Holger and I placed three dead men each in their two trucks. We started the trucks and drove them about two hundred yards off the road. We cut the fuel lines on both trucks and lit them on fire, burning the trucks and the bodies.

We came back to Arturo and decided to bury him a few yards off the road in a deep grave, hoping to prevent any wild animals from digging him up. We placed a few large rocks over his grave, and I said a small prayer.

"God, bless this man who graciously befriended us and got us this far on our journey. May he rest in peace."

Holger and I returned to Arturo's truck and weighed our options.

I looked at my watch. It was close to 3:00 p.m. As we stood there next to the truck in thought, I looked west and saw a lone mountain off in the far distance. It had to be Nevado Sajaman. We decided to drive in a westerly direction, targeting the mountain, until we ran out of gas. According to the gas gauge on the old truck, we had half a tank of gas left.

Holger volunteered to drive, and we hopped in the truck. Holger worked the ignition, and the truck came to life after a few pumps of the gas pedal. We kept our guns and extra ammo in the cab while driving silently. We both were trying to take in everything that had just happened. I had also taken Arturo's rifle and ammunition. We were well-armed in the event we encountered any more bandits. Arturo would never return home to his family. My heart broke for them.

After traveling two hours, it was close to 5:00 p.m., and the sun was beginning to dip in front of us. Our gas was quickly running out. A thought occurred to me. As I had lain in the back of the truck, I recalled smelling gasoline. At the time, I figured it was just Arturo's old truck emitting gas fumes. Now, it may have been gas cans placed under the straw. There were no gas stations anywhere nearby. Arturo may have had backup gas for the long drive west.

I asked Holger to stop the truck and turn off the engine. I got out of the truck and moved around to the truck bed. I moved the straw around the back of the truck and dug around a bit. I soon found four cans of gasoline tied to the side of the truck bed. I could not believe it.

I removed the cans and carefully poured the gas from all four cans into the truck's tank. I then hopped back into the truck.

"Well, Allen, three-quarters of a tank. Nice job," Holger said as he started the truck again.

We traveled for another three hours. The sun, by then, had set in the western skyline. Nevado Sajaman was much closer. I estimated it was less than twenty-five miles to the mountain's base. If possible, the landscape had become even more desolate in western Bolivia.

We drove another thirty minutes and, for the first time, saw a few tiny homes nestled off the road on either side. I did not want to risk Rickert being alerted by the people around the mountain's base. Even though the people occupying these tiny homes may not have known Rickert or he was living on the mountain, I could not afford to take that chance.

I asked Holger to find a place to hide the truck. He found a batch of trees about two hundred yards off the road. He left the road, parked the truck in the middle of the trees, and cut the engine.

There was an eerie silence. We heard nothing except the wind blowing from west to East. We got out of the truck with our weapons. If we were going to find and ultimately kill Rickert, we had to be rested, so we decided to sleep for a few hours in the back of the truck. The straw that was left would keep us warm. We were both hungry, but eating would have to wait. We felt relatively safe in our present location.

I slept hard for just over four hours, surprising even myself. Over my military career, I have slept in some problematic areas and positions. Still, that night, I was relatively comfortable, as I could lie in a stretched-out position and had plenty of straw to keep me warm.

I left the truck and found a place to relieve myself within the limited tree line. Holger and I had little water left in our canteens and zero food. Securing water and food would be our first two priorities that morning.

Walking back to the truck, I noticed that one of the tiny homes we had passed the evening before was close. The home had smoke coming from its chimney. I took that to mean someone was already up and possibly cooking breakfast. If we could secure a meal, gather some intelligence on Rickert and filling our canteens would be an excellent start to the day.

Holger was a little hesitant to approach the house, thinking we could accidentally knock on Rickert's door and invite a shot to the chest or even worse. I finally convinced him that Rickert would not live in plain sight like that and that we had limited options for food and water.

We left the truck and walked to the nearby house, covering about a mile. We saw movement inside the house. I knocked on the door, waiting for someone to answer. I knocked again, and I got the same result.

The house was situated against the mountain's base, and I could hear water running nearby. I motioned Holger to join me, and we both searched for the running water. We walked around the backside of the house. Just a few yards behind it was a creek. I knelt by the creek and lapped up some of the running water in my hands. The water was cold and refreshing. We both filled our canteens.

We decided to head back to the house and try again to get someone to come to the door. Our third time did the trick. A petite, elderly lady came to the door. To my surprise, she spoke English.

"Good morning, gentlemen. What brings you to my door this morning?" she said.

"We are two hikers who want to climb Nevado Sajaman. I am from America, and my friend, Holger, is from Germany. My name is Allen," I replied.

"Greetings to you both. My name is Maria. My husband died just over a year ago. We lived in this home for over forty years, but now I live alone. My husband built this home for us just after the turn of the century. I could never have any children, but we loved each other and enjoyed many happy years together," Maria said.

"I am sorry for your loss, Maria," I replied.

"Thank you, Allen. I was afraid to answer the door when you knocked earlier. We only get a few visitors to this mountain. I was wondering if you were here to rob me or not. I knew you were harmless after I saw you both fill your canteens at the creek behind my home. Can I treat you both to a warm breakfast? I have plenty to share. Would some eggs and potatoes, washed down with coffee, sound good?"

Before I could reply, Holger interjected, "Yes, we would love to share a breakfast with you, Maria. Thank you."

We followed Maria into her tiny home. Meeting Maria and entering her home, along with the smell of breakfast cooking, immediately brought back memories of when I visited my Grandmother Lucille's home in western New York. Whenever I visited her and my grandfather Maurice, she cooked a massive breakfast, telling me to keep eating because I was too skinny.

Breakfast was soon ready. We all sat down and ate at Maria's little table. It was a simple breakfast, but the eggs and cooked potatoes were plentiful, and they tasted amazing. The coffee was hot and felt good going down.

As much as I wanted to sit by the warm fire and sip coffee, I knew Holger and I had to get going. I thanked Maria for her hospitality, and as we left her home that morning, I asked her a simple question, hoping to get feedback on a possible location for Rickert Pagel.

"Maria, as we hike the mountain this morning, will we encounter anyone that lives there?"

"Not too many people live here by the mountain, but those of us that do live at the base," Maria said. "The mountain is not very hospitable, with little foliage or trees. I only know of a handful of people that live on the mountain. There is one man who recently moved here from Germany. I don't know him, but I understand he had logs shipped in from eastern Bolivia and had a cabin built close to the top of the mountain, just above the snow line."

"Thank you, Maria. Maybe we will have a chance to meet him. As you know, Holger is from Germany and may be from the same region of the country as Holger," I replied, hating to lie to Maria.

With that, we thanked Maria again and said our goodbyes.

We now had something to go on. I had learned the mountain was just over 21,000 feet in elevation, and snow typically does not melt above 15,000 feet in summer. We would have our work cut out for us, climbing just about three miles upward, taking in less air with every step we took.

Holger and I returned to where we had left Arturo's truck the night before. We gathered our weapons, ammo, and remaining supplies.

We had yet to determine what side of the mountain Rickert had built his cabin on, but at least we knew the approximate elevation. We began our ascent.

The mountain rose sharply as soon as Holger and I cleared the tree line where we had slept the night before. The steep incline forced us to hold on to rocks and brush as we climbed. The climb was labored, and we had to be careful not to lose our footing, or we would fall back down the mountain.

After climbing for about ninety minutes, we noticed a drop in the temperature. The snow line appeared to be about two more miles away.

Holger and I stopped to rest, positioning our backs against a large rock. We took a few sips of water from our canteens and absorbed the view, which was spectacular. We could see for miles. The landscape was desolate but peaceful.

"If we find Rickert, how do you plan to kill him, Allen?" Holger asked.

I paused for a minute before answering, "Quickly and painfully."

"Sounds like you are frustrated and eager to see this mission behind you," Holger said.

"I am, Holger. I miss my girlfriend, Alice, and I am sick and tired of being away from her. I feel like all I have done for the last twenty-plus years is live and operate outside the United States. I am so envious of your wife and family," I replied.

"I cannot relate, Allen, but I, too, miss my wife and look forward to seeing her again soon," Holger said.

We rested a few more minutes, took in the view, and started our ascent again.

After another sixty minutes, we hit the snowline. Neither of us felt the effects of the reduced temperature due to the physical exertion we had just undertaken.

I saw no evidence of civilization anywhere. At that elevation, there was little vegetation, rocks, or brush. Rickert would see us coming from a mile away. We followed the snowline around the mountain until we found Rickert's cabin.

We walked for about an hour. Our view changed dramatically. Looking west, I could see what I thought was the Pacific Ocean way off in the distance. I was unsure if my eyes were playing a trick on me. I knew we were very close to Chile, so the Pacific Ocean was not far away.

As I took the view, I felt Holger tugging my right arm. I turned around, and he gestured for me to get down on one knee. He quickly directed my attention to the left and pointed slightly down the mountain. Approximately five hundred yards off and down to my left was a small log cabin with smoke billowing out of its chimney. It had to be where Rickert was living. I had one picture of Rickert with me that would allow me to confirm we had the right Nazi.

After considering our options regarding our approach to the cabin, we split up and approached it from the north and south. The cold temperature was beginning to make us both uncomfortable. I was concerned that if we had to wait until nightfall, our senses would be dulled, and our reaction time slowed.

We planned to draw Rickert out of his cabin to confirm his identity. We would kick the door down if we could not do that. Simple but effective.

I volunteered to approach from the south; Holger would come from the north. I walked down the mountain about one mile, then started working my way back toward the cabin. Holger had to work down the mountain about five hundred yards.

I made my way up to about fifty feet from the cabin. I could not see Holger at all. A gunshot rang out, echoing for several seconds. Had Holger fired his weapon? Had Holger been shot? I immediately hit the ground and waited for a few seconds. Holger soon appeared around the side of the cabin. He raised his hands in a way that told me he was okay and did not know where the shot had come from, either.

I quickly concluded the shot had to have come from inside the house. I got back up and crept the remaining few feet to the cabin. I peered in a window by the front door and saw a man's body lying on the ground. He held a German Luger pistol in his right hand. His legs were moving a little bit, obviously from discomfort. Blood oozed from his head onto the cabin's wooden floor.

I opened the front door, and Holger and I stepped in. I quickly determined there was no one else in the cabin. I approached the man on the floor, placed my knee on his right wrist, and removed the pistol from his hand. The man groaned in pain.

I repositioned the man onto his back; the man on the floor was clearly Rickert. He had tried to kill himself with a gunshot to the head but had not done an excellent job. He had seen us approaching the cabin and decided to end his life rather than be killed or captured. Due to the isolation and lack of foliage, we'd had no real chance of sneaking up on him.

Rickert had shot himself, but in his haste, he had fired at his head at an upward angle and more or less scalped himself instead of shooting himself in his temple. He was bleeding profusely but was not dead yet. I grabbed a nearby towel and pressed it on his head, attempting to stop the bleeding. I wanted to extract intelligence from him on the whereabouts of his fellow Nazis.

I sat Rickert up and spoke to him in German softly and calmly, hoping his confused state would allow me to get the information I needed faster than I would if I took the interrogation route.

"Rickert, mein Name ist Alfred. Ich bin aus Berlin und ich bin hier, um Ihnen und Ihren Mitbürgern hier in Südamerika zu helfen. Ich muss wissen, wo sie sich befinden. Kannst du mir erzählen?" *Rickert, my name is Alfred. I am from Berlin and I am here to help you and your fellow Nazis here in South America. I need to know where they are located. Can you tell me?*

It took Rickert a few seconds to get his bearings, but he eventually replied.

"I am the only Nazi on this mountain. My fellow Nazis are scattered far and wide here in South America. Warner Weltzin was in Argentina, but he was recently shot and killed by an unknown assailant. Walter Rauff is the last I heard somewhere in Chile, and Eckerd Jacobsen is in Brazil."

Now I understood why he had attempted to kill himself. He was concerned he would share the same fate as Weltzin.

I now had details on the last remaining Nazis I was hunting. I laid Rickert down again. He was still bleeding. I stood up, picked up his Luger pistol, and walked outside the cabin. Holger joined me. I threw the pistol as far away as possible into the deep snow.

"I am going to finish what Rickert started and put a bullet in his head. We now have information on the two remaining Nazis. I am not wasting any more time. Let's get this over with," I said to Holger.

I walked back into the cabin, straight to Rickert lying on the floor, and in German said, "You deserve to burn in the hottest part of hell for what you did to the Jewish population during the war, Rickert. You will die today." He looked up at me with his glazed eyes wide open and gasped.

I pulled out my Colt 45 handgun and shot a bullet squarely in the middle of his forehead. The bullet penetrated his head and was embedded in the wooden floor of the cabin. Even more blood spilled all over the floor.

I left the cabin and sat down on the small, makeshift porch. I felt no remorse. I had visited the concentration camps during the war and had seen the brutal Nazi atrocities. I was halfway through with my mission and closer to getting home to Alice. I looked out that afternoon and admired the view: two Nazis down, two to go.

CHAPTER 7

Into the Void

"This is no time for ease and comfort. It is time to dare and endure."
Winston Churchill

After I killed Rickert, Holger and I placed his body outside the cabin. We decided we would take advantage of the safety and warmth of his cabin for the night and come off the mountain the following morning. Rickert, being German, had plenty of dried meat and potatoes in his cabin, so we did not go hungry.

I let Holger have Rickert's bed for the night, seeing as Rickert no longer needed it. I found a few extra pillows and crafted a makeshift bed on the floor. I was warm and comfortable. The cabin had a large fireplace, and we ensured it burned overnight. It was probably the best sleep I had gotten in some time.

Over a limited breakfast the following day comprised of more potatoes and dried meat, Holger and I discussed our options for getting off the mountain and securing transportation to our next targets. We also discussed the two remaining Nazis on my list. Which would we first hunt down, Walter Rauff in Chile or Eckerd Jacobsen in Brazil? We could not tell either of them was where they were supposed to be. Argentina, Chile, and Brazil were large countries, and finding either of my targets would be challenging without additional information. The question before us was, where would we get that information?

Before leaving Rickert's cabin, we went through all his belongings to find something that could lead us to Rauff or Jacobsen. Rickert had very few possessions, but what he did have a lot of were letters and newspapers. Some of his newspapers dated back to the late 1930s and early 1940s. As I scanned them, I figured he kept them as souvenirs. Rickert had been written about and even pictured in many papers, especially during the war years.

While I scanned the newspapers, Holger rifled through Rickert's large volume of letters. As it turned out, Rickert had recently corresponded with Rauff and Jacobsen. The letters were not long, but one from Rauff mentioned Warner Weltzin's killing and Rauff's concern over Jewish or American assassins infiltrating South America.

Other letters by Jacobsen and Rauff spoke about their missing Germany and the old days of the Nazi Party. I joined Holger in reviewing the letters. A letter from Rauff stated that he was living in Mejillones, Chile. I was shocked. In that letter, Rauff described fishing in the port city on the western shores of central Chile. None of the letters from Jacobsen gave any indication of his exact location in Brazil. Since we now had something more to go on regarding Rauff, he would be our next target. We were ready to get off the cold mountain and secure immediate transportation to Mejillones, Chile. We packed the letters and took them with us. We filled our canteens with snow and began our descent.

The only way down the mountain that morning was the same way we came up, walking. It took us a little under four hours to descend to the mountain's base. It was good to be in a warmer elevation again. I had not shaved in days and was craving soap and a hot shower, but that would have to wait. First, we had to secure transportation.

We had come off the mountain in a southwesterly direction. The goal was to be heading in the general direction of Mejillones. We found the backside of the mountain to be even more desolate than we had experienced on our approach to the mountain two days earlier.

Holger and I wasted no time as we continued to walk in a southwesterly direction. I wanted to avoid risking Rauff relocating, as that would leave us no clear direction on finding him. Time was critical. It would be hard enough to find him with the bit of information we had, but it was enough to go on for now.

After walking for three long days, practically fifteen hours a day,

Holger and I decided to take a break, rest for half a day, and eat the rest of the dried meat we had secured from Rickert's cabin.

As we sat there that early afternoon, the sky was clear, and I saw a hawk flying high above my head. It was a beautiful sight to see. For a moment, I forgot I was in southwestern Bolivia, deep in South America, hunting Nazis.

My thoughts were interrupted by a train whistle off to my right. I looked at Holger, who stood up and looked off to the right. We concluded the whistle had come from the southwest. As desolate as the landscape was, it had rolling hills, and it was hard for us to see the western horizon. We gathered what few belongings we had and ran toward the sound of the train whistle.

We reached the top of a nearby hill, and what came into view was astonishing. Way off in the distance, we could see the Pacific Ocean. I estimated it was at least ten to twelve miles away, but only two miles below us was a train barreling down the tracks in a southerly direction.

We could not catch that train, but we knew a train station had to be nearby. We worked our way down toward the train tracks and soon found a small train station. The sign on the station said Arica. There were a few buildings outside selling food and clothing.

We had pushed ourselves to get this far by walking, and it was essential to secure lodging for the night and acquire some fresh clothes and food. Holger agreed. We walked into the small town of Arica. The Pacific Ocean soon came into view. It had been almost a year since I had seen the Pacific Ocean since returning to the United States at the end of World War Two. A slight breeze came off the ocean that morning, and it was refreshing.

We soon found a small hotel near the beach and secured two rooms for the evening. We dropped our limited belongings in separate rooms and hid our weapons under the mattresses. We then ventured out to find some fresh clothes and food.

Food was easy to secure with our limited currency; the clothing was a different story. I had to barter the watch my father had given me when I left for Army basic training. I struggled when I had to hand it to the street vendor, but we had to have fresh clothes. The watch secured us both two new pairs of pants and shirts. The clothing was rugged and would be sufficient. The watch was valuable enough that I got some currency back.

The sun was setting and broke over the Pacific Ocean in bright orange and yellow colors. It was beautiful to see. My mind raced back to Alice, wishing she was there with me to see it.

We made our way back to our hotel. I showered and put on a set of my new clothes. Holger and I then ventured out and found a small restaurant. We used the currency we had acquired from the street vendor to pay for a good meal that night. That evening, I slept well simply because I had a comfortable bed, a good meal, and a shower.

The following day, Holger and I packed and walked back to the Arica train station, secured tickets, and waited for the 9:00 a.m. train to take us south. The train would take us to Mejillones, approximately two hundred and twenty miles south of our current location. We did not have to wait long. We heard the familiar sound of the train whistle off in the distance. The train soon came into view, and not long after, it arrived at the station. Train travel, for me, had become so commonplace and familiar. I was a creature of habit and secured a seat in the second car, sitting on the right side of the car. Holger and I never sat next to each other, doing our best not to draw attention.

Our train headed south for the next eight hours, stopping at small stations along the way. More people boarded the train the farther south we traveled. By the time we neared Mejillones, every seat on the train was taken. Two people who boarded drew my attention. Several rows before me were two Caucasian males who had boarded the train a few stops earlier. They appeared to be German, and as soon as I heard them speak to each other in German, my suspicions were confirmed. They spoke openly about reuniting with someone from the homeland. I made it a point to pretend I was sleeping, propping my head against the window. They never mentioned Rauff by name, but I figured they would meet him.

Upon reaching Mejillones, I waited for the two Germans to disembark before Holger and I got off the train. He had noticed the two Germans, as well, and agreed with me that they were most likely headed to meet Rauff. One option was to follow them to locate Rauff quickly. The other option was to avoid them and later locate Rauff on our own. We opted for the second option. The simple fact that Rauff, unlike Rickert and Weltzin, would not be alone and would have two people assigned to protect him gave me pause for concern.

Holger and I were in dire straits. We had no money left, nothing to barter with, and nowhere to lay our heads that night. Upon exiting the train, we could not see the two Germans anywhere. They had left the train station and vanished into the city streets.

As Holger and I stood on the street with the train station behind us, we thought long and hard about what to do next. There were very few cars on the streets. Suddenly, a car pulled up to us and stopped.

An overweight Caucasian man stepped out of the car and hollered at us, "You chaps in need of a lift?"

The large man was British and appeared harmless. "Yes, we do, sir," I said.

The man exited his vehicle and opened his trunk. We placed our bags in the trunk. Holger climbed in the car's back seat, and I took the front passenger seat.

"What brings you two gentlemen to Mejillones?" he asked as we pulled away from the train station.

"My name is Allen Voigt and I am from New York. Where are you from, sir?" I asked.

The man suddenly pulled over to the right side of the street and slammed on his brakes.

"Allen Voigt with the United States Office of Strategic Services?" he asked.

"Yes, that is correct, sir, Colonel Allen Voigt. How do you know that?"

The man looked at me incredulously. "You probably do not remember me, but during the war, I was a member of the British Army stationed in Washington, D.C. I was often at the White House, conferring with various cabinet members and Army and Navy personnel. I clearly remember seeing you there on several occasions and even attending some of the same meetings you had with the late President Roosevelt. I cannot believe you are now sitting in my car!"

I was stunned that out of all the people here in Mejillones, Chile, I had found the one person who knew me. I did not remember him at all, though.

"I'm sorry, but I don't remember you. What is your name?" I asked. "I am retired Colonel Sam Randell. I do not expect you to remember me as I sat in the back of the room during those White House meetings. I was always jealous of your role in the United States military. The missions you had behind enemy lines and in all those foreign countries must have been an exhilarating experience."

"I am not sure I would call those experiences exhilarating," I answered, "but I am glad I was able to play a small part in the Allied victory over Germany and Japan. God surely had his providential hand of protection on me."

Holger sat in the back of the car all this time, bewildered at the rapid exchange between the retired British Colonel and me. During a pause in the conversation, I looked back at Holger and noticed he was shaking his head in bewilderment.

"What in the world brings this hole-in-the-wall city to you, Allen?" the Colonel asked.

"Believe it or not, from one Colonel to another, we are here hunting a particular Nazi that escaped Germany after the war, Walter Rauff," I replied.

"Walter Rauff? He has also been on the British radar," the Colonel said. "You are telling me that Rauff is hiding here in Mejillones?"

"Our sources tell us he is hiding here," I said. "On the train here, we witnessed two German men who disembarked with us and most likely were going to meet Rauff. I'm surprised you don't know that a German is milling about Mejillones. He is not afraid to show his face about town as our sources tell us he likes to fish. Why, exactly, are you here, Colonel Randell?"

Colonel Randell laughed, put his car back into drive, and pulled out onto the main street. He navigated the streets efficiently but waited to answer my question.

Finally, after what seemed like an eternity, he answered me.

"During the 1941 German bombings of London, my family was killed. I was at the British War Ministry building when my family's apartment building in East London was heavily damaged. My wife and three children took the brunt of the bombing. Our entire apartment was destroyed, and my family was buried under the rubble. I received word of the bombing that night and was allowed to leave the War Ministry and return home. I supported the attempt to rescue them, working throughout the night, removing brick by brick, timber by timber until we found my young daughter. She had survived the blast but was caught in the building's collapse. She was in a balled-up position, clutching her doll. We soon found my two sons and wife. They must have taken the brunt of the blast, as their bodies were mangled."

He paused for a moment, then continued. "I just sat there in the rubble and cried. My life took a dramatic turn that day. I later buried my family and eventually asked the War Ministry to transfer me away from London. They obliged, and I was assigned to the White House. I worked closely with your Harry Hopkins and the British Ambassador to the United States, Lord Viscount Halifax. That is why I was sometimes in the same room with you at the White House. You were not there often, but when you visited, the British government was aware of your missions, and we always offered our unwavering support."

The Colonel navigated a tricky turn, then spoke again. "After the war, I became very disillusioned and wanted to escape. I had nothing to return to in London and nothing keeping me in the United States. I resigned from the British Army and made my way down here. I spent time in Central America, Columbia, Brazil, and Argentina, all before arriving here in Mejillones just a few weeks ago. I have bought a small restaurant on the northern outskirts of the city. We get a lot of military members from various countries that occasionally port here in Mejillones. I have always liked to cook, as you can probably determine from my robust figure. I am hoping to bring a little bit of British-style cooking to South America. I am opening the restaurant tomorrow."

I was utterly surprised by Colonel Randell's story. It now made sense to me why he did not know Walter Rauff lived here in Mejillones.

"I am sorry, Colonel, about your family," I said. "Thank you, Allen," he replied.

Holger then spoke up from the back seat. "Colonel Randell, my sincere condolences in the loss of your family. My name is Holger Hartmann. I am a retired German soldier. I'm here supporting Allen in the hunt for my fellow Germans who were members of the horrific Nazi Party but have now escaped here to South America."

I expected Colonel Randell to offer a derogatory response to Holger's introduction.

Instead, he did the opposite, saying, "Pleased to meet you, Holger. I was wondering who you were. I hold no ill will against you. Our countries were at war, and war was evil. I had to forgive Germany for what they did to my family, but mainly, I had to forgive myself. I was upset with myself that I was not there with my family on the night of the bombing. I kept rehashing that night in my mind over and over again, thinking there must have been a chance that I could have gotten them out of the building when the first air raid sirens sounded."

We then rode in silence as Colonel Randell continued to drive. We finally pulled up to a small building in the northern part of the city. There on the building was the restaurant's name, Randell's Runaway.

"Allen and Holger," the Colonel said, "I assumed you don't have a safe place to stay this evening. I live on the second floor of this building. I have three rooms upstairs, and you are welcome to have two. Let's get inside, and let me scrounge up some dinner for you."

The turn of events was incredible. Holger and I had arrived in Mejillones, wondering how we would secure food, let alone put a roof over our heads. We had chosen to travel to Mejillones as soon as possible. Our resources had been expanded, and our options were limited. Colonel Randell was a godsend.

The rest of the evening was spent conversing and eating. Not much was said about the war we had all actively participated in or even about Walter Rauff. We chose to talk about family, sports, and politics. It was a nice change, and we were an odd combination of men to have such a discussion. In the middle of South America, a German, a Brit, and an American discussed various topics as if we had been best friends our entire lives. The evening was a nice respite from the breakneck pace Holger, and I had been keeping since arriving in South America.

As I went to bed that night, my mind naturally drifted to thoughts of Alice and what lay ahead of me the next day. I knew we had to locate Rauff quickly, especially since we had seen the two German men on the train. I was confident that they would conclude I was there in Mejillones for some reason other than vacation. Valuable time was being wasted. The risk of Rauff being warned by the two Germans was real.

I did not sleep well, tossing and turning all night, thinking about our plan to locate and eliminate Rauff. The only positive thing about not being able to sleep was that I could formulate a plan.

Mejillones was a small town. It was spread out and did not have many tall buildings, trees, or natural landscapes to conceal an approach. Our best option was to approach at night. We planned to use the grand opening of Colonel Randell's restaurant to ask his patrons if anyone new to town would like to eat there. Someone could provide a vital clue to Rauff's location. Upon locating Rauff, we would approach at night, capture him, and extract as much information from him as possible as to the location of Eckerd Jacobsen before killing him. It was a loose plan but the best I could come up with.

The following morning, I was dragging. I was mentally spent and not at the top of my game physically. I was thirty-eight years old, and my body reminded me of that.

Colonel Randell went above and beyond in his hospitality to us. Not only did Holger and I get a warm breakfast downstairs at his new restaurant, but we also received fresh clothes and new shoes. I felt horrible that I had no money to pay him for it.

Colonel Randell had indeed been a friend in our hour of need. As Holger and I shared our breakfast with the Colonel, I discussed my plan for finding and eliminating Rauff. I was not proud of the plan, as it did not give us the best chance of success, but we had to start somewhere. The longer I talked, the quieter the table became. Holger and the Colonel sat there and did not offer any feedback.

Upon outlining my plan, Holger offered up one word of reply, "Okay." Colonel Randell then gave me his opinion.

"Allen, your plan is more of a run-and-gun approach, but I wonder if you have that many other options to choose from. The restaurant opens in two hours at 10:00 a.m. sharp. My five new employees will be arriving within the hour. I'll ensure they know to ask our guests many questions throughout the day. My workers don't know what's happening, so they won't give anything away. Let's regroup here at 7:00 p.m., and I'll share any information we have gathered. It's best if you and Holger keep a low profile by either staying upstairs today or hiring a boat and going fishing. I clearly understand the urgency of your mission, Allen, and will do all I can to support it."

The Colonel's comments were genuine, and he was exactly right.

Holger and I could not risk exposing ourselves more than we had already. The risk of losing Rauff was real.

We soon parted ways. It would be an exciting day for Colonel Randell with the opening of his new restaurant.

Holger and I wouldn't be able to stay upstairs all day. We decided to take the Colonel's advice and go fishing. I had never been saltwater fishing, nor had Holger. We looked at the opportunity as an adventure.

We snuck out of the restaurant's back door and walked toward the ocean. It didn't take long to get there, only about thirty minutes. We soon found a dock with several boats tied to it. We were in luck. It took talking to three boat captains before we finally got our fishing request across. The third captain was named Jose, and his boat was named *Solitary*. He spoke English and welcomed us aboard.

We arranged with the captain to give him every fish we caught as payment for letting us fish with him. He agreed and welcomed the extra help. He told us he relied on his daily catches to support his family. Upon returning to the dock daily, he sold most of the fish he caught to a local market; the rest he kept for his family.

The sun rose quickly in the eastern sky. It would be a hot day, but the ocean breezes kept it tolerable. Jose's boat was much like a tugboat I had seen in New York City near the submarine docks before the war. Jose, his deckhand, Holger, and I headed to the open water. The ride was relatively smooth. The shore faded quickly from view. Having never fished in the ocean, I asked Jose how far out we would go. His answer surprised me.

"We will travel forty miles or so. We like deep water because that is where the big fish are. We are looking for silver sea trout, red grouper, and Almaco Jackfish. They bring the best price at the local market, plus they taste good," Jose said.

I had been on, over, and under the world's oceans, but this was an entirely new experience. We finally reached what Jose called his favorite fishing spot. The shoreline was gone, and I saw nothing but blue water around us.

To my and Holger's embarrassment, Jose and his deckhand had to show us everything, like how to cast a fishing line, bait it, reel a fish in, remove it from the hook, and store it on ice. Their occasional chuckle told me they were slightly surprised about our lack of fishing knowledge. They took it in stride, and soon Holger and I were fishing.

Before too long, I caught my first fish. It was more of a struggle to reel it than I imagined. It felt like I was pulling up a truck tire from the bottom of the ocean.

What I reeled on board turned out to be a twenty-pound red grouper. I was shocked at the size of the fish. You would have thought I had given Jose a pot of gold. He was ecstatic at the type and size of my first fish. Over the day, I caught six more fish of various kinds. Holger was even more fortunate than me; he caught sixteen fish. Jose was so excited that these two novice fishermen managed to double his daily volume of fish. Between the four of us that day, we caught over fifty fish. By 4:00 p.m., we headed back to the shore. The water was choppier on our return. I started to get seasick as the boat rode the waves up and down.

I lost what little lunch I had eaten that afternoon. Fortunately, I threw up over the side of the boat and not where I had been sitting.

The seas became calmer as we got closer to shore, and my nausea subsided. It took us nearly two hours to return to the dock in Mejillones. While the sun set, Holger and I helped Jose and his deckhand unload all the fish into his nearby truck.

We said our goodbyes to Jose and his deckhand and thanked them for an adventurous day. It was not a day I ever expected to have during this mission. Regardless, it was a nice change, and even though I ended up getting sick, I found the day enjoyable.

Holger and I walked back to Colonel Randell's restaurant. The restaurant was packed with guests, a good sign for the Colonel. We waited in our respective rooms until the Colonel came and got us at 7:00 p.m.

Holger, the Colonel, and I all sat at a small table in my room.

The Colonel shared the information he had secured from his patrons that day.

His news was detailed and much more than I had ever expected. He had confirmed that a German man lived about a mile from the beach. He also learned several new German men had arrived in town over the last twenty-four hours and had been seen with this particular German. All this information had been collected from one patron who said he lived near this German man and suggested he and his friends might like Colonel Randell's style of European cooking.

This differed from how intelligence was gathered, but this was not an ordinary mission. The details provided supported the idea that the two German men on the train were there to help Rauff. It also supported the information in Rauff's letters about his fishing habits. The fact that he lived near the ocean made sense.

We were also given an address, and I made it clear to Holger and the Colonel that we would plan to capture Rauff that night.

The Colonel then fed us, and we spent the next two hours checking our weapons and looking at a city map that the Colonel had given us. The Colonel planned to drive us to within a half mile of Rauff's home. We would depart the vehicle at 1:00 a.m. and approach the house from the rear, hoping to meet only minimal resistance.

The Colonel then offered to leave immediately and conduct a drive-by of Rauff's residence to give us a visual of the number of floors, windows, and doors.

Holger and I had to wait patiently as it took the Colonel several hours to return. We wondered anxiously about what was taking him so long. When the Colonel returned, it was close to 10:30 p.m. The restaurant had cleared out, leaving us alone at a table. The Colonel could not sit still as he talked. He whipped up some sandwiches for us and passed out some cold bottled Coca-Cola.

The Colonel talked about how he had driven around the house multiple times. I could sense from his excitement that he was happy to contribute to my mission. He finally began to describe the details of the house. It was a two-story residence with a door in the front and one in the back. What had taken the Colonel so long was that he'd ended up parking a hundred yards down the street from the house. He'd observed the comings and goings of the house and neighborhood. He had seen two German-looking men enter the home around 9:00 p.m. and have yet to come back out. That was the only activity he had witnessed.

I concluded that we must eliminate the two Germans to capture Rauff alive. The plan was to interrogate Rauff in his residence, eliminate him, and leave all three bodies in the house. Holger and I would work our way back to Colonel Randell, resupply, and board the earliest train out of Chile.

I was tired of being on the run. I had been moving from town to town almost my entire military career. My missions during the war had taken me all over the world and into harm's way. Regardless of how my mind and body felt at this moment, however, I would have to work hard to stay sharp and focused if this mission would succeed. The risks of this portion of the mission were very high due to the lateness of the hour, the unknown surroundings, and the multiple targets.

It was time to go. I checked my weapons one last time and counted my ammunition. I had thirty rounds of Colt forty-five ammo left. I would only carry my handgun and knife.

Before Holger and I departed the Colonel's residence, we reviewed our strategy for this late-evening mission one last time. Upon a quick last-minute review, we both agreed we were ready.

The Colonel drove us to within one mile of Rauff's residence. It was nearing 1:00 a.m., and no other cars were on the streets. We said our goodbyes to Colonel Randell and began walking the last mile to our target through the alleys running throughout the small city.

The streets were dimly lit, and a lot of cloud cover blocked out any moonlight. These factors certainly worked to our advantage in our approach to the residence.

Holger and I successfully navigated within fifty yards of Rauff's house and moved around to the backside. A small, white dog approached us and started barking repeatedly. I was concerned we would wake Rauff and the surrounding neighbors if the dog continued to bark. I tried to pick up the small, yapping dog, but he kept barking away whenever I approached him.

A light in a nearby house illuminated a window. I had a real fondness for dogs, but if the dog's barking did not stop soon, I would have to consider smothering it with my body or killing it with a knife. The next thing I knew, Holger knelt and held out his hand with food, offering it to the dog. Suddenly, the dog stopped barking, approached Holger, and took whatever was in his hand. Holger petted the dog and picked him up. Looking at the two of them, you would have thought they were best friends. I had no idea what Holger gave him, but it worked.

Fortunately, the dog stopped barking. Unfortunately, a nearby neighbor came out of his back door and just stared at us. It was the same house the light had come on in a few seconds earlier. The little dog that

Holger was still holding became excited at the sight of the neighbor, and it became clear that the man looking at us was the dog's owner. Holger put the dog down, and immediately, it ran over to the man in his bathrobe staring at us. The man picked up the dog and gave us one last stare before entering his house and shutting the door behind him. The light went out in the house, and once again, the alley became quiet. Holger and I said nothing as we stood there, ensuring no additional movement was in the alley. I looked over at Rauff's house and saw that nothing was happening. I motioned Holger to follow me as we walked closer to Rauff's back door. I tried the back door handle, and to my surprise, it turned. I glanced at Holger and slowly and quietly pushed the door open. The door opened to a dark hallway. At the end of the hallway, I could barely make out a set of stairs on the left. I had no idea of the interior layout of the house, other than that it had two floors.

Holger and I entered the hallway, and I shut the door behind us. The house was quiet. We both stood there in the darkness. I motioned to Holger that I would take the ground floor, and he could take the top floor. I had yet to learn where the bedrooms were in the house, but by each of us taking a floor, we could take out multiple targets simultaneously. Our handguns were drawn and ready to fire at a moment's notice.

Suddenly, a quick flash illuminated the hallway. It was gunfire, and it was close. Holger fell immediately to the floor. I quickly fired five successive shots from my handgun, directing my fire down the hallway in the direction of the flash. In the darkness, I heard a body drop to the floor. I then knelt to assess Holger's wounds. He was making a gurgling sound and spitting up blood. I had seen this type of wound before during the war, inflicting it on both German and Japanese soldiers. The noise always meant a fatal wound. He had taken the bullet right in his throat. The bullet had entered his upper throat and exited the back of his neck. There was not much else to assess. I tried to ease Holger's suffering by holding his hand. He looked up at me with a scared look, and then he was gone. He died there in the hallway, with his eyes still open. I closed them. I momentarily lost all sense of my surroundings. My heart broke for Holger; his wife would now be a widow, and his children back in Buenos Aires would be fatherless.

I turned away from Holger and quietly stood. I walked over to the body at the end of the hallway. In the darkness, my eyes strained, but I could see that the body lying there on the floor bleeding was not Rauff's. It belonged to one of the two Germans I had spotted on the train the day before. He had taken four of my shots, three in the chest and one in his upper right thigh. He was dead.

I was not out, but I put a fresh eight-round clip into my handgun. I was upset over Holger's death but kept my emotions in check and proceeded to check the rest of the downstairs. There were two rooms. One was a bedroom that the now-dead German had just exited. The second room was a small kitchen. The downstairs was clear of anyone else.

I assumed that the other German from the train and Rauff were upstairs and now wide awake. I decided to go back over to the front door, open and close it, simulating my leaving the house. I then quietly walked over to the base of the stairs and stood there, motionless. I listened for any movement coming from upstairs. I waited for six minutes before I heard anything. I backed away quietly from the base of the stairs and waited. The movement I originally heard upstairs became silent again.

Suddenly, there was a knock at the back door. The figure behind the door spoke rapidly in Spanish. As best I could make out, the man asked if the house's occupants were okay. Most likely, it was the man we had seen earlier in the alley with his dog.

There was movement again upstairs. Someone approached the stairwell.

Was it the German from the train or Rauff?

Rauff was the key to finding Jacobsen in Brazil. I could not risk killing him immediately. As hard as that was in the darkness, I had to wait to identify the individual approaching the stairwell.

I backed even further away from the stairwell, which gave me close to ten feet of distance. I waited, and soon, the individual emerged from the stairwell. He turned toward the back door with his back to me, not allowing me to make out who it was. He stepped over Holger's body and then opened the back door. I only had one picture of Rauff, and I could not tell who the person was.

As the door opened, the hallway was slightly illuminated. The man I had seen earlier with his dog was, in fact, the man now standing at the back door, still holding his small, white dog in his left arm. He immediately started speaking rapidly in Spanish to the person with his back to me. I could not make out anything he was saying, but the tone of his words clearly expressed his concern over hearing gunfire.

Suddenly, the man holding his dog noticed Holger's body lying on the hallway floor. The unknown man with his back to me had not said a word yet. The neighbor started speaking even faster in Spanish, pointing at Holger's body lying there in a pool of blood.

To my surprise, the man with his back to me asked the other man, in German, to leave immediately. He didn't know any Spanish, but he knew the situation was escalating at the back door. The neighbor put his dog down and instructed the dog to go home. I saw the dog walk away. With both hands-free, the neighbor became even more animated at the unknown German.

Without hesitation, the unknown German grabbed the neighbor by his bathrobe with one hand and pulled him into the hallway. With the other hand, he pulled out a large knife and cut the man's throat from ear to ear. The German man held the neighbor up in a standing position as he bled out, just staring at him until he died. The German then threw the man to the floor, watching his body fall next to Holger's. It was a vicious act.

Before shutting the door, the unknown German just looked down at the two men lying dead near the back door. I could finally make out the identification of the unknown German. It was, in fact, Rauff.

I immediately saw another flash and felt a bullet enter the right side of my body. I was knocked to the floor, but in the same motion, I got off a round from my handgun back in the direction of the flash, then fell to the floor, still conscious.

Looking up from the floor, I saw the other German from the train fall from the stairwell and into the hallway. My shot had been accurate. My bullet had entered his right eye and exited out the back of his head.

I was beginning to fade, but I saw Rauff turn and look at me. He paused and then fled out the back door. I tried very hard to get to my feet. I was bleeding profusely from my right side, but I was determined to get Rauff. I used the right side of the hallway wall to prop myself up. I then stumbled down the hallway that was now littered with four bodies. Blood covered the floor and walls. It took me over a minute to reach the back door. I exited the door and looked left and right. There was no sign of Rauff. By this time, more neighbors were turning on their lights. No one dared to step out of their homes, though.

Due to my severe wound, I decided to go back to Colonel Randell's restaurant. I staggered down the alley and used the walls of the surrounding houses to keep myself upright. I managed to make it out to a main street. I paused, leaning against the corner of the building. There were no passing cars and no sign of Rauff. I must have passed out.

Several hours passed before I opened my eyes again. I was back in my second-floor room at Colonel Randell's restaurant. I was propped up in my bed. My shirt was off, and I had a large white bandage wrapped around my stomach and lower ribs. The right side of the bandage was a little bloody. It hurt to breathe, mainly from my diaphragm being wrapped so tightly.

I heard a light knock on the bedroom door. An older man entered the room, accompanied by Colonel Randell.

"Allen, this is Dr. Sanchez. He has been taking good care of you," Colonel Randell said.

"How was I brought back here, Colonel?" I asked.

"I found you bleeding on the street," the Colonel said. "After waiting almost two hours here at the restaurant for you and Holger to return, I decided to go find you. I knew something must have gone wrong. After driving down several streets, I found you lying on the ground, bleeding. I patched you up the best I could with what I had and then put you in the backseat of my car. I drove you here and put you on a restaurant table. I then ran down the street and banged on Dr. Sanchez's door. He came right away and assessed you. The bullet entered your right side, between two ribs, then exited your back, missing your spine by an inch. From what the doctor can tell you did not seriously damage any organs. He cleaned your wounds and stitched you up. You are a fortunate man, Allen."

"Thank you, both, for your kindness," I replied.

"I am sorry about Holger, Allen," the Colonel said. "He was a good man."

"How did you know he died?" I asked.

"I was not sure at first. Your well-being was front and center for me. Upon getting you back here, I immediately dispatched a male employee that I trusted to take my car and return to Rauff's house. I armed him with a handgun and asked him to find Holger and bring him back here.

He was warned to shoot and ask questions later in case Rauff returned. I also asked him to search the house for any paperwork. He got into the house and secured Holger's body, but as he was leaving, the police showed up, and he was not able to search the house. I'm sure neighbors spotted him as he carried Holger's body over his shoulder. Holger is lying in the next room with a sheet over his body. I promise, Allen, to properly bury his body," the Colonel said.

"Thank you, Colonel," I said. "That was a noble gesture on your part.

Can I ask even more of you, sir?" "Anything, Allen."

"I would like to have Holger's body transported back to his family in Buenos Aires," I said. "I would escort him back, but I plan to hunt Walter Rauff to the ends of the earth and kill him."

"You need to focus on healing first, Allen. We have no idea where that Nazi has gone. I will make sure Holger's body is prepared for transport, and I will have the same employee who carried him back here escort his body home to his family. You have my solemn promise," the Colonel replied.

I was glad we had met the Colonel and relieved that Holger's body would be cared for and returned home.

While I was talking, Dr. Sanchez changed my bandages and cleaned my wounds. After he finished, he and the Colonel left the room. I put my head back on my pillow and closed my eyes.

I must have slept the rest of the day; at 7:00 p.m., another knock on my door awakened me. It was the Colonel with a tray of hot food and cold water. A young Chilean man accompanied him.

"You need to eat, Allen. The restaurant has prepared a hearty meal for you," the Colonel said as he placed the tray beside my bed.

"This young man is Rafael Hernandez. He is the employee who retrieved Holger's body. I have asked him to accompany Holger home. Holger's body has been prepared, and Rafael will leave late tonight on the 10:00 p.m. train to Buenos Aires," the Colonel said.

"Thank you, Colonel, and thank you, Rafael. I am forever in your debt," I said.

Both men left the room. I did not know if Rafael understood what I was saying, but I was confident the Colonel would tell him how thankful I was.

I spent the next hour eating everything on my plate. I had not eaten in almost twenty-four hours. Upon finishing my meal, I got out of bed and slowly walked down the hall to the bathroom. I then made my way back to a chair in my room. With much effort, I grabbed a shirt and got it over my head and upper body. I sat there, put my head in my hands, and pondered what had happened over the last eighteen hours. Where had I gone wrong? I also thought of Alice, wishing she was with me to care for me. I was upset over it all.

I must have drifted off to sleep again. I woke up the following day in bed with my shirt off and fresh bandages applied. They had taken good care of me.

What would happen next? How would I find Walter Rauff? Would I heal well enough to finish my mission? I had a lot of unanswered questions.

It was October 8, 1946. I had been in South America for ninety days and managed only to kill two Nazis on my list. How much longer would it take to kill the other two?

CHAPTER 8

Demise of Sanity

"Insanity is often the logic of an accurate mind overtasked."
Oliver Wendell Holmes, Sr.

I spent weeks healing from my gunshot wound. My patience wore thin. I was cooped up in one of the Colonel's upstairs bedrooms for over two weeks. By the third week, I walked more freely and even down to the beach to regain my stamina. Dr. Sanchez took good care of me. He even picked up a few words of English, and my Spanish slowly improved.

It was November 2, and Dr. Sanchez gave me a clean bill of health. I prepared to continue my hunt for Walter Rauff. Colonel Randell confirmed that Rafael returned Holger's body to his family in Buenos Aires.

On my behalf, the Colonel told Rafael what to tell Holger's family about his death and what had happened. I felt tremendous guilt that I was not there to console Holger's family, hug his wife, and shake Rudolph's hand. I couldn't begin to imagine what they were going through.

After much debate with Colonel Randell, I convinced him I needed to return to Walter Rauff's house and search for clues that might lead me to him. The police had canvassed the entire city, looking for information on what led to the deaths of the four people at the Rauff residence. According to the Colonel, they had no solid leads. The residence had been wiped clean. Rumor had it that Rauff's belongings were still in the house because his body was not among the dead. Neighbors informed the police that Rauff had not been seen in several weeks. He was not considered a suspect in the deaths, though. I would have to break into the house to search for anything that might lead me to Rauff.

The night of November 2, I decided to walk the five miles to Rauff's house. I needed to build my endurance, and walking was the best way. I left for Rauff's house at 11:30 p.m. It took me close to three hours to walk the five miles. I was winded when I approached Rauff's back door at about 2:30 a.m. This time, there was no barking dog. I wondered to myself what had happened to that little white dog.

There was a sign on the door written in Spanish that I concluded said, "Do Not Enter." Ignoring the sign, I used my knife to pry open the door lock and enter the residence. I had come prepared to encounter Rauff or anyone else who might be at the house. My handgun was by my side. Here I was again, entering the dark hallway, the very same one where I saw Holger die and where I killed the two Germans from the train.

This time, I carried a flashlight that Colonel Randell had given me. I turned it on, and to my surprise, there was still a significant amount of dried blood covering the floor and walls. Whoever had cleaned the home had done a poor job.

I first surveyed the downstairs bedroom and kitchen. I found a few letters bundled together with a string in a kitchen cabinet. A small suitcase was stowed in the downstairs bedroom, but nothing significant was stored there. I placed the letters from the kitchen in a shoulder bag and walked upstairs. The upstairs had two mostly empty bedrooms. The Germans from the train had barely had enough time to unpack. One room belonged to the German who shot me. He had left behind a suitcase on the floor and a few pairs of shoes. A few pairs of pants and shirts were also hanging in the closet. The German's suitcase contained a few files that I grabbed and placed in my bag.

The other room belonged to Rauff. I could tell he had been in the home for a while, simply from the kitchen letters and the fact that his bedroom had a few family pictures. One picture appeared to be of his son, who was in uniform and looked like he had been an S.S. officer.

Rauff had a small desk in his room; I found more letters and miscellaneous paperwork. I took everything and crammed it into my bag. I also took all the German's clothes and shoes from the other upstairs bedroom. I slammed it all into the suitcase the dead German had brought with him and headed out. Hopefully, I had secured something that would be of use in my hunt for Rauff.

I walked back downstairs and out the back door. None of the neighbors' lights had come on, and I was confident I had not been seen. I walked back to Colonel Randell's residence, arriving back at 5:30 a.m. The sun would be up soon.

Upon entering the restaurant's back door, I saw that Rafael was already up and starting breakfast for patrons coming in soon. In my limited Spanish, I thanked him for getting Holger's body back to his family. I asked him if the family had said anything to him. He just said there was a lot of crying. He had not remained long in Buenos Aires, catching a train back to Chile the same day he arrived.

As I headed upstairs to sleep, Rafael handed me a glass of grapefruit juice and a napkin full of cooked bacon. I was too tired to go through all the paperwork I had secured. I crashed on the bed and slept for a few hours. I awoke around 11:00 a.m. and spent the next three hours going through every letter and piece of paper I had collected the night before. Much of the correspondence I had secured from the upstairs German spoke to his instructions. It was straightforward, directing him to travel to Chile, locate Rauff, and protect him. He had lived in Essen, Germany, and had traveled thousands of miles to meet his death. I assumed the first German I killed was probably from Essen or a nearby town, like Dusseldorf. Neither man would be returning home.

The documents I collected from Rauff's room did lead to some valuable clues. He had corresponded with other Germans who had fled to South America. None of these other Germans were on my mission list, and I was unsure of their roles in the war. The cities where these other Germans lived were all in southern Chile. There were various letters received from Santiago and Valdivia, Chile. My best action would be to travel immediately to those two cities.

I spent the rest of the evening sharing with Colonel Randell what I had found and details about the two cities in southern Chile that were the best possible locations for finding Rauff.

The Colonel was concerned that I might not be physically fit to make the journey. He was right, but I would not argue with him.

I knew my wound would slow me down. I was nowhere near as

physically fit as I had been during the war. However, I wanted desperately to get home to Alice and be through with this mission. That desire alone propelled me to push forward and ignore any obstacles in my way, whether they were physical or mental.

I would not waste any time. My goal was to leave sometime over the next twenty-four hours. I packed one suitcase with a mixture of my newly-acquired clothes provided to me by Colonel Randell and the dead German. I prepared a second bag that contained my handgun, knife, ammunition, and a few extra pairs of shoes.

Before leaving the following day, I wrote a heartfelt letter to Alice. This time, I did not care what military protocol I broke. I shared with her everywhere I had been since leaving her. I even told her where I was about to go. I did not go into gory detail about the killings but told her I was still under the United States Army's direction and hoped to be home to her by late spring or early summer of 1947. I also did not tell her I had been shot. My letter turned out to be five handwritten pages. The Army was stringent on censoring during the war. I knew my mission was secret, but at that point, I did not care plus no one was around to censor it. I would miss Thanksgiving with Alice again. In the best-case scenario, it would be another six to eight months before I saw her again. She had no way of reaching me, either. I prayed my letter reached her.

I gave the letter to Colonel Randell, along with Alice's address, and asked him to make sure it got to her. As with Holger, he was fully committed to my request. He told me that he felt like he was an actual member of the OSS since meeting me and supporting my mission. I just smiled and patted him on the back.

The following afternoon, I said my goodbyes to Colonel Randell and Rafael. I told the Colonel that I might never see him again but thanked him for all the support he had given me. In the short time since our paths had crossed, he had sheltered, fed, supplied, given me intelligence, and saved my life. I was forever in his debt.

The Colonel later dropped me off at the Mejillones train station. We said our goodbyes, and I firmly shook his hand. My train to Santiago, Chile, was leaving soon. The trip would take two days, covering close to 874 miles. Once again, I was boarding a train. I found my seat and settled in.

For the first time in several months, I was on my own. Until this particular mission, that was how I had been trained and operated covertly and on my own. Regardless, I missed Holger. We had established a bond that soldiers often do. We had not fought on the same side during the war, but we had both spilled blood to defend our country, and because of that, we shared a bond.

The train trip to Santiago, Chile, was uneventful, except that the train tracks hugged the western coastline of Chile and offered some fantastic views. I found the country to be very picturesque. Despite the recent carnage I had witnessed, I kept my perspective looking forward and took the time to notice God's creation.

My train arrived in Santiago during the early evening of November 5. Colonel Randell had graciously provided me with two hundred Chilean dollars. I was still a member of the United States Army, but my monthly checks could not reach me in South America. The Army was not supplying me, and I was alone during this mission. The money given to me by the Colonel would be helpful.

I found a cab outside the train station to deliver me to the Hotel Villafranca. Rafael had recommended this hotel to me. He was originally from Santiago and said his family ran that hotel. He said all I had to do was check in and state that I was his friend and that they would take good care of me.

Rafael's promise was true. Upon checking in, I mentioned his name and was given an upgraded room on the top floor of the five-story hotel. My room was discounted, and I was told I would eat for free during my entire stay.

I spent that first evening in Santiago unpacking and reviewing all the letters Rauff had received from the address in Santiago. The name of the person Rauff was communicating with was Jorge Schmidt. The unusual name told me that the individual was probably born in South America but was possibly the child of a German father.

The content of the letters exchanged between Rauff and Schmidt spoke about refuge and support that would be offered in the event Rauff needed to leave Mejillones. From what I could gather, Rauff and Jorge's father had known each other in Berlin. The father was never named in the letters, but indications were that he was now dead, and Jorge was keeping up the communication with Rauff as a promise to his late father.

After eating a hearty breakfast the following morning, I wasted no time. I reviewed some city maps the hotel provided me and found the approximate location of the Schmidt family's address. The street was on the opposite side of town. The hotel was in southeast Santiago; the Schmidt residence's street was in the city's northwest section.

While reviewing the maps in the hotel lobby, a young man walked up to me.

"Allen, my name is Julio, and I am Rafael's cousin. I work nights here at the hotel. Are you looking for a particular address on those maps, or are you looking to sightsee?" Julio asked.

Julio spoke English very well. I saw this as an opportunity and replied, "It is nice to meet you, Julio. You speak English much better than your cousin Rafael!"

Julio laughed and quickly said, "My cousin was not very good in school. We both went to Catholic school here in Santiago. We had a great nun from America who offered to teach us English. I spent time with her every day for two years. All Rafael did was the basics and never put in the extra effort. He was just good at manual labor."

Julio's comments about his cousin made perfect sense to me in light of what Rafael had recently done for me, escorting Holger's body back to his family.

"Julio, if I paid you, would you consider driving me around the city, dropping me off, and picking me up at various times? I need a flexible driver who can work odd hours. I don't want to interfere with your job here at the hotel, though," I said.

"My mother is my boss at the hotel, and you are already a critical guest. Rafael would only refer an extraordinary person to us. All I have to do is ask my mother permission to leave, but I am confident she'll let me help you," Julio said.

"Well, that is great news," I said. "If you work nights at the hotel, I bet you are heading home. Would you be available later today?"

"Yes," Julio answered. "I can meet you back in the lobby at 3:00 this afternoon. Will that work?"

"That will be perfect, Julio," I replied.

Julio said his goodbyes and left out the front door of the hotel. Selfishly, I wanted him to drive me immediately to the northwest side of the city so that I could find and check out the Schmidt residence. I would have to be patient. I could easily take a cab but wanted greater flexibility with coming and going. Meeting Julio and establishing a local connection was a good start.

I spent the rest of the morning and into the early afternoon exploring the streets around the hotel. I had to continue to build up my endurance after spending almost three weeks on my back recuperating from my gunshot wound. I was way behind concerning my overall conditioning. My side still hurt, but I did my best to ignore it. During the entire war, I had managed to avoid getting shot, yet here I was in South America after the war, and I had managed to get shot by a German, nonetheless.

Santiago was an ancient city full of unique architecture. The city was vibrant that morning, with many local merchants selling their goods. You would have thought every street vendor had a great deal for me as they all tried passionately to sell me something.

As I wandered in and out of the vendor's areas, I thought that I should stop and buy something for Alice.

Then, it hit me like a ton of bricks. If I counted all the time Alice and I had spent together since meeting in Zurich many years ago, it would not amount to three months of combined time together. I did not even know what she liked. It was embarrassing. I was hopelessly in love, and I knew she loved me. I could buy her anything, and she would like it. She was undoubtedly not a needy person. That was one of her endearing characteristics. She was a down-to-earth girl. I wanted to talk to Alice as I walked through the city, but it would have to wait.

After a few hours of wandering that section of the city, I returned to my hotel and waited for Julio to pick me up. Like clockwork, Julio pulled up at the front of the hotel at 3:00 p.m. sharp. I hopped into his car, and off we went.

"Julio, thank you for your willingness to pick me up and take me around the city as needed. What I will be doing will probably not make much sense to you, but trust me, it's vital work," I said.

Julio quickly said, "You are very welcome, Allen. I figured you were not here in Santiago for vacation."

Julio's reply surprised me. I did stand out.

I gave Julio the address of the Schmidt residence, but I have yet to tell him anything else. It took us about thirty minutes to reach our destination. When we arrived, I asked him to pull over and park within two hundred feet of the address.

I had no idea what Schmidt's son, Jorge, looked like. I knew what my target looked like, though, and all I wanted to do was see if he was there. I would have to approach the house eventually, but I did not want a repeat of what happened in Mejillones. No more innocent people needed to die.

I asked Julio to turn off the car. I told him which house I was watching and asked him to keep his eyes open for an older Caucasian man. I took a chance and shared a little with him about my actions. Julio did not question me in the least.

We sat in Julio's car for the next three hours. No one entered or exited the house. I had to know if we were even watching the right house. At 6:00 p.m., I left the car, but not before telling Julio that if he heard shots fired, he was to drive away immediately. His eyes widened, and he gripped the steering wheel tightly.

I casually approached the house, walked up the front sidewalk, and knocked on the door. After a few seconds, a young man opened the door. His skin tone immediately told me he had mixed parents, so I assumed he was Jorge from the letters.

In German, I asked him if he was Jorge Schmidt. He looked at me in surprise, and German replied that he was. He asked me who I was.

I continued speaking in German and told him I was a friend of his father and Walter Rauff. I told him my name was Fritz Greiner, my alias from my early military career in Germany and the very same name I had initially been given Rudolph as we traveled to Buenos Aires from Casablanca. In a soft voice, I asked Jorge if either his father or Walter was there.

As I suspected, Jorge told me his later father, Timo, had passed away about a year earlier from cancer. He shared with me that he had never met Walter Rauff but knew of him, having written him a few times as a courtesy to his late father. I took this as a sign that Jorge was telling the truth about Walter and that Walter was, in fact, not there.

I thanked Jorge for his time and left. As I returned to Julio's car, I was glad I had the right house but frustrated that Rauff had not yet surfaced in Santiago.

When I sat back in the car, Julio did not say anything. Nothing was said between us on the drive back to the hotel. I was quiet because I was frustrated that Rauff was still eluding me. Julio was quiet and confused, afraid to ask me what was happening.

Upon reaching the hotel, I finally spoke up. "Julio, I know you are confused, but if you agree to take me back to the same house tomorrow, I will share more with you about what is happening."

"Thank you, Allen," Julio replied. "I am confused, but knowing is not my business."

We parted ways. Julio went to work at the hotel; I went to my room. Before retiring for the evening, I reviewed all the written correspondence I had secured from Rauff's house, looking for more clues to help me find him. Nothing new surfaced. Frustrated, I went to bed.

The next day and for the following three weeks, I had Julio drive me to Jorge's residence, and I monitored the comings and goings. Most days, I asked Jorge to drop me off. Each day, I situated myself nearby at a café or public park, or I asked Jorge to loan me his car and had him take a taxi back to the hotel. It was a dull and tedious process, and as each day passed, I became more frustrated.

It was November 28, 1946, Thanksgiving Day back in the United States. I was depressed. My depression centered on Alice having to spend Thanksgiving alone and the fact that Rauff still eluded me. I hoped Alice had received my heartfelt letter and that she took some solace in the fact that I would be home relatively soon. I decided to postpone my search for a few days.

Somehow, word got back to the hotel staff that it was Thanksgiving. They surprised me with a traditional Thanksgiving dinner with turkey, mashed potatoes, cranberries, stuffing, and pumpkin pie. I was shocked. Several of the staff joined me that evening as we ate the surprise meal in the hotel kitchen. We had a great time as I tried my best to explain to them what a pilgrim was and all the traditions of Thanksgiving. The red wine served at dinner helped soften my depression and put me in a better mood.

The next day, I visited some other sections of Santiago. I visited some old churches, sat in the empty pews, and lit candles near the altars. I used this time to clear my head.

Julio invited me to spend the weekend at his family's home. His mother and father were very hospitable. They must have been a family of means, as their home was on the beach. The view of the Pacific Ocean was incredible, and the sunsets were spectacular. It was a nice break, and it recharged my batteries, but I would pay a significant price.

As Julio and I departed his parent's home on Sunday night, December 1, I asked Julio to drive by Jorge's residence one last time so that I could knock on his door again and inquire about Rauff.

It took us about forty-five minutes to arrive back at Jorge's neighborhood. I asked Julio to park down the street, as usual. The sun was setting rapidly. I had hidden my handgun and knife in Julio's car, next to the passenger seat. I secured both and began the quick walk to Jorge's residence. I was walking up the sidewalk when a shot rang out inside the house.

I wasted no time. I ran to the front door; it was locked. With my gun drawn, I kicked the door open. I heard a flurry of activity coming from the back of the house. After clearing the home's front portion, I turned left and charged down a narrow hallway. There lying on the floor was Jorge, dead from a bullet to the head.

I heard more noise coming from a room to my right. The house had no lights on, and it was hard to see. I immediately moved to the room, a bedroom, and saw Walter Rauff climbing out the window. He cursed at me in German, telling me that I would never catch him alive. I raised my gun and fired off a shot, hoping to slow him at least down. For an older guy, he moved fast. He cleared the window. I was not sure if I had hit him or not.

I ran to the window. My shot must have hit its mark as I saw a blood trail and a backpack lying on the ground. I crawled out the back window, picked up the backpack on the ground, and followed the blood trail.

The sun had set by then, and the back alley where Rauff had disappeared was very dark. I did not have a flashlight, and very few surrounding homes had turned on their exterior lights. I listened for any sound, but there was none. I quickly made my way back to Julio, as I was concerned that Rauff might commandeer Julio's car and kill Julio in the process.

I was relieved when I saw the car with Julio sitting safely inside. He wore a look of sheer terror on his face. I jumped in the front seat passenger side of the car, threw the backpack I had just secured in the backseat, and asked Julio to circle the neighborhood with his headlights off.

As he drove around, I explained that what he had just witnessed was my hunt for an escaped Nazi from Germany. I told him I had chased Rauff to Santiago and desperately needed to find him.

Julio and I searched for hours, but no sign of Rauff appeared. I was so upset with myself. We decided by 4:00 a.m. to head back to the hotel.

As Julio drove back to the hotel, my sanity was at its limit. If I had not taken the weekend off by spending time with Julio's family, I would have seen Walter Rauff enter Jorge's residence. Jorge would still be alive if I had approached the house tonight differently and had not been seen. I strongly felt that Walter Rauff had killed Jorge simply to silence him, to leave no trace of being there. Here again, another innocent civilian had died senselessly.

I was upset over the fact that, for a second time, Rauff had escaped my capture. I was an experienced soldier in the United States Army. Things like this did not happen to me. What could I have done better?

I did not sleep well that night. I tossed and turned, upset and tired of chasing what seemed to be a ghost.

The following day, I searched the backpack that Walter Rauff had left behind when he escaped out the bedroom window. The backpack contained more correspondence with his contacts in Valdivia, Chile. The absolute goldmine in the backpack, though, was another detail that provided the location of Eckerd Jacobsen in Brazil. He was living in Porto Alegre, Brazil, and working on a fishing boat. My day suddenly got a lot better, and my mood brightened.

I made immediate arrangements to travel to Valdivia, Chile, to make one last attempt to find and kill Rauff. I would then travel to Porto Alegre, Brazil, and attempt to do the same to Jacobsen.

I quickly packed my clothing and secured my weapons and ammo.

I approached the hotel's front desk and asked for my bill so I could check out. The young lady at the front desk asked me to wait a minute while she went to the hotel office in the back.

While waiting, Julio found me and asked me where I was going.

"I am leaving immediately to try and locate our escaped Nazi in Valdivia," I replied.

"Valdivia? I have an uncle who lives there. I haven't seen him in a while. Let me see if I can get permission to drive you there. Would that be okay, Allen?" Julio asked.

I had estimated that the distance from Santiago and Valdivia was five hundred and thirty miles. That was a tall order to ask anyone.

"Julio," I said, "I sincerely appreciate your willingness to drive me, but I need you to stay at the hotel and work. My friend, I have taken too much of your time and resources."

He was disappointed with my reply, but I think he understood. My real reason for turning him down was that I didn't want any more innocent people to die. I needed to go alone.

The young lady managing the front desk returned and told me that Rafael's family had covered my bill. I was shocked but was very appreciative of the kind gesture. I quickly left the hotel.

I headed straight for the Santiago coast by taxi and, upon my arrival, started searching for a charter boat to take me to Valdivia. The money I saved at the hotel could be used to secure passage on a boat.

As luck would have it, I found a boat service that ran every other day from Santiago to Valdivia. I bought a ticket at the last minute and boarded just before the boat exited the dock. I quickly found a seat in the top section of the boat. The ride would take a total of twenty-four hours. We would be served two meals, but there were no sleeping quarters. I had to take what I could get.

For the next twenty-four hours, the boat traveled south, hugging the western coast of Chile. Even though the shoreline was in sight the entire trip, the seas were rough. Many people on the boat became sick and lost their meals over the ship's side. I managed to power through by eating less. The food did not look that good, anyway.

Mid-morning on December 4, the charter boat docked in Valdivia, Chile. I disembarked and found a small hotel near the docks. With my minimal Spanish, I checked in without a hitch and dropped my belongings in my hotel room. For the rest of the day, I studied maps of Valdivia that the hotel had lying around. I located the address with which Walter Rauff had been corresponding. The residence was within walking distance of the hotel, only two miles south of my current location. I would set out the next day.

I secured my weapons and ammo the following day and placed them in Rauff's backpack. I ate a quick breakfast and left the hotel. I felt much healthier. The pain from my gunshot wound was practically gone, and I walked the two miles to the residence in about thirty minutes. I found a café that faced the front door of the residence. I sat down at the café and sipped strong coffee for the next four hours. No one came or went from the house.

I repeated this same activity for the next three weeks. During that entire time, I saw no one enter or exit the house. I decided to give my surveillance three more days. On the third day, the very last day I decided to spend in Valdivia, an old lady walked up to the house's front door, pulled out a key, opened the door, and walked inside.

That morning, the individual entering the residence made sense to me because the written correspondence between the residence and Rauff appeared to come from a woman. The letters spoke of missing each other and said it had been years since they had seen each other. Was this elderly woman possibly the missing Nazi's mother? Was Rauff in the house all this time, and was his mother caring for him?

I returned to my hotel and decided to return that evening under darkness. I was not going to be seen approaching any residence again in daylight.

That night, close to 10:00 p.m., I approached the backside of the house. There was a dim light on, and I peered in a window. Sitting in a small chair was the elderly woman I had seen enter the home earlier that day. She was reading a book. I looked in a few more windows and saw no one else in the home. I went around to the front of the house and knocked. It was December 24, Christmas Eve.

Before too long, the woman opened the door. I greeted her in German. I told her I was a friend of Walter's from Germany and hoped to see him. I asked if he was there.

Her reply to me in German was different from what I was expecting.

"Du bist der Mann, der meinen kleinen Walter jagt Wenn ich jünger war, würde ich ein Messer durch dein Herz legen. Walter ist nicht hier und er wird nie hier wegen dir sein."

I stepped back away from the door and took a deep breath. In a very calm voice, she told me that she knew I was the man hunting her little Walter. With her finger pointed at me, she said that if she were younger, she would put a knife through my heart. She said that Walter was not there and that he never would be as a direct result of my actions. She continued to tell me that I would never find him.

Somehow, word had gotten to her that I might be here, and she was expecting me. I quickly concluded that this woman posed no threat to me. I walked up to her, pushed her aside, and informed her in German that I would search the house.

Entering the home that evening, I saw a picture of Walter Rauff in his Nazi glory days. One picture had him standing next to Adolph Hitler and Hermann Goring. Nazi swastika banners were hanging on one of her walls, and to top it off, she had a bust of Hitler's head on her coffee table. She was a full-fledged Nazi.

Searching the house for any sign of Rauff, I listened as the old woman berated me in German.

I quickly concluded that Walter had not been there. In a calm voice, I asked the woman to sit down. She sat down, and I did, as well. For the next few minutes, I asked her everything from her name to where she lived in Germany to how many children she had. My goal was to calm her down with the hope of soliciting valuable information.

She told me her name was Sarah and that she and her husband had lived in Heidelberg, Germany. Her husband was a veteran of World War One and had been killed in the battle of Verdun in December 1916. She told me that her only son, Walter, had been born in 1905 and was eleven years old when his father was killed. When Hitler came to power in the 1930s, Walter rose quickly in the German Army. She said that, late in the war, Walter saw the storm coming and asked his mother to move to South America to escape the carnage. Sarah had moved to Valdivia, Chile, in 1943, joining several other families from Heidelberg. She had only seen Walter once since he escaped to South America in late 1945.

I told Sarah about all the atrocities that her son Walter had performed during the Second World War, telling her how he had been responsible for killing thousands of Jews. I told her I first ran across Walter during my activity at Auschwitz, participating in construction work and gathering intelligence. Walter had visited the camp one afternoon to gather more supplies. I told her I saw him curse at the Jewish inmates who were working nearby, even spitting on one of them as he waited for his trucks to be loaded.

Sarah kept a stoic face the entire time I talked to her.

I wrapped up my conversation with her by saying I was going to kill Walter if I ever found him, and I wanted her to know that. He would brutally go to his grave if I had anything to do with it.

Sarah rose from her chair and started screaming at me, pushing me toward her front door. I let myself out.

I walked the two miles back to my hotel, mulling over what had happened. I concluded that I was wasting my time trying to find Walter Rauff. He had left a trail of chaos and destruction in his wake. I would travel to Brazil the next day and locate Eckerd Jacobsen.

I packed and left my hotel in Valdivia, Chile, the following morning, Christmas Day. I hoped never to see the country of Chile again. My time there had not been good at all. I lost a friend and saw several other innocent people die at the hands of Walter Rauff. I thought of Alice, what she would be doing, and where she would be that day. I assumed she would spend the day with her parents. I missed her and was still hoping she had received my letter.

The worst part of my three-week journey was the water transportation up the western coast of Chile. I had to take a series of four ships up the coast. We left Valdivia, and after four separate ships, we finally docked in Valparaiso, Chile. It was the final ship that caused the real issue. The ship's steam engine failed. This meant the ship drifted further out to sea, away from the coast.

When I boarded the ship, I wondered how it would even float. The ship was full of rust, and I spotted holes in the upper sections of the stern. The crew appeared nonchalant and seemed unconcerned about preparedness.

I boarded, anyway, because I had become impatient with the time it took me to reach Porto Alegre.

Something was wrong when the ship no longer produced wash from its rudders. The horn on the ship blew, and I heard several phrases in Spanish over the ship's loudspeakers. From what I could tell, the ship was not operating under its power, and we were drifting. I watched as the ship's crew tried to lower the starboard and port anchors, but they were not lowering. The crew cursed at the anchors and banged on the large chains with sledgehammers.

I had been through so much over my long military career, but this problem with the ship did not worry me. I was frustrated that it was happening, but I was not worried overall. We were floating, and that was the most important thing.

The ship drifted for two days before another ship radioed from our ship's captain caught up with us. Large ropes were lashed to our ship's port side. The two ships were brought together, and our passengers were transferred to the new ship. The crew from the ship that rescued us appeared more competent, and they lowered the stricken ship's anchors, allowing the crew to remain with it and wait for another ship to come with the parts required to repair it.

After boarding the new ship, it took us two and a half days to reach the port of Valparaiso, Chile. After that, the train trips commenced. It took me a series of five trains to reach Porto Alegre, Brazil, where I was hopefully one step closer to Jacobsen. If I had my way, I would never take another train ride for the rest of my life. Three of the five trains had been canceled, forcing me to wait several days to secure passage on the next train. Periodically, the tracks were blocked by livestock or fallen trees.

On January 16, 1947, I arrived by train in the eastern coastal city of Porto Alegre, Brazil, at close to 9:00 p.m. I quickly found a hotel and settled in for the evening. It was refreshing to take a shower and shave.

I took in the sunrise from my hotel room balcony the following morning. From what I could see, Porto Alegre was a beautiful port city. If I was an escaped Nazi-like Jacobsen, I would have chosen a city like Porto Alegre, Brazil, and tried to blend in.

My attention quickly turned to locating this fourth escaped Nazi and getting back home to Alice. Later that morning, I verified with the hotel the location of his address. The address turned out to be inland, in the middle of the city. I was told the approximate distance between the hotel and Jacobsen's address was four miles. I was very close.

I felt out of sync the last few months and highly frustrated. Factors like Holger's unnecessary death, my inability to capture Rauff on two occasions, and being shot. On top of all that, all the movement within the South American continent was taking its toll on me. I had to quickly refocus and concentrate on the final stage of my mission. Jacobsen was in my sights. This Nazi was not going to get away. Late in the morning, I secured my weapons in my newly-acquired backpack, walked out of the hotel, and quickly found a cab to transport me to Jacobsen's residence. The ride took about twenty minutes. Porte Alegre was bustling at the late-morning hour. People hurried down the sidewalks as cars and buses sped down the streets. The city was not on the scale of Santiago, Chile, but it appeared vibrant. I asked the cab driver to drop me off a mile from Jacobsen's address.

I paid the driver, hoisted my backpack around my right shoulder, and walked toward the address. I had one black and white photo of Jacobsen that I had studied carefully the night before.

Within a few minutes, I was very close to the address. A small outdoor vegetable market covered the remaining one hundred yards to the address. There, looking over the vegetables, stood Eckerd Jacobsen. He had aged considerably since my photo of him had been taken. He did not look like he was in good health.

I took this as a perfect opportunity to approach him. I walked right up to him and introduced myself in German.

"Guten Morgen mein Herr. Wie sehen die gemuse heute aus?" *Good morning sir. How do the vegetables look today?*

Jacobsen looked up and over at me and said with emphasis, "Abgestanden!"

He was telling me the vegetables were stale, and he was unhappy. I went on, pretending to be interested in the vegetables. I also began complaining in German, making sure Jacobsen could hear me. I went so far as to say the vegetables in my hometown of Berlin were always fresh, even during the war years. This comment perked Jacobsen up, and he started to engage me in conversation.

He asked me what part of Berlin I had lived in. It was easy for me to talk about Berlin, as I had recently been there to study the very man who stood next to me. It was also easy because I had lived there in the mid-1930s as an undercover United States government attaché, the precursor to my OSS activity.

Jacobsen came around to express his concern over the fact that there was no other educated German he could speak to in Porto Alegre. He said there was a pocket of Germans living in the city, but they needed to be educated. I laughed in response, attempting to keep him engaged in conversation.

What happened next took me by surprise, but it would eventually make my job of eliminating him that much easier. Jacobsen asked if I would like to join him for lunch at his nearby home. I accepted.

As we walked the last hundred yards to his home, he asked me what brought me to Porto Alegre. I informed him that I was backpacking through South America to recover from the toils of war back in Germany. I came right out and asked him what brought him to Porto Alegre.

There was a long pause. We had reached his home by then. His home was part of a duplex right off the street. When Jacobsen spoke, he answered honestly, to my surprise.

He told me he knew why I was in Porto Alegre and why I had approached him on this very day. He knew I was there to kill him. I was not surprised he knew that, as he and Rauff had been corresponding, but for him to come right out and state that, even inviting me into his home, was a big surprise.

Jacobsen did not break stride or change his voice when he invited me in. He asked me to sit as he went into the kitchen to make lunch. I fully expected him to grab a weapon or come out of the kitchen as fast as he could and attempt to kill me where I sat. As he prepared lunch, he continued to talk, however. I listened, but not before removing my handgun and placing it in my right hand down between my right thigh and the seat.

Jacobsen then told me what I already knew. He said he and his death squad were directly responsible for executing Jews in their own homes.

I was astounded by his brutal honesty. He told me he was sick with cancer and was not expected to live more than another four to five months. He brought the lunch he had prepared into the small living room where I was sitting. He placed the liverwurst sandwiches and freshly cut pickles on the nearby table and motioned me to eat. He had no threatening demeanor or weapons on him and appeared harmless.

As we ate, he talked more and more. He expressed that he missed his home in Berlin. He told me he had left Berlin with several other lower-ranking German officers shortly before the Russians overtook the city. They traveled in a convoy of three trucks into southern Germany, slipping past all the Allied troops. They traveled through northern Italy into Switzerland and eventually through Spain and Portugal. They traveled to South America on a German submarine out of Lisbon, Portugal. I was amazed.

He told me he had been in Porto Alegre for fifteen months and knew that he was sick, even before leaving Germany. He paused before continuing.

By this time, we had finished our lunch. Jacobsen looked at me and asked me if I would kill him quickly. I informed him that he had two choices. Tell me where Rauff was, and I would kill him quickly, or refuse to tell me, and I would kill him slowly.

Jacobsen did not hesitate to tell me that Santiago, Chile, was the last place he knew where Rauff had lived. I told him I had recently been there to find him. I told Jacobsen all the places I had been in my attempt to capture him and that I had come close on two occasions. I even told him that I had met Rauff's mother in Valdivia, Chile and that she had refused to give him up. I knew well that she pretended not to give him up, but she had no idea where he was.

I concluded from our dialogue that Jacobsen also needed to find Rauff's location. I had to let Rauff go. I wanted to get home to Alice. I knew the sooner I eliminated Jacobsen, the quicker I could return to the United States.

Jacobsen was sitting in front of me, a shell of a man. I almost felt sorry for him, but not for too long. This old man had killed hundreds of thousands of innocent Jewish men, women, and children. The entire time he spoke, he never showed any remorse. He knew he was dying and now he had no reason to live. Part of me wanted him to die alone, in agonizing pain from his cancer.

My hatred for the Nazis and my desire to get home propelled me to finish what I came to South America to do. I picked up my Colt 1911 handgun that was by my side. I already had a bullet in the chamber. I stood and walked over to Jacobsen. He never flinched or rose from his chair.

I put my gun to his forehead and said, "Brenn in der Holle Nazi."

Burn in hell, Nazi.

I pulled the trigger and blew the back half of Jacobsen's head off. Blood and chunks of his brain matter splattered against the wall behind him. It was a quick death but brutal.

I knew that the gunshot probably alarmed Jacobsen's neighbors. I quickly searched his tiny home for any intelligence on Walter Rauff. I rifled through some letters and documents Jacobsen had on his nearby coffee table. I didn't expect to find anything on Rauff that I did not already have, but something told me to check anyway.

As I looked through the paperwork, I noticed a handwritten letter dated two weeks earlier, January 5, 1947. The signature or the need for an actual signature at the bottom drew me to the letter. In big, bold letters, where a typical signature would be, were simply the letters "A.H." Could this be a letter from Adolph Hitler himself?

Rumors had circulated that Hitler had escaped his Berlin bunker in early May 1945. After the war, no natural confirmed body was ever revealed. The Russians claimed they found it but never showed it to the United States Army.

So many Nazis were never captured, and one that I was surprised was not assigned to me back in Berlin was Adolf Eichmann. Eichmann had been the main organizer and orchestrator of the Holocaust. Some in the United States military thought that both Adolph Hitler and Adolph Eichmann could have escaped together to South America.

I quickly read the letter. The letter spoke specifically about being careful and watchful of Americans and Jews who were hunting escaped Nazis in South America. The author of the letter talked about him being safe and being careful not to be seen, referring to a cattle ranch in Junin, Argentina, that was harboring him. The letter wrapped up with the author referring to raising the fourth Reich and for Jacobsen to remain patient for that to happen.

Adolph Hitler clearly wrote the letter. I was shocked, at first, that he was indeed alive. The rumors were true, after all. Second, I could not believe I was holding a letter that Adolph Hitler had written.

I placed the letter and my handgun in my backpack and left. I walked back down the street, right by the outdoor vegetable market where I had just met Jacobsen. After a short distance, I hailed a cab back to my hotel. That morning, I had considered my mission would end if I could find and kill Jacobson. Things had changed dramatically with my finding a letter that provided evidence that Hitler was still alive and determined to raise a Fourth Reich.

CHAPTER 9

No Penance

"Speak softly and carry a big stick; you will go far."
Theodore Roosevelt

Upon finding evidence that Adolf Hitler was alive and living in Argentina, I decided I couldn't let this new development go unchecked. I had not been assigned Adolf Hitler as a target, but only because the majority of the United States military and government believed he'd killed himself in the bunker. I'd believed that, as well.

I thought for a moment about what to do. Hitler would undoubtedly be surrounded by people loyal to him and his cause. The other four targets I had been assigned had not been guarded, more or less on their own and on the run.

The evidence now pointed to a vast network of Nazis in South America. They were warning each other of people targeting them and encouraging each other to remain steadfast and committed to keeping the Nazi ideology alive. I decided to capitalize on this new development and attempt to locate and kill Adolph Hitler.

Upon returning to my hotel, I quickly packed and arranged to travel to the Porto Alegre train station. I found a train that would take me to Junin, Argentina. The city was west of Buenos Aires but smaller and remote. My train left at 2:00 p.m. The date was January 17, 1947. My journey would last all afternoon and night, covering almost nine hundred miles. As I sat in my seat on the train, I was taken back to those times I had come across

Adolph Hitler in Germany back in the 1930s. I found myself becoming angry over what Hitler had orchestrated and his treatment and elimination of a large segment of the Jewish population. I was not afraid to confront him or to kill him. I was trained to kill, and I would not hesitate.

I thought about the possible ramifications of killing him and the news that his death would create worldwide. I accepted the risks and was determined to take advantage of this opportunity to kill Adolf Hitler.

My train arrived at the Junin, Argentina, train station at 10:15 a.m.. I disembarked and entered the small train station. I found a large map of Junin on the train station's wall. The map was vital in helping me study the city, but more importantly, it helped me identify two cattle ranches surrounding the small city.

Adolph Hitler's letter revealed he was hiding out on a cattle ranch in Junin. One of the ranches was located west of the city, while the other was south. I opted to first go to the cattle ranch west of the city. If I were lucky, Hitler would be at this one; if not, I would visit the second one. I estimated the cattle ranch to the west was approximately eight miles outside the city.

I knew a daylight approach for a target of this caliber would be out of the question. I would have to wait until dark. I found a small hotel not far from the train station. I checked in and was assigned a room on the second floor of the three-story building. I spent most of the afternoon planning my approach to the ranch and what I would do if I were able to find and kill Adolf Hitler.

I treated this mission as any other I had undertaken up to this point, staying level-headed. I set aside a few hours for sleep, as I anticipated I would be awake most of the coming night.

I awoke at 8:00 p.m. I checked my handgun and ammo. I had three clips of ammunition left, giving me twenty-four rounds. I cleaned and sharpened my knife. That was all I would need that evening. I inserted one ammo clip into my handgun and placed it in my backpack. Before closing the pack, I placed the other two ammo clips and knife inside.

I left my hotel room at 8:30 p.m. I found a small restaurant near the hotel where I ate a quick meal, paid the waiter, and left.

I caught a cab near the restaurant. In my limited Spanish, I tried to explain to the driver that I wanted him to drive me west of the city toward the cattle ranch. Somehow, he figured out where I wanted to go. I noted his odometer reading as we pulled away: 1,482 miles. I knew I didn't want him to drive me to the ranch's front door, about eight miles away. I would let him drive me six miles, at which point I would ask him to pull over to the side of the road and let me out. I would walk the remaining two miles to the ranch in the dark.

There was no conversation in the car that evening. The farther we got from the city, the darker and more remote it became. It felt like we were driving off the edge of the earth. The sky must have been cloudy because I saw no moon or stars. I hadn't seen it this pitch-black in a long time.

I carefully watched the odometer as the cab driver drove west. One mile traveled quickly turned into five. When the odometer had increased by six miles, I tapped the driver on the shoulder and motioned for him to pull over to the side of the road. He was surprised at what I asked him to do but still pulled over. I got out with my backpack and motioned for him to drive away. The driver was concerned but eventually pulled away and drove back toward Junin.

I waited until his taillights disappeared in the darkness and listened intently until his car's engine sound faded. I turned and looked west. I stood motionless, listening for anything. It was eerily quiet and very dark. I could only see a few yards in front of me as I started to walk in a westerly direction. All I heard was the sound of my feet hitting the pavement.

After walking about half a mile, I noticed the pavement stopped and gravel began. After another half-mile, the gravel disappeared entirely. I peered into the darkness and noticed a few lights from a stationary object. I knelt on my right knee and tried to discover what I saw but could not.

The ground was now covered in short grass, and I could smell cow manure. I could creep as the grass dampened the sound.

I walked approximately a mile and a half before I could make out the source of the lights. They were coming from the windows of three tiny, one-story houses. A wooden fence surrounded the buildings to keep cattle away from the houses. Once the lights and buildings became visible; I decided to sit in the grass and observe. I estimated I was still half a mile away from the structures.

Before too long, I noticed a man with a rifle on his shoulder roaming the property. He appeared to be guarding the area, but he did not seem to be on alert. He kept looking at the ground as he walked.

I saw no other guards patrolling the property that night. I also looked at the windows, which were covered by thin curtains that prevented me from seeing any movement inside the houses. I waited until the guard walked behind the houses, then rose and started to walk in a large arc in the direction of the left side of the house. I walked back around the house and eventually came up behind the guard. The guard was so distracted with his thoughts that he did not see me quietly come out of the darkness. I put my left hand around his mouth and, with my right hand, reached around his body and plunged my five-inch knife between his ribs and into his heart. It was a quick death. The guard fell to his knees and stopped breathing. I gently placed him on the ground face-down. I gingerly pulled off his rifle and searched his coat pocket for ammunition.

I was pleased to see the rifle was a German-made Mauser, a fine rifle I had seen a lot of them in Germany. I found two clips of ammunition, each containing five bullets. I looked up at the three tiny houses directly in front of me. Only one of the houses had a window on the backside, and it was not illuminated.

Through the darkness, I managed to make out the time on my watch; it was 2:15 a.m. I began working around the house on the right in a crouched position. I soon propped myself against the corner of the house and listened for any sound coming from inside. I heard nothing.

Standing there, I could not believe what I was about to attempt. So many of Hitler's people had tried to kill him during the War and failed. The Allied bombardment from countless air raids had not managed to kill him, either. Here I was in the middle of Argentina, about to kill one of the most evil men alive and end any chance of his resurrecting a Fourth Reich. Hitler was fifty-seven years old, not a young man of any sort. I was not concerned that he would outrun me and escape. No doors were on either side of the three tiny houses or the backside. I would attempt a front entry on each house and hopefully find my infamous target. It was time to finish this.

I left the corner of the house and walked past the illuminated window and to the front door. I pulled out my handgun and chambered a round. I paused for a second or two and then, with my right foot, kicked the wooden door open. I quickly entered the small structure. Sitting at a small table were two men, who I assumed were guards. They played cards with a bottle of whiskey on the table between them. Surprised, They looked up at me in alarm as I rapidly fired four rounds.

One man fell forward and landed face-first on the table, knocking over the bottle of whiskey, which poured onto the table and then onto the bare concrete floor. The other man had started to stand when I shot him. The concussion of the two bullets that hit him knocked him back and onto the floor.

I walked over to both men and confirmed they were dead. I surveyed the small area. There were no bedrooms; it was simply a four-walled structure that contained two sleeping cots, a table, and a small armoire. I rushed out the door and ran to the next house, this one slightly larger.

There was also a light coming from its window. I carefully tried to peer through the thin curtain but could not find any figures inside the house.

I proceeded to the front and kicked the door, but it did not open as quickly as the previous one. I tried again but had no luck. I pulled the Mauser rifle off my right shoulder and fired three shots at the handle area of the door. That did the trick. This time, I quickly kicked the door open. I paused before entering, fearing gunshots might riddle the door in my direction. That is precisely what happened. Five shots rang out, splintering the door. I waited a brief second and then ducked my head inside the house and back out again.

There, sitting in a chair facing the door with a smoking German luger pistol in his right hand, was Adolph Hitler. Knowing there could be eight rounds in a German luger, I waited before entering the house. A small lamp was turned on and sitting on a table next to Hitler. At that point, I didn't know if anyone else was in the house. There was another window on the left side of the door, but it was not illuminated. I carefully bypassed the door and walked over to the window. I ejected the spent Mauser clip from the rifle and inserted the last clip. I fired all five rounds from that clip into the dark window, firing in several directions, hoping to hit anyone who might be in the room.

After firing all five rounds into it, the window was shattered; I cleaned out the glass with the rifle and then dropped the rifle on the ground. I pulled out my handgun, inserted a fresh clip into it, and then crawled into the window, not knowing what awaited me on the other side.

The room was partially lit from the open doorway to the main room where Hitler was sitting. I cleared the room and found no one. I assumed it was Hitler's bedroom. I then walked over by the door to the other room, and three more shots rang out in my direction, missing me by only inches. I knew then that the clip in Hitler's Luger was spent. I rushed through the door and came face to face with the monster.

He still held his luger in his right hand, but I knew he had no more bullets. I walked closer to him, never taking my eyes off him. What happened next shocked me.

Hitler placed his luger on the table and said, "Fritz Greiner, why are you here to kill me?"

I could not believe he remembered the alias name that I had given him when I last saw him north of Berlin; when we met at the concentration camp I was helping to construct, I had told him I was from Austria.

"I clearly remember you, Fritz, as you told me you were from Austria. How could I forget that? I do not understand why you are here now. How did you find me?"

I did not answer him at first. I walked over to the table, pulled out the remaining chair, and sat facing Hitler.

"Are there any more people on the property?" I asked him. "No, the last house is simply for storage," he replied.

For some strange reason, I believed him.

Before asking Hitler any additional questions, I explained to the madman that I was a member of the United States Army and that it would be by my hand that he would meet his death. Then, I continued with my questions for him.

"How did you escape Berlin in May 1945 and return to Argentina?" I asked.

Hitler then confirmed the rumors about what happened. He managed to exit the bunker through a series of tunnels, making it underground to Berlin Tempelhof Airport. Hitler had a pilot fly him south, stopping twice to refuel the plane at secured German runways scattered in southern Europe. He finally was delivered to Sines, Portugal, where he boarded a German submarine that safely delivered him to the coast of Mar del Plata, Argentina. There, a small boat picked him up and delivered him to a secure beach where devout Germans transported him to numerous locations throughout Argentina. He told me he had only been at his current location for three months.

I had many more questions for Hitler, but I was done talking. I spotted a camera on a nearby bookshelf. It suddenly occurred to me that none of my superiors would believe that I had located and killed Hitler unless I took pictures. I rose from my seat, grabbed Hitler's luger, and placed it in my jacket pocket. I then walked over to the table and grabbed the camera. I checked it for film and snapped pictures of Hitler sitting in his chair.

I sat back down in my chair, faced Hitler, and said to him, "How do you want to die, coward? You managed to draw your country into a long, bloody war and then left them there for the Russians to pillage and rape."

Hitler took a deep breath, placed his hands on the table, and said, "By my hand. Please give me back my luger pistol."

"I will not give you that satisfaction," I replied.

I pulled out my faithful Colt 45 handgun and placed it on the table. "I will photograph you after I kill you so that the entire world will know you died alone here in Argentina. I hope you burn in hell for all your brutal crimes against humanity."

I then picked up my handgun and fired a bullet into Hitler's forehead, right between his eyes. His head snapped back and then slumped forward. I then fired two more bullets into his chest.

I put my gun away and took a series of photographs of Hitler's dead body. I also photographed the inside of the house, the two dead guards inside the first house, and the dead guard outside. Lastly, I took pictures of the three houses, although I was not sure if they would come out due to the darkness.

I left the bodies where they fell and left. I couldn't believe what had just happened. I had managed to kill Hitler and his three bodyguards. I was fortunate to come away with no wounds and was thankful. I walked the eight-plus miles back to my hotel in downtown Junin. The walk took me under three hours and gave me time to clear my head and focus on my next steps. I glanced at my watch when I walked in the hotel's front door; it was 4:00 a.m. I got to my room, fell into bed, and slept hard for three hours.

Just after 7:00 a.m., I awoke, showered, and gathered my belongings, especially ensuring I had the camera. I checked out of the hotel.

I could not return home immediately, as there was something I needed to do. After spending only one night there, I checked out of my hotel in Junin. I had been very fortunate to quickly find and eliminate both Eckerd Jacobsen and Adolph Hitler in a matter of only a few days. Hitler had been a valuable additional target to my mission, making it all worthwhile.

The Junin train station was within walking distance of my hotel. I carried my suitcase and backpack and went to the train station to purchase a ticket to Buenos Aires, Argentina.

I needed to visit Holger's family and pay my respects. His death had affected me, and I felt like I had not had ample time to grieve. It had been several months since his death, and I'd had zero correspondence with his family. His body had been returned home, accompanied by a stranger. Holger's father, Rudolf Hartmann, had been a valuable resource to me during the early stages of my mission. His kindness and hospitality were incredible, and I felt I owed him. The very least I could do was visit the family and pay my heartfelt respects.

The train ride only took about three hours, taking me east to Buenos Aires. At the Buenos Aires train station, I arranged to have a cab driver take me to the Hartmann estate. Having visited the estate many times last year, I felt comfortable directing the cab driver where to go.

It took the cab driver about ninety minutes to navigate the narrow roads. We finally arrived at the front gate of the Hartmann estate. I placed my suitcase and backpack next to the car, paid the driver, and sent him on his way. As the driver pulled away, I turned and grabbed my bags. I could see the large house off in the distance. I took a big breath and began my walk up to the house.

I lifted the unlocked gate handle, walked through it, and shut it behind me. It was early afternoon, and the sky was void of any clouds. I started the half-mile walk towards the house.

Before too long, I heard a dog barking in the distance. Soon, Augustus came running in my direction. I was concerned that he had forgotten me after all these months and might be intent on biting me. When Augustus came upon me, he slowed to a walk, and I knelt. He came right up to me and covered me with licks, literally knocking me down with his excitement. He was so glad to see me.

I stood up, grabbed my scattered bags, and walked the rest of the way to the house. Augustus stayed by my side the entire way.

As I approached the first step of the large front porch, the front door opened, and Holger's wife, Ruth, came out to greet me. I climbed the remaining steps of the porch and could not tell from her demeanor if she was going to slap me for allowing her husband to be killed or hug me for coming to visit. She took the latter approach. She walked up to me, and before I could even drop my bags, she embraced me and just held on to me. I spoke to her in German, saying, "I am so sorry for your loss. I counted Holger as my close friend. I miss him dearly. I am upset I could not save him."

Before letting me go, she spoke to me with her head still buried in my chest.

"Allen, I miss him so much. It is not your fault. Holger was a German soldier who knew the risks of combat. He always spoke highly about you and considered you like a brother."

At that time, Holger's real brother, Matthias, his family, Rudolf, and Elsa, came out to greet me on the porch. Lots of hugs and handshakes were passed around. I was welcomed inside the home as if I had never left.

Over the next few hours, we all reminisced about Holger. I heard many stories about his childhood from Rudolph and Elsa. Ruth shared how they had met and where they were married. Later that evening, we talked even more over a large dinner that had been prepared.

After dinner, Rudolph motioned for Matthias and me to follow him to the house's back deck. I had a strong feeling as to what he wanted to discuss.

Rudolph handed me a glass of bourbon and a cigar and said, "Tonight, we toast my son, Holger!"

We lit our cigars and sipped on our bourbon for a minute before Rudolph spoke again.

"Allen, tell me how my son died."

I knew Rudolph wanted to talk to me about this when he motioned me outside, away from Elsa's listening ears.

"Do you want to know each detail, sir, or just the fact that he died quickly?" I asked.

Rudolph looked at me momentarily, took his cigar out of his mouth, and said, "From one solder to another, Allen, I want to know everything. Did you get to kill the bastard responsible for killing him?"

I started by telling Rudolph that I had killed the man who killed his son. I then reviewed the backstory about how we located Walter Rauff and how we had approached his house that late evening back in Mejillones, Chile. It took me about an hour to share all the details. Rudolph was persistent with his questions, often stopping me mid-sentence to clarify a point. He had me share exactly how Holger was killed. I had difficulty telling him that part, but I got it out. I told him that Holger had been killed by a Nazi who was protecting Walter Rauff. I had to share how Rauff had escaped and how he had escaped again in Santiago, Chile. I did not want Rudolph to think his son had died in vain. Matthias stood there listening to what I had to share about his brother. He never said much any time I was around him. He only shared a few words.

"Thank you, Allen, for killing the man who killed my brother."

I did not reply to Matthias; I shook his hand firmly. Nothing else needed to be said between us.

We wrapped up our somber conversation that evening. I was given my familiar bedroom in Rudolph's home. I had a clean bed and fresh sheets and slept well that night despite the intricate details I had shared earlier with Holger's family.

The following day, I was given a robust breakfast and lots of hot coffee, which I shared at a table with Matthias. We exchanged pleasantries, and as usual, it took a lot of work to get much out of the man in terms of conversation.

Upon finishing our breakfast, I asked Matthias a heartfelt question. "Matthias, will you take me to Holger's grave in Buenos Aires? I would very much like to pay my respects."

Matthias paused, looking down at his empty plate and then at me. He said, "Holger is buried right here on the property. Dad built a cemetery in his honor about a mile from the house. I'd be happy to take you there, Allen."

Matthias and I soon left the house's back door, but only after grabbing some rifles to take with us. The groundkeepers had warned us that a few mountain lions had been spotted on the property. That brought back the memory of Augustus taking down the mountain lion several months earlier when he and I had taken a late afternoon walk. This time, Augustus did not join us.

As we walked, Matthias surprised me by sharing additional memories of Holger, precisely when they used to hunt in the woods in Germany as teenagers. The walk to Holger's grave took about twenty minutes. Upon reaching the cemetery, I saw Holger's grave, the only one in the newly created cemetery. The cemetery was approximately twenty by twenty yards, surrounded by stone walls roughly five feet in height. A large iron gate allowed easy access to the cemetery.

Holger had a dark granite headstone that listed his name, date of birth and death, and a quote. The quote read, "Go with God, Son. You loved and were loved by all. Rest in Peace."

I found the headstone fitting for Holger.

I took my rifle off my right shoulder and set it on the ground. I then knelt on my right knee in front of Holger's headstone. I placed my left hand on the top of the headstone and looked at his name. I then spoke to him. "Holger, I am here, my friend. I want you to know that I killed the man that took your life that night in Chile. I found and killed all but one of the Nazis on our list. Walter Rauff got away twice, and I cannot forgive myself for allowing that to happen, especially knowing it was at his home that your death occurred. I am so sorry that this happened to you. I value our friendship, and I want you to know that you are missed not only by me, but by your brother, wife, and entire family. I will never forget you, my friend. Rest in peace."

By then, Matthias had come over to where I was kneeling and put his right hand on my left shoulder. I then stood, turned, and left the small cemetery. My eyes had filled with tears.

Matthias and I decided to let off a little steam. We walked another mile into the property and shot some pigeons and anything else that moved. We left all the animals where they fell. In addition to the mountain lions, plenty of wildlife would benefit from the freshly killed pigeons, squirrels, and rabbits on the ground.

We felt better after squeezing off a few rounds. We then walked back to the house. It was lunchtime, and I had my last meal at the house that day with Matthias, his family, Ruth, Rudolph, and Elsa. I expressed my condolences to Ruth one last time. I shared with her that Matthias and I had the privilege of paying our respects that morning at Holger's grave. Ruth was most appreciative.

Rudolph had spoken to my superiors in Washington, D.C., specifically Major Joe Yates. He told him my mission was over, and I wanted to return. What Rudolph did not know and, as a result, did not share with my superiors was that I had located and killed Adolf Hitler. I found it best to keep this quiet until I returned to the United States. In addition, I wanted to get the pictures developed to provide my superiors with additional proof that I had killed the madman.

With the support of Rudolph, transportation was arranged for me to take a ship from Buenos Aires, Argentina, to Miami, Florida, and then a second ship from Miami to Baltimore, Maryland. From Baltimore, I could quickly secure transportation to Fort Meade. I was so ready to get back to Alice. I was also informed that President Truman wanted to meet with me. That was somewhat intimidating news.

I said my goodbyes to everyone in the house, especially Rudolph. I thanked him for his gracious hospitality and support for my mission. We briefly talked about the deaths of Joaquin and Holger and how their deaths had been avenged.

Lastly, I firmly shook Rudolph's hand, grabbed my suitcase, turned, and walked to a waiting cab parked down the hill outside the property's main gate. The only weapons I had decided to take back with me were my trusty Colt 1911 and my Army knife, keepsakes for sure. I had managed to fit them into my suitcase along with all the clothing I had obtained over the last few months.

Just as I reached the main gate, Augustus ran in my direction. I crouched down, rubbed his head, and patted him several times.

"It is good to see you, my big protector. Thank you for saving me from that mountain lion and providing company when needed. You are a good dog, and I will miss you," I said.

I motioned Augustus to return to the house. He just sat down on his hind legs and stared at me. I felt horrible leaving him. I went up to him one last time and rubbed his head.

"It is time for you to return to the house, Augustus," I said. He just sat there and stared at me.

I had to go. I turned and stepped through the gate. I threw my suitcase onto the cab's back seat and got in. As we pulled away, I saw Augustus just staring at me.

He remained in the same position until I lost sight of him. It was a heartbreaking sight. Upon returning to the United States, I would have to get a dog like him. Alice loved dogs as much as I did. I was confident she would agree.

The cab ride to the Buenos Aires shipping docks took about two hours.

The trip was slowed by cattle crossing the road occasionally.

I barely had time to check in with the ticket office and obtain my ticket and cabin assignment. I had to run up the gangplank to board my ship bound for Miami, Florida. It was January 22, 1947.

CHAPTER 10

End of the Beginning

"We are not retreating – we are advancing in another direction."
General Douglas MacArthur

I found my cabin and dropped my suitcase on the bed. I wanted to be on the top deck when the ship left its moorings and headed to the open sea. I was so eager to get back to Alice. I had been away from her for nine months.

Once I worked my way up to the ship's top deck, I found a seat near the front of the ship's bow and settled in for the departure. I did not have to wait long, as most of the ship's passengers had boarded long before me. The ship's steam engines came to life. I watched the dockworkers loosen the mooring lines from the bollards and give the ship's captain the all-clear to move the ship away from the pier.

As the ship slowly worked out of the harbor and into the open water, I reflected again on how little time Alice and I had spent together since first meeting in a chocolate shop in Zurich, Switzerland, during Christmas 1932. Between that chance encounter and our next meeting nine years later during the December 7, 1941, Pearl Harbor, Hawaii, attack. Shortly after that reunion, we had to leave each other when I left Hawaii in early 1942.

I found out in late 1941 that General Donovan, the head of the newly formed OSS, wanted me back in Washington for meetings with him, President Roosevelt, and Secretaries Knox and Stimson during the second week of January 1942. My trip back east was arranged specifically by

General Donovan, and at that time, I took a submarine back. The USS *Tautog* (*SS-199*) was assigned to deliver me to Oakland, California, where I was to board an Army Air Corps plane back to Fort Meade.

As I'd started to board the submarine assigned to take me back to the mainland, I remember those next few minutes being extremely hard for Alice and me. I'd held Alice close, and we hadn't spoken. Soon, it was time for me to leave as sailors around us loosened the mooring lines.

I whispered into her ear before letting Alice out of my grip, "I promise to find you, Alice. Don't forget me. I love you."

Tears had flowed down her cheeks as she'd smiled and replied, "I know you will, Allen; I love you."

I had turned and walked up the gangplank. Just before I'd entered the sub's hatch and descended the ladder, I'd turned and looked back. Alice was still standing in the same spot, waving goodbye to me. I waved goodbye and descended into the sub.

I would not see her again until May 1942, when I was assigned to rescue a group of nurses supporting General Wainwright's troops on the island of Corregidor. Alice was among them. She had been determined to stay behind and tend to the wounded. I had left the island with seven nurses who had been selected to leave with me due to their health and age. I'd been devastated when I'd had to leave Alice on the island. The Japanese had been rapidly descending on the island, and the Americans were soon to be overrun.

Alice, along with General Wainwright and his troops, had later been captured and imprisoned for the rest of the War in a Japanese prison camp in Manila, Philippines. That was a very dark time for me. My heart had longed for her, and I'd repeatedly asked my superiors to stage a rescue mission, but my requests had been denied. I somehow had been able to get a letter to her. I'd received confirmation that the letter was successfully smuggled into the country and hand-delivered to her. I had not been able to receive a letter in response, but knowing Alice had received my letter was a relief. I had poured my heart out to her in that letter. She had known my intentions after reading it.

It was not until after the War when I was back at Fort Meade, that I received an update on Alice. On April 2, 1946, word finally arrived, and it was information that I had not expected. Senior OSS officials told me that the Army rescued the nurses in Manila a year earlier, in February 1945. Alice had suffered a head injury during an American bombing run over the city of Manila in December 1944. A section of the hospital roof had collapsed and killed several patients and nurses. Alice had survived but had been in a coma for over three months while the swelling in her brain subsided. She had come out of her coma sometime in March 1945, just before she and her fellow nurses had been transported back to the United States. The other nurses with her had cared for Alice during their trip back to San Diego, California.

To make matters worse, Alice had suffered from amnesia and did not even know her name, let alone remember me. She had been transported home to Jacksonville, Florida, to live with her parents with the hope she would eventually regain her memory. By then, she had been home with her parents for over a year. I was shocked.

With uncertainty, apprehension, and excitement all mixed up in my mind, I had secured a month's leave from the Army and traveled by train to Jacksonville in early April 1946. I did not know what to expect when I walked up the front steps. I had been wearing my Army uniform, hoping that would help bring some memories back to Alice. At that point, I had not seen Alice for four years. Would she know me? Would she still care for me?

The door opened, and an older man, presumably Alice's Dad, greeted me.

"May I help you, son?"

"Yes, Sir, my name is Allen Voigt, and I am a friend of Alice's. Is she home?" I replied.

"Are you making this up, son?" he asked.

I had paused for a moment before answering, thinking to myself, why would he think that? "Yes, I am Allen, the only Allen Voigt I know, Sir."

The man had motioned me in and asked me to sit on a couch in the living room. The house had been quiet except for the grandfather clock ticking in the corner. Before too long, I'd heard movement coming from the hallway. I'd risen to my feet and had seen Alice for the first time in a long while. She'd had no bandages on her head and shown no signs of head trauma.

My eyes had filled with tears when I walked up to her. She had looked at me and said, "Allen, is that you?"

"Yes, it's me, and I'm here right now," I'd replied as I pulled her into my arms. "I was afraid I'd lost you forever, Alice."

She had laid her head on my shoulder and said, "No, I'm right here."

"I'm never losing you again, Alice," I whispered.

I had spent the entire day with Alice and her parents. While Alice and I sat on her parent's couch, her parents told me she did not even know them when Alice moved back home. Three months before my arrival, Alice's memory had returned to the point that she remembered she had been a nurse, knew she had been overseas, and recognized her parents. She had mentioned to her parents that she had met a man named Allen during the War but could not recollect his last name. Alice also told her parents she remembered falling in love with him but could not remember much more. That explained why, when her father had greeted me at the door, he thought I was making things up.

I had found a nearby hotel and spent the next few weeks going back and forth to see Alice. Slowly, her memory returned, and we recalled our limited time together over the last fifteen years. She also had regained her ability to walk independently, which allowed us to go out on the town a few times, catching movies and dinners. I had been able to secure an Army post in Jacksonville, and we had spent as much time together as we could. We had walked on the beaches of Jacksonville, Florida, and watched the sunset many a night. We had been apart for so long but were making up for it.

Shortly after that, I had to leave for Berlin, Germany, on April 27, 1946.

I was finally returning to Alice, hopefully for good this time. The ship pushed through the waves. The air was warm since we were south of the equator, and I enjoyed milling about the top deck for several hours. Seagulls followed the ship for a few miles, and I could see dolphins diving up and down through the water as they swam parallel to our ship.

That night, I found a table in the dining room and joined two elderly couples for dinner. Both couples were American and had vacationed in Argentina for ninety days. One couple was from Sagaponack, New York, on Long Island out by the Hamptons.

The other couple was from Chicago, Illinois. The men had served together in the Army during World War One. I shared with them information about my father's service in the War and where he had been in Europe. It sounded like my father and these men shared some of the same dirt and time in the trenches.

It was clear, just by how these couples were dressed and where they were from, that they had a lot of money and were celebrating a leisurely life now. I was envious but enjoyed my conversations that evening with them.

The following morning was more of the same. I walked the ship's top deck over fifty times to get into even better shape. I will be seeing Alice! Ever since being shot a few months earlier, I had not kept my body in top physical shape. The walking certainly helped with my cardiac conditioning. I also took the time to perform sit-ups and pushups in my cabin each morning.

Over the next ten days, I repeated the same activity. There was not much else to do. For a few nights, I watched some movies in the entertainment section of the ship. I was a big fan of Humphrey Bogart and saw the movie *The Big Sleep* with him and Lauren Bacall. I also saw *My Darling Clementine*, a western starring Henry Fonda and directed by John Ford.

By February 2, 1947, we reached the port of Miami, Florida. It was good to see the United States again. I was excited to get off the ship and call Alice at her parents' home. I had not heard her voice in such a long time.

My ship from Miami to Baltimore was not leaving for twenty-four hours. I found a room at a small hotel near the port of Miami. The hotel had a lobby phone that I could use to call Alice.

I sat in a chair in the hotel lobby, looking out at the palm trees of Florida, watching various ships move in and out of the port. I connected to an operator who helped me get a call to Alice's parents' home. As the phone rang, I wondered to myself who was going to answer the phone and if anyone was going to be home at all.

The phone rang four times before the line was picked up. On the other end of the line, I heard Alice's voice.

"Hello," she said.

"Alice, it's Allen. I'm back in the United States and calling you from Miami. I have missed you so much. Did you get my letter? How are you?" I asked.

"Allen, I can't believe it's you. It is so good to hear your voice. I have missed you terribly. I got your letter and have read it every day since receiving it. Thank you for sending it to me," Alice said.

In the letter, I had not shared any news about my being shot, as I did not want to worry her about my condition. She was still trying to heal from her traumatic head injury.

I continued, "Alice, tomorrow I board a ship for Baltimore, Maryland. I have to report back to Fort Meade and later visit with President Truman. Would your parents give you money to take a train to Baltimore and meet me at Fort Meade?"

There was a slight pause on the other end of the phone.

"Allen, I can think of nothing better. I am a grown woman and have been holding down a job, working twenty hours a week at a local hospital in Jacksonville. I have saved up some money. When are you scheduled to arrive in Baltimore?"

"My ship, the U.S.S. *Tempest*, is scheduled to arrive on February 14," I replied.

For the next thirty minutes, I only asked Alice about her health and how her parents were doing. She made it clear that most of her memory had returned, and I knew that was the case when she brought up our meeting so long ago in Zurich. I was so relieved that she was feeling better.

We ended our call and agreed to meet in Baltimore, Maryland, when I arrived. I could not wait.

I spent my only night in Miami restless, eagerly anticipating boarding the ship to Baltimore. The following day could not come soon enough.

On February 3, I boarded the *Tempest*. The scheduled twelve-day trip directly resulted from the ship heading to Bermuda and the Bahamas to drop off passengers and pick up new passengers bound for the East Coast. We would have to spend three long days in Bermuda. After reaching Bermuda and the Bahamas, the ship would stop in Savannah, Georgia; Charleston, South Carolina; Wilmington, North Carolina; and Virginia Beach, Virginia, all before arriving in Baltimore.

It was the longest twelve days of my life because I wanted to get back to Alice. In retrospect, the last leg of my journey taking longer allowed Alice time to request her vacation from the hospital and travel to Baltimore.

The day finally arrived, February 14, 1947, Valentine's Day, believe it or not. I had my suitcase in my hand and was on the ship's top deck as it maneuvered into the Baltimore bay and subsequently docked. As the ship butted up against the pier, I scanned the large crowd standing on the pier, looking for Alice. I did not have to look long before I heard a shout from the crowd.

"Allen, here I am. I love you!" Alice shouted up at me as she waved her right hand at me.

She was the most beautiful woman I had ever seen. She looked amazing the day I first met her, but even after fifteen years, she looked better than ever.

I waved back at her and said, "I have waited eleven long months for this day. I love you beyond words!"

As the ship's gangplank was lowered, I positioned myself first in line, forgoing the protocol for women, children, or elderly folks. I felt terrible, but at this point, nothing was keeping me from getting off that ship as fast as possible.

I ran down the gangplank, almost tripping and dropping my suitcase into the water. I managed to right myself and made it down to the pier. Alice jumped into my arms the second my foot hit the concrete pier.

We both did not care at all who was around us. We kissed passionately and hugged for over a minute. I ran my fingers through Alice's hair and just stared at her. We later held hands as we walked down the pier and tried to find a cab.

Alice had come to the pier that morning straight from the train station. I carried her suitcase in my left hand and positioned my old suitcase up under my right arm. Nothing would prevent me from holding her left hand as we walked.

We soon found a cab and a friendly, cozy restaurant in downtown Baltimore to have lunch. It was like we had never left each other. We picked right up, reliving all the encounters and limited chances to see each other over the last fifteen years.

Before leaving for Fort Meade, we both made quick calls to our parents, letting them know we were together. I had not talked to my parents in over a year, and it was a complete shock to them that I was calling them. Alice had been kind enough to call them every month for me and check-in, especially when she got my letter a few months earlier, sharing all the updates.

Later that day, we arrived by cab at Fort Meade.

Upon reaching the front security gate, I rolled down the cab's window and said, "Captain Allen Voigt reporting."

The young Corporal attending the gate looked down at me from his guard station and said, "Are you the real Captain Allen Voigt, Sir? You are a legend in the Army. I have heard all about you. It is an honor to meet you, Sir."

I replied, "Yes, Corporal, it is me."

I smiled and saluted him. The young Corporal waved us through the gate. Alice looked at me and smiled, holding me close.

I directed the cab to my apartment on the base. I assumed it was still mine and that no one else had occupied it during my recent time away.

Alice and I were dropped off at the apartment. I had to find the base housekeeping staff to let us in, as I had lost my key somewhere along the way over the last eleven months.

Someone knocked on the front door not long after we entered the apartment. When I opened the door, the young Corporal stood holding a bottle of wine from the gate. He smiled and handed me the bottle, saluted and left.

Attached to the bottle was a card that read, "In honor of your return. Mission accomplished. Major Joe Yates."

I found a couple of glasses, opened the bottle, and poured each of us a glass of wine. We snuggled together on the sofa, drank our wine, and got to know one another again. We had so much to talk about and all the time in the world.

Night fell, and with it, the temperature. I lit a small fire in the fireplace to fight the chill. We ordered in and ate dinner on a blanket on the floor in front of the fireplace. Music played softly in the background on the radio.

After we finished eating, I stood and extended my hand to Alice. "May I have this dance?" I asked.

She smiled and said, "I thought you'd never ask."

She placed her hand in mine and rose gracefully from the floor. I pulled her into my arms, where she fit perfectly. We swayed gently to Benny Goodman and his orchestra. As one song eventually faded, a new one began and the introduction began with *"I Love You for Sentimental Reasons."*

Alice said, "I love this song."

She sang along softly, her cheek pressed against mine.

"I love you for sentimental reasons. I hope you do believe me. I'll give you my heart. I love you, and you alone were meant for me. Please give your loving heart to me and say we'll never part."

"This could be our song, Allen," Alice said.

I kissed her softly, took her by the hand, and led her to my bedroom. On that unforgettable night, I finally got to show Alice how much I loved her. We spent the next 24 hours in my apartment, wrapped in our little world.

The following morning, I called the base commander to tell him I was back on base and needed to make an appointment to meet with Major Joe Yates and President Harry Truman as soon as possible.

The base commander was already aware of my arrival and had been contacted by the Major. Things had been put in motion already. I was scheduled to meet them both at the White House the following morning for a full debriefing of my activity over the last eleven months. I decided to wait until I arrived at the White House to have the film developed. I did not want to risk having someone on the base find out that I had killed Adolf Hitler.

I asked Alice if she wanted to meet President Truman the following day. She was nervous about the idea but jumped at the chance. I have yet to meet the new President. All my meetings at the White House during World War II had been with President Roosevelt. After he died in April of 1945, I no longer visited the White House as my missions had me primarily overseas. I was somewhat surprised that Major Yates wanted to have the meeting at the White House. Why would the Major not just want to debrief me at Camp Meade? In retrospect, I was glad the meeting had been arranged at the White House, as the information I had to share was critical.

Alice and I were transported from Camp Meade to the White House via an Army staff car, the driver being the very same Corporal who had waved us through at the front gate the day before and delivered the bottle of wine. Based on his enthusiasm the day before meeting me, I bet he jumped at the chance to drive us.

Our drive that morning took about an hour, covering twenty-six miles to the White House. During the drive, I talked a lot with the young Corporal. I discovered his name was Scott Weber, and he was from Salt Lake City, Utah. Corporal Weber had only been in the Army since July 1945. He never participated in overseas action, as the War ended two months after his enlistment. I shared a few highlights of my missions during World War II with him.

Alice and I held hands during the entire ride, and she snuggled against me. She enjoyed my stories with Corporal Weber, as she knew little about what I had done and where I had been.

We finally pulled up to the White House and were quickly ushered through security at the east side entrance. Alice was looking all around, taking it all in. I had been there so often before that I could give tours if asked.

We were escorted to chairs located right outside of the Oval Office. It was at this point that we said our goodbyes to Corporal Weber. Alice and I were left there by ourselves. A female receptionist came over and asked us if we wanted any coffee. We obliged her by both saying yes. Sipping that hot coffee helped to calm our nerves. Even after visiting the White House before and meeting with former President Roosevelt, I never lost sight of the enormity of the office and the respect I had for it.

The Oval Office door opened, and Major Yates stood in the doorway. The last time I saw him was close to seven months before our brief time in Buenos Aires.

"Allen, is this Alice you have with you? You are out of your league!" Major Yates said.

"Yes, Sir," I replied. "This is Alice, the love of my life. Is it okay if she joins us for the debriefing?"

I was taking a big chance bringing her with me, let alone asking the Major and President Truman if she could listen in at the meeting.

"Allen, you and Alice have faithfully served our great country. You all have been away from each other far too much. By all means, she is invited. Both of you, please come in and meet the President."

We followed Major Yates into the Oval Office. There, sitting at his desk, was President Truman.

He immediately looked up and said, "Welcome, Allen and Alice."

I was surprised he knew Alice's name, mine, but there were few secrets in the Army.

He continued, "Everyone, please sit on the couches, and I will join you."

He pushed his chair back from his desk and stood. He walked over to the two couches prominently displayed there in his office. Alice and I sat next to each other on one couch. Major Yates and President Truman sat on the opposite couch, facing us.

The conversation started with the President thanking me for the mission I had just conducted, right on the heels of an exhausting set of missions before and during World War II. Major Yates had debriefed him. The extent of knowledge he had about my three kills in South America surprised me. I had yet to debrief Major Yates.

I filled in any gaps in timelines and confirmed which Nazis I had found and eliminated. I also apologized for the one I missed, Walter Rauff. The President and the Major expressed no frustration or disappointment that I had missed one. They were pleased with the three I had killed.

It had come to the point in the conversation that I needed to share my critical news about locating and killing Adolf Hitler. I was very nervous to share this news but simultaneously very eager to get the news out.

"Mr. President, Major Yates, I have one additional kill to report. After killing Eckerd Jacobsen, I rummaged through his written correspondence. Honestly, I was looking for more detail on my Walter Rauff. I was so frustrated he had gotten away from me on two occasions. It was a last attempt to find anything on him, with the hopes of locating him and killing him. As I read Jacobsen's paperwork, I discovered a handwritten letter he had recently received. The letter turned out to be from Adolf Hitler himself."

Both President Truman and Major Yates just looked at me with calm demeanors. Why were they not shocked?

"Allen, we knew Hitler was still alive, but this information was kept top secret," Major Yates said. "Only a small number of people knew that he had escaped the bunker in May 1945 and fled to South America, most likely to Argentina. The bad news since then has been that we had no idea where he was hiding. You were chosen specifically for this mission to hunt down and kill key Nazis that had escaped Germany at the end of the War. Our goal all along had been that you might find the whereabouts of

Adolf Hitler and eliminate him, as well. We had no interest in arresting him, bringing him back to the United States, and causing a worldwide firestorm. Realistically, we thought you had less than a ten percent chance of locating and eliminating him. Your news of finding and killing him is very welcome."

I then pulled out the roll of film I had brought back with me that provided absolute proof that Hitler was dead. I handed the roll of film to the Major.

"Major Yates, this film will provide you and the President with proof of my killing Adolf Hitler," I said.

The Major left the room immediately with the film.

The conversation suddenly shifted, with the President asking Alice about what she had done during the War and how we met. I knew her memory was back because she was very detailed about Zurich, Pearl Harbor, and Corregidor. Alice took close to thirty minutes to walk the President through the story. I was so happy she was with me and healthy again.

We wrapped up our morning meeting at the White House around 11:00 a.m. Major Yates met Alice and me outside the Oval Office as we said our goodbyes to President Truman. The Major took us to lunch near the White House, where we could talk further.

The Major thanked me for a productive mission, but more importantly, for the added intelligence on killing Hitler, especially for the film I had provided. He shared that the film had been in color. He also said that the photos were graphic but provided irrefutable proof that Hitler had indeed been captured and killed. He added more detail as we finished our lunch that day.

"Allen, the United States will keep your entire mission classified for several years. This secrecy also includes the killing of Hitler. We feel leaking this information will be detrimental to national security and could cause disruption in Europe. The continent of Europe, and especially Germany, is too fragile right now. The German Army, those not captured by the Russians, have disbanded and returned to their homes throughout Germany and surrounding countries. Any news of Hitler being located and killed, let alone news of him escaping Germany and living for over a year after the War, could cause unrest. Lastly, we are immediately sending a team to Argentina to dispose of Hitler's body, and the others you eliminated there outside the town of Junin. There can be no evidence of his killing."

The Major then turned to Alice and stressed the urgent need for her to keep everything she heard that day to herself.

I could tell all the secrecy had made Alice extremely uncomfortable. As she confirmed with the Major that she would keep everything she had heard to herself, she grabbed my leg and gripped it tightly.

We soon said our goodbyes to the Major, thanked him for lunch, and departed. Alice and I spent the remainder of the afternoon touring Washington, D.C., the memorials and parks. The trees were budding in beautiful colors. It turned out to be a great day. Nothing was said between us about the White House visit or lunch with the Major.

As I found out the next day, the bad news was that I had been ordered to remain at Fort Meade. I had to debrief Major Yates and others in more detail, almost with a blow-by-blow of my daily activity and time in South America. Alice had to leave two days after our White House meeting and return to Jacksonville, Florida. She did not want to leave me, and I did not want to see her go, but her job was essential to her, and I understood that.

For the next eight months, I traveled back and forth from Fort Meade to Jacksonville every two weeks to spend time with Alice. I also made a trip in April of 1947 to visit my parents in Buffalo, NY.

In November 1947, I asked Alice to marry me, something I regretted not doing during the time we spent together in Hawaii during the War. Looking back on it, I should and could have asked her, but it never felt right due to the dangerous nature of my assignments. We were married on Saturday, December 13, 1947, in Jacksonville, at the Riverside Presbyterian Church. Our honeymoon was spent in Naples, Florida, on the Gulf Coast.

Alice and I built a home near the beach between Jacksonville and St. Augustine, Florida. Time passed, and we raised a son and a daughter.

I retired from the Army in January 1948, serving faithfully for over twenty-one years. I never fully parted ways with the Army, as I spent another thirty years as a contract employee. I initially helped train young Army recruits heading off to the Korean War with counterintelligence and weapons training. By the fifties, the Cold War had escalated with the Soviet Union, and I was asked to train CIA personnel on how to blend into the society of a foreign country and maintain a false identity.

I made good money as an Army contract employee until 1978. Jimmy Carter was in the White House, and I had seen enough. For fifty years, I dedicated my life to the Army and the safety of the United States. It was time for me to concentrate on nothing but my wife, my now-grown children, and, by that time, my grandchildren.

The relationship I forged with Joe Yates and others was special to me, but they had all passed away by then. Joe died of a heart attack in the fall of 1962. Up to that point, we had managed to correspond over the years via letters.

After I heard the news about Walter Rauff's death that day, I got up from my chair and turned off the TV. That chapter of my life was now closed. It had always haunted me that I did not catch him back in 1946. His death was welcomed, and I was now able to have real peace. Death, indeed, was the final reckoning.

As I left the room, I glanced at the German Walther PPK Holger had given me. Lying next to it on the nearby table was the Hitler Youth knife. I always treasured those items to remind me of Holger and my last mission.

ABOUT THE AUTHOR

Tim Drake lives in Dahlonega, a city in north Georgia. He is a charter member of the National World War II Museum in New Orleans, a member of the Military Writers Society of America, and the 8th Air Force Historical Society. His passion for history, specifically World War II, started very young. He had two grandfathers who served in World War II and survived. Three other family members served but were killed in action. Tim has a deep passion for the Greatest Generation and keeping their service and memory alive. He speaks frequently on World War II and the Greatest Generation.

On the web, please visit www.inheritedfreedom.com. You can also reach Tim Drake at inheritedfreedom@comcast.net.

Printed in the United States
by Baker & Taylor Publisher Services